People have the power

I was dreaming in my dreaming
of an aspect bright and fair
and my sleeping it was broken
but my dream it lingered
in the form of shining valleys.
where the pure air
recified.
And my senses newly opened.
I awakened to the cry
that the people have the
power.
To redeem the work of fools.
upon the meek the graces shower.
its decreed — the people rule.

Where there were deserts I saw fountains
and like cream the water rose
and we strolled their together.
with none to laugh or criticize.
and the leopard & the lamb
lay together truly bound —
I was hoping in my hoping To
recall what I had found.
And I believe everything we dream,
can come to pass thru our union —
we can turn the world around —
we can turn the earth's revolution
for the people have the power —

一頁 folio

始 于 一 页 ， 抵 达 世 界

PATTI SMITH COLLECTED LYRICS 1970-2015

诗与歌：

帕蒂·史密斯

1970-2015

[美] 帕蒂·史密斯 著　　陈思安 译

GUANGXI NORMAL UNIVERSITY PRESS
广西师范大学出版社

·桂林·

图书在版编目(CIP)数据

　　诗与歌：帕蒂·史密斯：1970—2015：汉英对照 /(美) 帕蒂·
史密斯著；陈思安译. —— 桂林：广西师范大学出版社，2022.12
　　书名原文: Patti Smith Collected Lyrics, 1970–2015
　　ISBN 978-7-5598-5239-7

　　Ⅰ.①诗… Ⅱ.①帕… ②陈… Ⅲ.①歌词集—美国—现代—
汉、英 Ⅳ.①I712.25

　　中国版本图书馆CIP数据核字(2022)第156944号

著作权合同登记号桂图登字：20-2022-052号

SHI YU GE
诗与歌

作　　　者：[美]帕蒂·史密斯
责任编辑：黄安然
特约编辑：王韵沁
装帧设计：山川制本workshop
内文制作：燕　红

广西师范大学出版社出版发行

　　广西桂林市五里店路9号　邮政编码：541004
　　网址：www.bbtpress.com
出 版 人：黄轩庄
全国新华书店经销

发行热线：010-64284815

北京九天鸿程印刷有限责任公司

开本：889mm×1000mm　1/16

印张：26.625　　字数：800千字

2022年12月第1版　2022年12月第1次印刷

定价：168.00元

如发现印装质量问题，影响阅读，请与出版社发行部门联系调换。

In memory of Fred Sonic Smith,
1948–1994

纪念弗雷德·索尼克·史密斯[*]，

1948—1994

★ 弗雷德·索尼克·史密斯（Fred Sonic Smith，1948—1994），
美国音乐人，吉他手，著名摇滚乐队 MC5 成员。1980 年与帕蒂·史密斯结婚，两人育有一儿一女。

找 到 自 己 的 声 音

我们每个人都有一首歌。

这首歌自然而然地到来，表达着喜悦、孤独，用以驱散恐惧或展示小小的胜利。我们几乎留意不到自己正酝酿着它，当我们唱起它时，时常是独自一人，有一半儿是唱给自己听的。

是对自我内心词语的发现，引导着我们去歌唱。它可能是一曲赞美诗，是些叛逆的碎片，或是一个少年的祷告。我们有可能在被丢到车库角落里、床底下，或是挂在典当铺橱窗里的一把旧吉他里寻找到灵感。走着路时，在风儿捎给我们的一句话里找到它。在镜子中自己的映像里找到它。有时候，我们从别人的歌中认出我们自己的歌。这是流行歌曲的奇迹，这些歌受到广泛喜爱，通常是因为它们简单朴素。

这些小小的歌曲演化成为诗歌、即兴表演以及合作创作，产生出歌词，它们被带着极大的期待写出来，希望能够引起一些共鸣，触动听众，让他们在其中找到自己的意义，然后跟着一起唱。

我记忆中自己唱出的第一首歌是《耶稣爱我》[1]。我能在脑海中看到自己坐在芝加哥的一个小门廊前唱着这首歌，等待街头艺人牵着他的宠物猴子沿街走来。我能听到空气中的那些歌声。《天亮喽》[2]《捕虾船》[3]和《我心之心》[4]。我能听到父亲用口哨吹着"深紫"[5]乐队的歌，还有母亲哄我们入睡时唱出的歌声。

我还记得我的第一台唱机，只比午餐盒大那么一点点，还有我的两张唱片，一张红色的一张黄色的：《大号图比》[6]和《巨石糖果山》[7]。我喜欢看它们旋转，沉浸在它们所唤起的世界之中。但是引发我人生第一次激烈内心反应的歌，是由小理查德[8]唱出来的。

那是个星期天。我跟母亲手牵着手。她正带我去圣经学校上学。她戴着儿童手套，就像《爱丽丝梦游仙境》里那只白兔子。那副手套给她营造出一种特殊的氛围，我实在太喜欢它们了。我们路过男孩们的"俱乐部"——两只巨大的冰箱包装盒被剪开，拼凑在一起。里奇·格拉斯哥转着圈儿，从那扇手工切出来的窗户里飘出的东西（更像是用来被呼吸而不是被看到的）死死地阻止住我的脚步，这导致我非常突然地挣脱开母亲的手，把她的手套都拽掉了。

我不知道自己听到了什么，也不知道自己为何反应如此剧烈。那首歌不是《捕虾船》或《天亮喽》。那是某种新事物，尽管我无法理解是什么吸引了我，我仍然被它吸引住了。被一个孩子兴奋的舞蹈所吸引。那首歌是《什锦水果》[9]，那么陌生，却那么熟悉。那是小理查德。对我而言，那便是摇滚乐的诞生。

我们曾在费城住过一段时间。那里每个人都喜欢唱歌跳舞。妹妹和我会跳吉特巴舞[10]。人们在街角唱着阿卡贝拉。我九岁时，全家搬到了南泽西。我的音乐老师热爱歌剧。他把他的唱片带到班级里，给我们播放威尔第和普契尼的选段。我被这种音乐迷住了，尤其是被玛丽亚·卡拉斯所触动。她情感的强度。她如何从每一根纤维里汲取能量来创造出一声低吟。她的唱腔从唱机转盘上骤然升起——尤其是我最喜欢的，歌剧热门单曲《美好的一天》。有段时间我梦想成为一名歌剧演员，但我并未受到那种召唤，也缺乏自律，以及必要的体格。我的老师，感受到了我的渴望，交给我一项光荣的任务。他让我出演曼里科，演唱威尔第《游吟诗人》当中的摇篮曲。有那么一瞬间，我感受到了这位游吟诗人对他群山之中的家乡那份广博之爱。

我梦想成为像琼·克里斯蒂和克里斯·康纳那样的爵士歌手。梦想着用比莉·哈乐黛那种懒洋洋又充了电似的方式处理歌曲。[11]梦想着像罗特·莲娜[12]的《海盗珍妮》那样支持被压迫者。但我从未梦想过在一支摇滚乐队里唱歌。他们尚未出现在我的世界中。不过我的世界瞬息万变。

我有幸在一段鼓舞人心的精神与文化的革命性时期成长起来。音乐也成为一场革命，所有人都在其中找到了自己的声音，借由这声音我们联合在一起。我们的战场是俄亥俄、芝加哥，以及费尔摩。我们为"战士"这个词赋予了全新意义。我们在身上挂起一把电吉他而不是机关枪。

我挣脱了乡村生活的束缚。告别工厂、方块舞大厅、枯萎的果园。我出发到了纽约城。我心里想成为一个画家，借由这个追求我找到了自己声音的节奏与根基。站在被钉到墙上的大幅纸张面前，图像令我感到挫败，取而代之地，我绘制出了文字——韵律从纸页上流淌而出溢到灰泥墙壁上。这种绘制文字的身体行为渐渐演化成写下歌词。稍后，这一过程的精炼便导向了表演。

1969 年，我跟罗伯特·梅普尔索普 13 一起搬进了切尔西酒店。那时我已放弃了成为画家的希望。我得到了一份地下剧场的工作。这工作局限太多。我渴望与人切磋，去建立连接。罗伯特鼓励我表演自己的诗作。我参加了一些诗歌朗诵会，却发现那比剧场还要更加局限。鲍勃·纽沃斯 14 建议我把歌词的风格融入音乐中，山姆·谢泼德 15 在他的戏剧作品《疯狗布鲁斯》16 里面使用了我的两首作品。

1971 年 2 月 10 日，我举办了自己的第一场诗歌朗诵会，在包厘街的圣马可大教堂里为杰拉德·马兰加 17 做开场表演。因为想要投射出一种原始的能量，我招募了莱尼·凯 18。当我朗读《坏男孩之歌》时，莱尼用他的电吉他制造出的音浪诠释了一场改装赛车竞赛，我们一起把这场朗诵推向了高潮。这次表演在当时似乎有些消极影响。我把它当作一个积极的信号。

接下来的几年里，我开始研究汉克·威廉姆斯 19，搞来本鲍勃·迪伦的歌词集，拼命拨拉一台 30 年代的老吉布森吉他。我在一家书店里打工。我画画。我给罗伯特当模特。在我的笔记本里乱写乱画。我在 60 年代的废墟中穿行徘徊。有那么多的喜悦，也有不满。有那么多声音冒出来，接着又被压灭。我这一代人的遗产传承似乎已岌岌可危。

有些事情萦绕在我脑海中：艺术家的历程，自由之路的重新定义，空间的重新创造，全新声音的浮现。

　　而这些事情我是通过——尽管说出来有些尴尬——摇滚乐的形式来表达的。或许我一直只不过是个好斗的小兵，但我依然对自己所采取的行动心存感激。

　　向所有帮助我做出那些行动的人致敬。

1　"Jesus Loves Me"，最受欢迎的基督教赞美诗之一。

2　"Day-O"，牙买加传统民歌，以对唱形式讲述码头工人整夜搬运香蕉上船。最著名的版本为美国歌手哈里·贝拉方特（Harry Belafonte）于 1956 年发行的版本。

3　"Shrimp Boats"，美国 1950 年代流行歌曲。

4　"Heart of My Hearts"，作曲家本·莱恩（Ben Ryan）写了 1926 年的一首流行歌曲。

5　"深紫"（Deep Purple），英国摇滚乐队，成立于 1968 年。该乐队被认为是重金属音乐和现代硬摇滚的开拓者之一。

6　"Tuby the Tuba"，美国著名儿童歌曲，最早录制于 1946 年。"图比"是一只大号的拟人化形象。

7　"Big Rock Candy Mountain"，美国民间歌曲，讲述流浪汉对天堂生活的想象，最早录制于 1928 年。

8　理查德·韦恩·彭尼曼（Richard Wayne Penniman，1932—2020），艺名"小理查德"，美国创作歌手、音乐人。他最知名的作品诞生于 1950 年代中期，其充满活力的音乐和富有魅力的演出奠定了摇滚乐的根基，也对灵魂乐和放克乐产生了重要影响。

9　"Tutti Frutti"，"小理查德"录制于 1955 年的热门单曲。2007 年被英国《MOJO》杂志评选为"一百张改变世界的专辑"榜首，被认为是"摇滚乐诞生之作"。

10　20 世纪初流行于非裔美国人当中的一种舞蹈，融合了多种摇摆舞的风格特点。

11　琼·克里斯蒂（June Christy，1925—1990），克里斯·康纳（Chris Connor，1927—2009），比莉·哈乐黛（Billie Holiday，1915—1959），皆为 20 世纪美国重要爵士歌手。

12　罗特·莲娜（Lotte Lenya，1898—1981），奥地利裔美国歌手，活动家，演员。她曾出演布莱希特《二分钱歌剧》中的珍妮，并演唱了歌剧中著名的曲目《海盗珍妮》（"Pirate Jenny"）。

13　罗伯特·梅普尔索普（Robert Mapplethorpe，1946—1989），美国摄影师，帕蒂·史密斯的长期密友。

14　鲍勃·纽沃斯（Bob Neuwirth，1939— ），美国歌手、词曲作者、音乐制作人及视觉艺术家。

15　山姆·谢波德（Sam Shepard，1943—2017），美国剧作家、演员、编剧及导演。

16　"Mad Dog Blues"，两幕音乐剧，1971 年 3 月 4 日在农场圣马可堂（St. Mark's Church in-the-Bowery）的创世记剧场（Theatre Genesis）首演。

17　杰拉德·马兰加（Gerard Malanga，1943— ），美国诗人、摄影师、电影制作人及艺术策展人。

18　莱尼·凯（Lenny Kaye，1946— ），美国吉他演奏家、作曲家，帕蒂·史密斯乐团成员。

19　汉克·威廉姆斯（Hank Williams，1923—1953），美国乡村音乐及布鲁斯创作男歌手。

目 录

FIRST SONGS

AND

PERFORMANCE

PIECES

最 初 的 歌

及 表 演 作 品

Jesus died for somebody's sins	耶稣为别人的罪而死
but not mine	不是为我的
melting in a pot of thieves	熔在一锅贼里
wild card up my sleeve	狂野是我袖中王牌
thick heart of stone	铁石了心肠
my sins my own	我的罪我自己扛
I engrave my own palm	我在手掌刻下
Sweet black X	甜蜜的黑色 X
Adam placed no hex on me	亚当的魔咒对我没用
I embrace Eve	我搂着夏娃
and take full responsibility	为我熟练又灵活
for every pocket I have picked	偷过的每只口袋
mean and slick	担下所有罪
every Johnny Ace song I've balled to	伴着每首约翰尼·艾斯[1]的歌我狂舞
long before the church	早在教会把那些歌
made it neat and right	清理干净又正确之前
So Christ	所以基督
I'm giving you the good-bye	我要跟你说再见
firing you tonight	今晚就一拍两散
I can make my own light shine	我能让自己的光闪耀
and darkness too is equally fine	就算黑暗也无关紧要

you got strung up for my brother

but with me I draw the line

you died for somebody's sins

but not mine

你为我的兄弟被吊死

但我要跟你划清界限

你为别人的罪而死

不是为我的

1　约翰尼·艾斯（Johnny Ace，1929—1954），美国节奏布鲁斯歌手。1950 年代中期发表过一系列热门单曲。25 岁时死于自己造成的意外枪伤。

工作之歌

I was working real hard	我工作得实在卖力
to show the world	向世界展示
what I could do	我能做到什么
oh I guess	哦，或许
I never dreamed	我做梦也没想到
I'd have to	我不得不如此
world spins	世界旋转
some photographs	一些照片
how I love to laugh	当人群大笑起来
when the crowd laughs	我也爱跟着笑
while love slips through	而爱轻轻溜走
a theater that is full	穿过满座的剧院
but ooh baby	但是，哦，宝贝
when the crowd goes home	当人群四散归家
and I turn in	我上床入眠
and I realize I'm alone	意识到自己如此孤独
I can't believe, I had to	我无法相信，我不得不
I was working real hard	我工作得实在卖力
to show the world	向世界展示
what I could do	我能做到什么
oh I guess	哦，或许

I never dreamed	我做梦也没想到
I'd have to	我不得不
I had to	不得不
I had to	不得不
sacrifice	牺牲
you	你

A FIRE OF UNKNOWN ORIGIN	不明之火
A fire of unknown origin	一场不明之火
Took my baby away	带走我的宝贝
Fire of unknown origin	起因不明之火
Took my baby away	带走我的宝贝
Swept her up and off my wavelength	卷走她截断我的心波
Swallowed her up like the ocean	吞下她犹如一片深海
In a fire thick and gray	这场浓密灰沉的大火
Death comes sweeping	死亡穿过走廊
Through the hallway	扫荡干净一切
Like a lady's dress	像条淑女的衣裙
Death comes riding	死亡驶下公路
Down the highway	快马加鞭向前
In its Sunday best	穿着它最好的盛装
Death comes riding	死亡快马加鞭来了
Death comes creeping	死亡缓慢爬着来了
Death comes	死亡来了
I can't do nothing	我没有任何办法
Death goes	死亡走了
There must be something that remains	一定有什么东西留下来
Death it made me sick and crazy	死亡它让我恶心又疯狂
'Cause that fire it took my baby away	因为那场大火它带走了我的宝贝

7

goodnight Irene.

have you seen
dylans dog
its got wings
it can fly
if you speak
of it to him
its The only Time
dylan
cant look you in The eye

have you held dylans snake
it rattles/like a Toy
it coils in his hand
it sleeps in The ~~bed~~   he sleepin in the grass
dylans bed   he's the only one
its The only one   strikes out
sleeps near his head   when dylan comes

have you pressed
To your ~~ear~~ face
dylans bird dylans bird
it rolls on the ground   it rests on dylan hip
it sings dylans songs   it drops on dylans ground
its the one   it rolls with him
Who can hum like dylan hums   its the only one
                                   who can hum when dylan hums

have you seen
dylans dog   it Trembles with him
it's got wings
it can fly   it rests in dylans hump
then it lands   it Trembles inside of him
like a clown   it drops upon The ground
its The only thing allowed.   its the only one
look him in the eye   who can hum when dylan hums

DOG DREAM

狗梦

have you seen	你见过
dylan's dog	迪伦的狗吗
it got wings	它长着翅膀
it can fly	它能飞翔
if you speak	要是你跟他
of it to him	聊起这事
it's the only	那会是迪伦
time dylan	唯一无法
can't look you in the eye	直视你双眼的瞬间
have you seen	你见过
dylan's snake	迪伦的蛇吗
it rattles like a toy	它像玩具似的吱嘎乱响
it sleeps in the grass	它睡在草丛
it coils in his hand	盘卷在他掌心
it hums and it strikes out	嘶嘶叫着突然袭击
when dylan cries out	当迪伦大声叫喊
when dylan cries out	当迪伦大声叫喊
have you pressed	你让它紧贴过
to your face	你的脸吗

dylan's bird	迪伦的鸟
dylan's bird	迪伦的鸟
it lies on dylan's hip	它躺在迪伦屁股上
trembles inside of him	在他身体里打着战
it drops upon the ground	它跌下去掉到地面
it rolls with dylan 'round	它绕着迪伦转圈圈
it's the only one	它是唯一一个
who comes	只有迪伦出现时
when dylan comes	才会露面的
have you seen	你见过
dylan's dog	迪伦的狗吗
it got wings	它长着翅膀
it can fly	它能飞翔
when it lands	当它落地
like a clown	像个小丑
he's the only	他是唯一
thing allowed	获得允许
to look dylan in the eye	能直视迪伦双眼的

BALLAD OF A BAD BOY

Oh I was bad

didn't do what I should

mama catch me with a lickin'

and tell me to be good

when I was bad twice times

she shoved me in a hole

and cut off all my fingers

and laid them in a finger bowl

My mama killed me

my papa grieved for me

my little sister Annalea

wept under the almond tree

Oh I loved a car, car

and when I was feelin' sad

I lay down on my daddy's Ford

and I'd feel good

and you know that I got bad

robbed hubcaps from the men

and sold them to the women

坏男孩之歌

哦我是个坏男孩

没干我该干的事

妈妈暴揍我一顿

告诉我乖一点

当我又一次干坏事

她把我猛推进一个洞

剁掉我所有手指头

把它们铺进洗手盅

我的妈妈杀了我

我的爸爸哀悼我

我的小妹妹安娜莉亚

在杏仁树下流眼泪

哦我爱上过一辆车，车

每当我感到悲伤

躺到爸爸的福特车上

就会心情好起来

你知道我已变坏

抢劫男人的车轮毂

把它卖给女人们

and stole them back again

再把它们偷回来

and I got me a car

我给自己买了车

a Hudson Hornet car

一台哈德逊大黄蜂 [1]

and rolled the pretty ladies

载着漂亮姑娘四处晃

and often went too far

经常做得太过火

I went to Chicago

我去过芝加哥

I went to Kalamazoo

我去过卡拉马祖

I went to Nashville

我去过纳什维尔

the highways I flew

飞越过高速公路

I went to Salinas

我去过萨利纳斯

I rode to the sea

奔驰向海边

and the people all scolded

人们都在谩骂我

and pointed to me

指着我说

they said there's a bad boy

那是一个坏男孩

I was so bad boy

哥们，我坏到了这地步

they gathered their daughters

他们召集女儿们

I heard what they said

我听到他们说

steer away from him, honey

离他远一点，亲爱的

'cause that boy is bad

那个男孩是坏蛋

and tho' he's hung good	尽管他看上去还不赖
and flashes that loot	把宝贝亮出来给你看
don't slide by his side	不要溜到他身边
he rides a wrong route	他走的是错的路
'cause he's a bad boy	因为他是个坏男孩
I was so bad boy	哥们，我坏到了这地步
my mama killed me	我的妈妈杀了我
my papa grieved for me	我的爸爸哀悼我
my little sister Annalea	我的小妹妹安娜莉亚
wept under the almond tree	在杏仁树下流眼泪
And I wept on a stock car	我坐在改装赛车上掉眼泪
I captured the junkyards	我占领了垃圾场
and I sped thru the canyons	我飞速穿过大峡谷
though I never went far	却从未远离
from the wreckers mechanics	救险车的机修工
I worshipped these men	我崇拜那些人
but they laughed at me, man	他们却来嘲笑我，哥们
they called me mama's boy	他们叫我妈宝男孩
mama mama mama mama	妈妈 妈妈 妈妈 妈妈

Monday at midnight	周一午夜
Tuesday at two	周二凌晨两点
drunk on tequila	用龙舌兰灌醉自己
thinking of you, ma	想起了你，妈
I drove my car on, ma	我还在开我的车，妈
wrecking cars was my art	撞烂车子是我的艺术
I held a picture of you, ma	我握着你照片，妈
close to my heart	紧贴我心脏
I rode closed windows	我靠着关闭的窗
it was ninety degrees	外面有九十度
the crowd it was screaming	人群在尖叫
it was screaming for me	他们是因我尖叫
they said I was nonsense	他们说我胡说八道
true diver chicken driver	真潜水员弱鸡驾驶员
no sense	没道理
but I couldn't hear them	但我听不到他们
I couldn't see	我也看不到
fenders hot as angels	挡泥板火热得像天使
blazed inside me	在我体内燃烧

I sped on raged in steam heat   我在热腾腾的蒸汽中狂怒加速

I cracked up and rolled at your feet   大笑着在你脚下打滚

I rose in flames and rolled in a pit   我在火焰里上升在泥坑中翻滚

where you caught me with a tire iron   你用撬胎棒把我打倒在地

and covered me in shit   给我浑身盖满屎

and I coulda got up   我原本可以站起身

but the crowd it screamed no   但人群尖叫着不要

that boy is evil   那个男孩是恶魔

too bad for parole   他太坏了不能假释

so bad his ma cut off all his fingers   他太坏了他妈剁掉他所有手指头

and laid 'em in a finger bowl   把它们铺进洗手盅

His mama killed him   他的妈妈杀了他

his papa grieved for him   他的爸爸哀悼他

his little sister Annalea   他的小妹妹安娜莉亚

wept under the almond tree   在杏仁树下流眼泪

Oh I was bad   哦我是个坏男孩

didn't do what I should   没干我该干的事

mama catch me with a lickin'   妈妈暴揍我一顿

and she tell me

You be good

—for Sam Shepard

她对我说

你乖一点

——写给山姆·谢泼德

PICTURE HANGING BLUES

挂图布鲁斯

Don't hang me up Jesse James

Don't hang me up Jesse James

Too many men have hung me up Jesse James

别吊着我杰西·詹姆斯 [1]

别吊着我杰西·詹姆斯

太多男人都吊着我杰西·詹姆斯

I know the true story of sweet Jesse James

The picture you have of him is badly framed

He lived as an old man in exchange for his name

He lived in hiding in exchange for his fame

我知道关于甜心杰西·詹姆斯的真实故事

你那张他的照片装裱得太差劲

他用声誉换取活得像个老头子

他用名望换取活得隐匿无形

I laid waiting for him on that fateful night

Caring for him though it wasn't right

I knew he was alive

Alive and run free

Another man slain in his place for me

So he could come after me

So he could come and love me

宿命的夜晚我躺下来等候他

关心着他尽管这不太对

我知道他还活着

活着且逍遥法外

为了我，又一个男人替他挨刀

这样他就可以追求我

这样他就可以来爱我

So don't hang me up Jesse James

Don't hang me up Jesse James

Don't hang me up Jesse James

Too many men have hung me

所以别吊着我杰西·詹姆斯

别吊着我杰西·詹姆斯

别吊着我杰西·詹姆斯

太多男人都吊着我

It was Billy the Kid used to lay in my bed	曾经躺在我床上的是比利小子 [2]
He knew I loved Jesse	他知道我爱着杰西
It was something I said	这话是我说出口的
I balled Jesse but I had no shame	我睡了杰西但不觉得羞耻
I balled Billy but I called Jesse's name	我睡了比利但喊着杰西的名字
Billy traced Jesse	比利追踪杰西
Gun in his hand	火枪抓在手里
Said there's no use living	说这样活着没意义
Half of a man	只算半个男人
He begged Jesse kill him	他央求杰西杀了他
And take up his name	夺去他的名字
Jesse got the picture	杰西拿走那张照片
Love was to blame	爱是罪魁祸首
Billy just trembled	比利浑身战栗
Mouth full of fright	嘴中塞满惊骇
Jesse was left	杰西已经离开
Love blinding sight	爱是灼目景象
Jesse was hot	杰西很火辣
Billy was shot	比利被枪杀

Life was the last thing   生命就是比利最后

That Billy could give   能够献出的东西

So Jesse could love me   这样杰西可以爱我

Jesse could live   杰西可以活

Billy lay broken   比利躺着奄奄一息

Jesse came slow   杰西缓慢地靠近

And the last words were spoken   最后遗言终于讲出

Were Jesse James "go!"   杰西·詹姆斯说"走啊！"

And don't hang her up Jesse James   别吊着她杰西·詹姆斯

Don't hang her up Jesse James   别吊着她杰西·詹姆斯

Don't hang her up Jesse James   别吊着她杰西·詹姆斯

Too many men   太多男人

Yeah, too many men   是啊，太多男人

Jesse James is runnin'   杰西·詹姆斯一路逃亡

The outlaws all love him   法外之徒都爱他

They don't blame him   他们不会责怪他

They say he's a saint   他们说他是个圣人

A saint   一位圣人

I ain't sayin' he is

I ain't sayin' he ain't

Though he could live like a man

Love me like a woman

My Billy died like a snake

And Jesse James never came

我不能说他是

我不能说他不是

他能像个男人一样活着

像个女人一样爱我

我的比利像条蛇似的死去

杰西·詹姆斯再没回来过

Oh you hung me up Jesse James

You hung me up Jesse James

And too many men

Too many men have hung me

Up yours Jesse James

哦你吊着我杰西·詹姆斯

你吊着我杰西·詹姆斯

太多男人

太多男人都吊着我

去你妈的杰西·詹姆斯

1 杰西·詹姆斯（Jesse Woodson James，1847—1882），美国强盗，曾为著名强盗团伙"詹氏－杨格"中最有名的成员。去世后，被刻画成一个民间传说人物，不时被误描绘成一个枪法能手。

2 比利小子（Billy the Kid，1859—1881），美国著名枪手、西部传奇人物。

vera gemini

Oh your the kind of girl
Id like to find in my mirror
you have all the markings
of the devil girl
yet you are boned like a saint
with the conscience of a snake

Oh your eyes have shifted from me
everyone saw what you did
how you slipped from beneath me.
live a nervous squid
a little false and frigid
the whole crowd knew you did it

yes you have behaved treacherously
and in public too my vera marie
so i believe you'll have to pay

i said you be good or go to hell
in my arms ill be happy to sail you there
my lovely

Oh no more horses horses
Were gonna swim like fish
into the hole in which
you planned to ditch me

you have filled me with a vengence
and touched me with your breath
and planned to leave me cold
but you'll never get your wish
im gonna pull you from the dance
you writhe you ride so easily
im gonna gather up your reins in my fist
just me and you
one two
oh no more horses
horses horses

I was your victom
I was well decieved
hells built on regrets
and i hold to many
i love your naked neck
even the lies youve told me
a lily thats bend lying
white and bent and sick

Oh but you arent two faced
you have two faces
that will speak no more no more no more

Oh your the knid of girl
i found in my mirror
laughing
the way you laughed at christ
oh he fell on frid y
rose on monday
but when i take you down you wont rise

THE REVENGE OF VERA GEMINI

维拉·杰米尼的复仇 [1]

You are boned like a saint	你骨架如圣人
with the conscience of a snake	良知如毒蛇
You're the kind of girl	你是那种我想
I'd like to find	在我镜子里
in my mirror	找到的女孩
in my mirror	找到的女孩
Your eyes have shifted from me	你的目光从我身上移开
everyone saw what you did	每个人都看到你干的好事
how you slipped from beneath me	你是怎样从我脚下滑走
like a nervous squid	像条紧张的乌贼
a little false and frigid	有些冷淡和虚伪
the whole crowd	所有人
knew you did it	都知道是你干的
Oh no more horses horses	哦没什么群马了没有马
you're going to swim like a fish	你像条鱼似的游走
into the hole in which	钻进那个洞里
you planned to ditch me	打算在那儿甩了我

I was your victim	我是你的受害者
I was well deceived	被你结结实实给骗了
hell's built on regrets	地狱建在遗憾上
and I hold too many	这种遗憾我攒着太多
I love your naked neck	我爱你裸露的脖颈
and the lies you've told me	还有你对我说过的谎言
You aren't two-faced	你不是个两面派
you have two faces	你就长着两张脸
the face of an angel	一张天使之脸
with the mark of a devil	烙着恶魔的印记
You filled me with a vengeance	你让我被复仇的欲望填满
touched me with your breath	用你的呼吸抚摸我
planned to leave me cold	盘算着冷酷丢下我
but you'll never get your wish	但你永远无法得逞
I'm going to pull you from the dance	我要把你从舞会上扯出来
you writhe you ride so easily	你翻滚你骑马那么轻易
Gather up the reins with my fist	我用拳头把缰绳收起来
Oh no more horses horses	哦没什么群马了没有马

23

you're going to swim like a fish

into the hole in which

you tried to ditch me

my lovely Vera

你像条鱼似的游走

钻进那个洞里

打算在那儿甩了我

我可爱的维拉

1 本曲收录于"蓝牡蛎崇拜"（Blue Öyster Cult）乐队 1976 年的专辑《命运代理人》
（*Agents of Fortune*），帕蒂·史密斯为其创作歌词并参与了演唱录制。该专辑也
是"蓝牡蛎崇拜"乐队商业上最成功的一张。

CAREER OF EVIL

I plot your rubric scarab,   我画下你的红色圣甲虫 [2]，

I steal your satellite   偷走你的人造卫星

I want your wife to be my   我要你的老婆变成我的

Baby tonight, baby tonight   宝贝就今晚，宝贝就今晚

I choose to steal   你秀出什么东西

What you chose to show   我就偷什么

And you know   你知道

I will not apologize   我不会道歉

You're mine for the taking   你就是我的猎物

I'm making a career of evil   我投身于罪恶生涯

Pay me I'll be your surgeon   给钱我就帮你开个刀

I'd like to pick your brain   我很乐意挖开你大脑

Capture you inject you   抓住你给你打针

Leave you kneeling in the rain   让你双膝跪在大雨中

Kneeling in the rain   跪在大雨中

I choose to steal   你秀出什么东西

What you chose to show   我就偷什么

And you know   你知道

25

I will not apologize	我不会道歉
You're mine for the taking	你就是我的猎物
I'm making a career of evil	我投身于罪恶生涯
I'd like your blue-eyed horseshoe	我想要你的蓝眼睛马蹄铁
I'd like your emerald horny toad	我想要你祖母绿色的角蟾
I'll leave all that you value	我会把所有你珍视的东西
By the side of the road	全都扔到大街边
And then I'd spend your ransom money,	接着我要花光你的赎金，
But still I'd keep your sheep	还要霸占你的羊
I'd peel the mask you're wearing	我要剥掉你戴的面具
And then rob you of your sleep	还要抢走你的睡眠
Rob you of your sleep	抢走你的睡眠
I choose to steal	你秀出什么东西
What you chose to show	我就偷什么
And you know	你知道
I will not apologize	我不会道歉
You're mine for the taking	你就是我的猎物

I'm making a career of evil

—*recorded by Blue Oyster Cult*

我投身于罪恶生涯

——收录于"蓝牡蛎崇拜"乐队《秘密条约》

1 帕蒂创作这首歌的灵感来自法国诗人洛特雷阿蒙的《马尔多罗之歌》。2015 年，J. K. 罗琳将自己以笔名罗伯特·加尔布雷思创作的推理小说命名为与本歌同名的《罪恶生涯》，并在书中多处引用了"蓝牡蛎崇拜"乐队的歌词。

2 圣甲虫被古埃及人认为是太阳神凯布利的化身，常被雕刻用作护身符。

PISS FACTORY

Sixteen and time to pay off I got this job in a piss factory inspecting pipe Forty hours thirty-six dollars a week but it's a paycheck, jack. It's so hot in here hot like sahara You could faint in the heat but these bitches are just too lame to understand too goddamn grateful to get this job to know they're getting screwed up the ass.

All these women they got no teeth or gum or cranium And the way they suck hot sausage but me well I wasn't sayin' too much neither I was moral school girl hard-working asshole I figured I was speedo motorcycle had to earn my dough had to earn my dough.

But no you gotta relate, right, you gotta find the rhythm within Floor boss slides up to me and he says Hey sister, you just movin' too fast. You screwin' up the quota. You doin' your piece work too fast. Now you get off your mustang sally, you ain't goin' nowhere, you ain't goin' nowhere.

I lay back. I get my nerve up. I take a swig of romilar and walk up to hot shit Dot Hook and I say Hey, hey sister, it don't matter whether I do labor fast or slow, there's always more labor after. She's real Catholic, see. She fingers her cross and she says There's one

撒尿工厂 [1]

十六岁到了养活自己的时候我找到一份在撒尿工厂上班检查管道的活儿每周干四十小时拿三十六美元但这好歹是份儿薪水，杰克。工厂里太热了热得就像撒哈拉沙漠这热气简直能让你晕倒但这些婊子们太差劲了完全无法理解对能有这么个活儿干就他妈的感激不尽了她们不知道自己被耍得团团转。

这些女人要么没有牙要么没有牙床要么没有头盖骨还有她们吮吸辣香肠的方式简直了不过好吧我没什么太多可说的我也不是什么有道德的女学生勤奋工作的小混蛋我想我就是辆飞速小摩托必须赚我自己的票子必须赚我自己的票子。

但是不行你得把它们联系起来，好吧，你必须找到其中的韵律楼层管事儿的滑到我身边他对我说嘿小妹，你走动得太快了。你把配额都搞乱了。你把自己的活儿干得太快了。现在从你的"野马莎莉"[2]上滚下来，你哪儿也去不了，哪儿也去不了。

我躺下去。壮起胆子来。我吞下一大口止咳药走到牛哄哄的"点钩"身边我说嘿，嘿小妹，我干活儿快或慢都无所谓，因为总有更多的活儿等着要干。她是个真正的天主教徒，

reason. There's one reason. You do it my way or I push your face in. We knee you in the john if you don't get off your mustang, Sally, if you don't shake it up baby. Shake it up baby. Twist and shout. Oh would that I could will a radio here. James Brown singing I Lost Someone. Oh the Paragons and the Jesters and Georgie Woods the guy with the goods and Guided Missiles . . . but no, I got nothin', no diversion, no window nothing here but a porthole in the plaster in the plaster where I look down look down at sweet Theresa's convent all those nurses all those nuns scattin''round with their bloom hoods like cats in mourning oh to me they look pretty damn free down there down there not having to press those smooth not having to smooth those hands against hot steel not having to worry about the inspeed the dogma the inspeed of labor oh they look pretty damn free down there and the way they smell the way the way they smell and here I gotta be up here smellin' Dot Hook's midwife sweat.

I would rather smell the way boys smell oh those schoolboys the way their legs flap under the desk in study hall that odor rising roses and ammonia and the way their dicks droop like lilacs. Or the way they smell that forbidden acrid smell. But no I got a pink

明白吧。她手指挑玩着十字架对我说有一个理由。有一个理由。按我说的干要不我就把你脸塞进马桶里。要是不从你的"野马"上滚下来，莎莉，我们就把你塞进马桶里，要是你不赶紧听话宝贝儿。赶紧听话宝贝儿。扭动啊尖叫。哎要是能在这儿装个收音机该多好。詹姆斯·布朗[3]唱的《我失去了某个人》。噢还有"十全十美"乐队还有"杰斯特"[4]乐队还有乔吉·伍兹[5]那个有好货的人还有《跟踪导弹》[6]……但是没有，我什么都没有，没有消遣，没有窗户这里什么都没有只有石膏墙上的一扇舷窗在石膏墙上在这儿我向下看向下看到好心的特蕾莎修女的修道院所有那些护士所有那些修女戴着她们花哨的头套走来走去就像一群披麻戴孝的猫哦我看她们相当他妈的清闲在这下面在这下面不用把它们压平整不用对着灼热的钢管抛光那些手不用操心速度和教条不用操心干活的速度哦在这下面她们看上去相当他妈的清闲还有她们闻起来那味道那味道她们闻起来那味道在这儿我不得不在这儿闻"点钩"身上接生婆似的臭汗味儿。

我宁愿去闻男孩们身上的臭味儿哦学校自习室里的男孩儿们双腿在桌子底下拍拍打打气味随之腾起是玫瑰混杂着氨气的味道他们的小鸡鸡耷拉着就像紫丁香花。或是他们身

piss factory

16 and time to pay off. I got this job in a piss factory
inspecting pipe. sweating my balls off in this hot like
sahara with no windows xxx real bullshit but its a paycheck
you could faint with the heat but the bitches are too lame
to understand they're getting screwed up the ass too god damn
grateful to get this job them with no teeth gripping gum
or cranium.nothing upstairs the way they suck hot sausage
but then i wasnt saying too much neither.i was moral asshole
hard working school girlgotta earn my doe. no. you gotta
play by the rules find the rythumn within them you got to
relate. floor boss says hey you did your piecework to fast
quit screwing up the quota get off your mustang sa,ly you
aint going nowhere.i swig some romalar and get my nerve up
and put it to hot shit Dot Hook, say hey sister i get bored
it dont matter whether you do labor fast or slow theres always
more after. shes no catholic she says there is ONE REASon
chicken do it my way or i push your face in. we may knee ya
in da john if you dont shape up baby. shake it up baby slow
motion inspection is driving me insane. no windows no diversion
would i could will a radio james brown singing I lost someone
hy lit georgie woods the guy with the goods and guided missles.
nothing here save a porthole in the plaster overlooking sweet
teresa convent. nuns in bloom hoods scatting like sats in
mourning. to me they look pretty damn free out there lucky
not to smooth those hands against hot steel free from the
dogma the in-speed of labor. every afternoon like the last
one like re-run lapping up Dot Hooks midwife sweat some
sound track I prefer the way fags smell and spades and dagos
school boys in heat. the way their legs flap under the desk
in study hall and that forbidden acrid lean amonia smell lilacs
the way they droop like dicks.how long am i condemned to pump
my nostrils full of clammy lady. me i refuse to sweat all i
got under my armpits are a few salt lick hairs peeking like pubes
peeking from my sleeveless I refuse to sweat its 110 degrees
in here i refuse to faint they're all waiting but i aintgonna
faint see the monotany is even more brutal hour after hour
in this piss factory more than ever my fists are assembled I
refuse to lose nothing here to hide save desire hide here save
desire. lucky i lifted rimbauds illuminations from the paper
back forum. it was the face on the cover see rimbauds hair
his sailor face. faire than any boy on the block i was seeing.
my salvation my nosegay the words rocked sex smells coming on
like my brothers sheets before the bath what did i care what
he was saying it was the sound the music the way he was saying
it his words over and over in my skull when I was pumping stel
and she was pumping steel we looked the same but i was getting
my first brain fuck illuminations my salvation oh stolen book
no crime since has been so sweet no perfume ever to fill my nose
no snow no more light then the simple knowledge of you rimbaud
sailor face stolen book hidden inside my blouse so close
to my breast.

clammy lady in my nostril. Her against the wheel me against the wheel Oh slow motion inspection is drivin' me insane in steel next to Dot Hook oh we may look the same shoulder to shoulder sweatin' hundred and ten degrees But I will never faint. They laugh and they expect me to faint but I will never faint I refuse to lose refuse to fall down because you see it's the monotony that's got to me every afternoon like the last one every afternoon like a rerun next to Dot Hook and yeah we look the same both pumpin' steel both sweatin'.

But you know she got nothin' to hide and I got something to hide here called desire I got something to hide here called desire. And I will get out of here you know the fear potion is just about to come. In my nose is the taste of sugar and I got nothin' to hide here save desire And I'm gonna go I'm gonna get out of here I'm gonna get on that train and go to New York City and I'm gonna be somebody I'm gonna get on that train and go to New York City and I'm gonna be so bad. I'm gonna be a big star and I will never return never return no never return to burn at this Piss factory. And I will travel light Oh watch me now.

上的味道那股被禁止的刺鼻味道。但是不要啦我鼻眼儿里塞着一个粉红色的黏湿淑女。她靠着机轮我靠着机轮哦慢动作的检查真要把我逼疯了靠近"点钩"的铁管旁哦我们可能看起来是一样的肩膀靠着肩膀汗流浃背一百一十华氏度 [7] 但我绝对不会晕倒。他们嘲笑我他们盼着我晕倒但我永远不会晕倒我拒绝失败拒绝倒下去因为你看是这种单调乏味让我崩溃每一个午后都像上一个午后的重演都要回到"点钩"身边是啊我们看起来都一样都在泵着钢水都在流着汗。

你知道她没什么好隐藏的然而我在这儿有些东西要隐藏它叫作欲望我在这儿有些东西要隐藏它叫作欲望。我会离开这里的你知道那治疗恐惧的药水马上就要到手了。我鼻子里是糖果的味道除了欲望我没什么好隐藏的我要走了我要离开这里我要搭上火车去纽约我要出人头地我要搭上那辆火车去纽约我要变得特别厉害。我要成为超级明星我永远不会回来永远不回来不永远不回到这座撒尿工厂里被烧焦。我要轻装离开哦现在就看我的吧。

1 《撒尿工厂》最早是帕蒂创作的一首诗,讲述自己青少年时期在一家婴儿车工厂做暑假工赚钱的经历,她渴望逃离这样的生活,去纽约实现自己的梦想。1974年11月,帕蒂发布处女单曲专辑《嘿,乔》(Hey Joe),在这张专辑的B面,加入了重新修订及编曲的《撒尿工厂》。

2 美国著名爵士乐歌手迈克·莱斯(Mack Rice)曾于1965年创作并推出单曲《野马莎莉》("Mustang Sally")。

3 詹姆斯·布朗(James Brown,1933—2006),美国著名歌手、作曲家、唱片制作人,有"灵魂乐教父"之称,对20世纪流行乐有极深影响。他于1961年发行了著名单曲《我失去了某个人》("Lost Someone")。

4 "十全十美"乐队(The Paragons),1960年代的牙买加慢摇滚队。"杰斯特"乐队(The Jesters),1950年代末的美国的一支嘟·喔普(Doo-wop)乐队,嘟·喔普是一种节奏布鲁斯音乐风格。

5 乔吉·伍兹(Georgie Woods,1927—2005),美国著名电台广播主持人,听众昵称他为"有好货的人"。

6 "Guided Missiles","袖扣"乐队(The Cuff Links)发布于1956年的单曲。

7 约43.33摄氏度。

THE ALBUMS

HORSES

群 马

*Three chords merged with
the power of the word.*

三个和弦融合词语的能量。

1975年11月10日，《群马》问世。少有艺术家像帕蒂·史密斯一样，在首张专辑便展露出如此野心。那是朋克摇滚形成雏形的年代。在此背景之下，《群马》在音乐上使用相对简单的和弦进行，结合即兴演奏，凭借与先锋和其他音乐风格的碰撞打破朋克传统。帕蒂大声读出她的诗、故事及向偶像的致敬之词，吉他手莱尼·凯指导乐队的演奏。两人初识于1971年《爵士与流行》（Jazz & Pop）杂志的一场分享会上。此后在帕蒂的邀请下，帕蒂与莱尼开始了长达三十余年的音乐合作。他们从最初的两人到逐渐组成一支完整的乐队，而这支乐队，后来站上了70年代纽约下城包厘街上的传奇朋克俱乐部 CBGB 舞台，一举获得关注。也正是以此为契机，帕蒂与卢·里德所在的爱丽斯塔唱片公司（Arista Record）签约，开始了第一张专辑《群马》的录制。

这样的即兴演奏并不像人们所想的简单。在2011年《独立报》（The Independent）的一篇采访中，莱尼回忆，"那是具有对抗性的，一股不可改变的力量与一个不可改变的物体。但依旧，一些创造性的东西诞生了。在推拉之间。"

在歌曲内容上，《群马》是私人的。帕蒂写下《雷东多海滩》，在与妹妹琳达发生了一场激烈争执后。琳达从她们合住的公寓夺门而出，直到第二天才回来。《金伯莉》写给帕蒂最年幼的妹妹，歌里，帕蒂再度将金伯莉搂在臂弯。《天降横财》一曲中，帕蒂回忆在新泽西贫苦的童年，母亲常常幻想赢得彩票。

而《群马》亦是开阔的。歌词中，帕蒂向摇滚、文学偶像致敬。她在一场通往诗人吉姆·莫里森墓地的梦之后，与"电视"乐队主唱汤姆·维莱恩写下《打破它》，向吉姆高喊，要"打破"困住他的巨石。《悲歌》录制于摇滚乐手吉米·亨德里克斯去世五周年纪念日。她将好友威廉·巴勒斯的小说《野孩子》中的男孩约翰尼带至她的《大地》，也在那里呼喊诗人兰波。

在滚石杂志评选的五百大专辑中，《群马》名列44位。问世以来，它影响了无数摇滚乐队，在首年售出近20万张。人们称它为第一张"真正"的朋克专辑。

IN EXCELSIS DEO

Jesus died for somebody's sins but not mine	耶稣为别人的罪而死不是为我的
Melting in a pot of thieves wild card up my sleeve	熔在一锅贼里狂野是我袖中王牌
Thick heart of stone my sins my own	铁石了心肠我的罪我自己扛
They belong to me. Me	它们只属于我。我
People say beware but I don't care	人们说要当心但我不在乎
The words are just rules and regulations to me. Me	这些话对我只是陋习陈规。对我
I walk in a room you know I look so proud	我走进房间你知道我看上去多骄傲
I move in this here atmosphere where anything's allowed	我踏入这里氛围变成一切无所禁忌
Then I go to this here party but I just get bored	接着我闯进这个派对但只感到无聊
Until I look out the window see a sweet young thing	直到望向窗外我看到那甜美的年轻尤物
Humping on the parking meter leaning on the parking meter	后背顶着停车码表身体斜靠着停车码表
Oh, she looks so good. Oh, she looks so fine	哦，她甜蜜极了。哦，她美好极了
And I got this crazy feeling that I'm gonna make her mine	我冒出个疯狂念头要把她占为己有
Oh I put my spell on her here she comes	哦我对她施下魔咒她来了
Walking down the street here she comes	沿街走过来她来了
Coming through my door here she comes	穿过我的大门她来了
Crawling up my stair here she comes	爬上我的楼梯她来了
Waltzing through the hall in a pretty red dress	身穿美丽红裙跳着华尔兹穿过大厅
And oh, she looks so good. Oh, she looks so fine	哦，她甜蜜极了。哦，她美好极了

And I got this crazy feeling that I'm gonna make her mine

我冒出个疯狂念头要把她占为己有

Then I hear this knocking on my door hear this knocking at my door

忽然我听到一阵敲门声听到一阵敲门声

And I look up at the big tower clock and say oh my God it's midnight

我抬头看眼大塔钟说哦老天午夜已到

And my baby is walking through the door laying on my couch

我的宝贝穿过大门躺在沙发上

She whispers to me and I take the big plunge

她对我轻声耳语我冒险坠入她怀抱

And oh, she was so good. And oh, she was so fine

哦，她那么甜蜜。哦，她那么美好

And I'm gonna tell the world that I just made her mine

我要告诉整个世界我刚刚将她占为己有

It was at the stadium. There were twenty thousand girls

体育场里。站着两万个女孩儿

Called their names out to me Marie Ruth but to tell you the truth

冲我大喊她们的名字玛丽·露丝说实话吧

I didn't hear them. I didn't see. I let my eyes rise to the big tower clock

我听不见。我看不见。我的眼睛爬升到大塔钟

And I heard those bells chiming in my heart going ding-dong

听到钟声在我心里齐鸣奏响 叮——咚

Ding-dong ding-dong ding-dong ding-dong ding-dong ding-dong

叮——咚 叮——咚 叮——咚 叮——咚 叮——咚 叮——咚

Ding-dong. Calling the time when you came to my room

叮——咚。准点报时你来到我的房间

And you whispered to me and we took the big plunge

你对我轻声耳语我们冒险坠入彼此怀抱

And oh, you were so good. Oh, you were so fine

哦，你那么甜蜜。哦，你那么美好

And I've got to tell the world that I made ya mine made ya mine

我必须告诉整个世界你是我的了你是我的

Made her mine made ya mine made her mine made ya mine

她是我的你是我的她是我的你是我的

G-L-O-R-I-A Gloria

G–L–O–R–I–A 格洛莉娅

"Gloria" was bred by crossing the poem "Oath," written in 1970, with the Van Morrison classic. "Gloria" gave me the opportunity to acknowledge and disclaim our musical and spiritual heritage. It personifies for me, within its adolescent conceit, what I hold sacred as an artist. The right to create, without apology, from a stance beyond gender or social definition, but not beyond the responsibility to create something of worth.

G-L-O-R-I-A Gloria

G-L-O-R-I-A Gloria

When the tower bells chime

ding-dong they chime

I said that Jesus died

for somebody's sins

but not mine

G-L-O-R-I-A 格洛莉娅

G-L-O-R-I-A 格洛莉娅

高塔上钟声响起

叮——咚 齐鸣

我说耶稣为

别人的罪而死

不是为我的

《荣归主颂》的创作灵感来源于我 1970 年写作的诗歌《誓言》，以及范·莫里森[2]的经典歌曲《格洛莉娅》。这首歌给了我一个机会去认可同时摒弃我们的音乐以及精神遗产。对我而言，在青春期的自负中，它代表了我作为一个艺术家所持守的神圣理念：拥有去创造的权利，无须道歉，超越性别或社会规范的立场，但不推卸需要创造有价值之物的责任。

---

1 荣归主颂（拉丁语：Gloria in Excelsis Deo），或译"大荣耀颂"，天主教称"光荣颂"，是基督宗教用于礼仪的一首诗歌，是礼文的一部分。歌词是从《圣经·新约》的《路加福音》第 2 章第 14 节衍出的赞词，在 2 世纪中已开始流传，并由教宗西玛克最先把它放入重大节庆的弥撒之中。

2 范·莫里森（Van Morrison，1945—），北爱尔兰著名音乐人，1993 年入选摇滚名人堂。

REDONDO BEACH

雷东多海滩 [1]

Late afternoon dreaming hotel	接近傍晚在梦想的酒店
We just had the quarrel that sent you away	我们吵了一架你生气离开
I was looking for you are you gone gone	我在四处找你你真走了吗走了吗
Call you on the phone another dimension	打电话给你像打去另一个次元
Well you never returned oh you know what I mean	好吧你再也不回来了哦你明白我意思
I went looking for you are you gone gone	我四处去找你你真走了吗走了吗
Down by the ocean it was so dismal	在海边真是太凄凉了
Women all standing with shock on their faces	女人们满脸震惊地站在那里
Sad description oh I was looking for you	悲伤的描述哦我在四处寻找你
Everyone was singing girl is washed up	人人都在唱歌那女孩从海里漂到了
On Redondo Beach and everyone is so sad	雷东多海滩所有人都伤感
I was looking for you are you gone gone	我在四处找你你真走了吗走了吗
Pretty little girl everyone cried	美丽的小女孩人人都在哭泣
She was the victim of sweet suicide	她是这场甜蜜自杀的牺牲品
I went looking for you are you gone gone	我四处去找你你真走了吗走了吗
Down by the ocean it was so dismal	在海边真是太凄凉了

Women all standing with shock on their faces	女人们满脸震惊地站在那里
Sad description oh I was looking for you	悲伤的描述哦我在四处寻找你
Desk clerk told me girl was washed up	前台服务员对我说那女孩从海里漂上来
Was small and angel with apple blonde hair now	身体小小的，现在是个长着苹果色金发的天使
I went looking for you are you gone gone	我四处去找你你真走了吗走了吗
Picked up my key didn't reply	拿起钥匙我没说话
Went to my room started to cry	回到房间我开始流泪
You were small and angel are you gone gone	你是小小的天使你真走了吗走了吗
Down by the ocean it was so dismal	在海边真是太凄凉了
I was just standing with shock on my face	我满脸震惊地站在那里
The hearse pulled away	灵车渐行渐远
The girl that had died it was you	刚刚死去的那女孩就是你
You'll never return into my arms	你永远无法回到我的怀抱
'Cause you are gone gone	因为你真的走了走了
Never return into my arms	永远无法回到我的怀抱
'Cause you are gone gone	因为你真的走了走了
Gone gone gone gone	走了 走了 走了 走了

Good-bye   永——别——了

1 雷东多海滩，美国加利福尼亚州洛杉矶下属的一座海滨城市，美国著名休闲城市。
帕蒂在接受《纽约客》杂志采访时谈到，这首歌词写作于 1971 年，当时她的妹
妹琳达正借住于帕蒂和罗伯特租住于纽约切尔西酒店的公寓内，一个下午，帕蒂
与琳达发生了罕有的争吵，琳达离开公寓彻夜未回。帕蒂乘坐 F 线火车独自前往
科尼岛，在那里的一片小海滩上坐了一整夜直到天亮，回家后写出了这首歌词。
琳达随后回到公寓，帕蒂给她看了这首歌词以后，她们再也没有争吵过。

the women were singing
of a girl who was watched

...Veins full of existance —   sad description /but oh I was
...like the son of a neck   Rilke   You   listening for

Shape of a young man dressed in a coat of
milk.

(Telling

Redondo Beach   the women were talking
it was late afternoon   They turned to tell me
dreaming Hotel   This girl was washed
we had just had the quarrel   up/on Redondo Beach
that sent you away   and everyone was so
I was looking for you—ou   sad—
and you were gone gone   pretty little girl
                                 everyone cried
called you on the phone   she was the victim
Johnny no answer   of sweet suicide
she never returned
oh you know what I mean mon   The desk clerk told
I was etc.   me
                                  The girl who
down by the ocean it was so dismal   called Johnny
women standing w/ shock on their faces small and
sad description /but oh I was looking   angel
for you—   w/ apple blonde
                                  hair
                        she

BIRDLAND

鸟园 [1]

His father died and left him a little farm in New England.

All the long black funeral cars left the scene.

And the boy was just standing there alone

Looking at the shiny red tractor

Him and his daddy used to sit inside

And circle the blue fields and grease the night.

It was as if someone had spread butter

On all the fine points of the stars

'Cause when he looked up they started to slip.

Then he put his head in the crux of his arm

And he started to drift, drift to the belly of a ship

Let the ship slide open, and he went inside of it

And saw his daddy behind the control board

Streaming beads of light.

He saw his daddy behind the control board

And he was very different tonight

'Cause he was not human, he was not human.

The little boy's face lit up with such naked joy

That the sun burned around his lids and his eyes were like two suns

White lids, white opals, seeing everything just a little bit too clearly

父亲死后给他留下新英格兰的一座小农场。

所有长长的黑色殡仪车都离开了。

只有男孩自己孤独地站在那里

看着那辆发亮的红色拖拉机

他和父亲曾经一起坐在里面

在蓝色的田野中旋绕，滑润着夜晚。

仿佛有人在星辰的所有

细微之处都涂满了黄油

因为每当他抬头看时它们便溜走。

他把脑袋藏进肘窝

然后他开始飘荡，飘向飞船腹中

舱门滑动着打开，他走进去

看到爸爸站在控制台后面

涌动出点点珠光。

他看到爸爸站在控制台后面

爸爸今晚看着很不一样

因为他并非人类，他并非人类。

小男孩脸庞被赤裸的喜悦点燃

日光灼烫着他的眼睑，双眼宛如两轮太阳

白色眼睑，白色猫眼石，万物看起来太过清晰

And he looked around and there was no black ship in sight

No black funeral cars, nothing except for him the raven

And he fell on his knees and looked up and cried out

No, daddy, don't leave me here alone

Take me up, daddy, to the belly of your ship

Let the ship slide open and I'll go inside of it

Where you're not human, you are not human.

But nobody heard the boy's cry of alarm.

Nobody there except for the birds around the New England farm

And they gathered in all directions, like roses they scattered

And they were like compass grass coming together into the head of

A shaman bouquet. Slit in his nose and all the others went shooting

And he saw the lights of traffic beckoning like the hands of Blake

Grabbing at his cheeks, taking out his neck, all his limbs

Everything was twisted and he said:

I won't give up, won't give up, don't let me give up

I won't give up, come here, let me go up fast

Take me up quick, take me up, up to the belly of a ship

And the ship slides open and I go inside of it

Where I am not human.

他四处环顾，视线内并没有黑色飞船

没有黑色殡仪车，除他和渡鸦外什么都没有

他双膝跪地抬起头来大声呼喊

不，爸爸，别把我一个人丢在这里

带我走吧，爸爸，去你飞船的腹中

舱门滑动着打开，我会走进去

在那儿你不是人类，你不是人类。

然而无人听到男孩惊恐的哭喊。

除了绕着新英格兰农场飞翔的群鸟外这里空无一人

它们从四面八方聚集，如散落开的玫瑰花瓣

它们像沙茅草般聚拢在一起钻进

萨满花束的头顶。钻进他鼻子的狭缝，其他的流弹般散去

他看到车流的亮光冲他召唤仿佛布莱克的大手

捏住他脸颊，掐住他脖子，他四肢

万物都在扭曲而他说道：

我不会放弃，不会放弃，别叫我放弃

我不会放弃，过来吧，让我快速飞升

快带我走，带我走，去那飞船的腹中

舱门滑动着打开，我会走进去

在那儿我不再是人类。

I am helium raven and this movie is mine

So he cried out as he stretched the sky

Pushing it all out like latex cartoon

Am I all alone in this generation?

We'll just be dreaming of animation night and day

It won't let up, won't let up and I see them coming in

Oh, I couldn't hear them before, but I hear them now

It's a radar scope in all silver and all platinum lights

Moving in like black ships

They were moving in, streams of them

And he put up his hands and he said:

It's me, it's me, I'll give you my eyes, take me up

Oh now please take me up, I'm helium raven

Waiting for you, please take me up, don't leave me here.

The son, the sign, the cross, like the shape of a tortured woman

The true shape of a tortured woman, the mother standing

In the doorway letting her sons, no longer presidents but prophets.

They're all dreaming they're going to bear the prophet

He's going to run through the fields dreaming in animation

It's all going to split his skull, it's going to come out

我是氦气渡鸦这部电影属于我

他大声呼喊，把天空抻展开

像乳胶卡通片那样把它全部推出去

这一代人只有我是这样的吗？

日夜沉浸在漫画的梦境里

它不会停止，不会停止，我看到它们进来了

哦，之前我无法听到它们，现在我听见了

全银色的雷达显示器，散发着铂金色的光

像黑色飞船驶过来

它们驶过来，湍流不断

他举起双手然后说道：

是我，是我，我把眼睛给你们，带我走吧

哦现在就请带我走吧，我是氦气渡鸦

在这等着你们，请带我走吧，别把我丢在这里。

儿子，符号，十字架，仿如一个受尽折磨的女人

一个受尽折磨女人的真正面目，那母亲站在

大门口任由她的儿子们，不再成为总统而是先知。

他们都在做梦，他们要承受先知的命运

他将奔跑穿越田野，热烈地做梦

这会割开他的头骨，从里面奔涌而出

Like a black bouquet shining, like a fist that's going to shoot them up

Like light, like Mohammed Boxer, take them up up up up up.

Oh, let's go up up take me up I'll go up I'm going up I'm going up.

Take me up, I'm going up, I'll go up.

Go up go up go up go up up up up up up up

Up, up to the belly of a ship. Let the ship slide open.

We'll go inside of it where we are not human, we are not human.

Where there was sand, there were tiles

The sun had melted the sand and it coagulated like a river of glass

When it hardened he looked at the surface, he saw his face

And where there were eyes were just two white opals, two white opals

Where there were eyes there were just two white opals

And he looked up, and the rays shot, and he saw raven coming in

And he crawled on his back and he went up up up up up up up.

Sha da do wop da shaman do way sha da do wop da shaman do way

Sha da do wop da shaman do way sha da do wop da shaman do way

We like birdland.

像一捧闪耀的黑色花束，像一只赶尽杀绝的拳头

像光线，像拳击手穆罕默德[2]，带他们飞升 飞 飞 飞 飞 飞。

哦，我们飞升吧飞升带我飞升我将飞升我在飞升我在飞升。

带我飞升吧，我在飞升，我将飞升。

飞升 飞升 飞升 飞升 飞 飞 飞 飞 飞 飞 飞

飞，飞到那条飞船腹中。舱门滑动着打开。

我们会走进去在那里我们不是人类，我们不是人类。

哪里有沙子，哪里就有瓷砖

烈日融化沙土，凝结成玻璃之河

当河变得坚硬他看着那河面，看到自己的脸

那里有两只眼睛只有两只白色猫眼石，两只白色猫眼石

那里有两只眼睛只有两只白色猫眼石

他抬起头，光线射出，他看到渡鸦飞进来

他匍匐着爬行然后就这样飞升起来 飞 飞 飞 飞 飞 飞。

Sha da do wop da shaman do way sha da do wop da shaman do way

Sha da do wop da shaman do way sha da do wop da shaman do way[3]

我们喜欢鸟园。

1 《鸟园》的灵感来源于美国心理学家、弗洛伊德主义代表人物威廉·赖希（Wilhelm Reich, 1897—1957）的传记《梦想之书》（*A Book of Dreams*），由他的儿子彼得·赖希撰写。书中写道，在父亲死后不久，彼得坚信父亲会开宇宙飞船将自己带走，但发现自己以为的不明飞行物实际上是一群黑鸟。帕蒂读后深受触动，写作了这首歌词。帕蒂曾提到，她四五岁时相信自己是外星人，因为她又高又瘦，跟身边的人甚至家人都很不一样。此外，"鸟园"也是纽约一家著名的爵士乐俱乐部的名字。该俱乐部创办于 1949 年，是纽约五大爵士乐俱乐部之一，也曾是美国"垮掉派"作家诗人热衷聚会的地点。

2 指穆罕默德·阿里（Muhammad Ali, 1942—2016），美国著名男子拳击手。

3 这段拟声唱词出自美国摇滚歌手恰比·却克（Chubby Checker）1962 年发行的歌曲《鸟园》（"Birdland"）。

FREE MONEY

Every night before I go to sleep

Find a ticket win a lottery

Scoop the pearls up from the sea

Cash them in and buy you

All the things you need

Every night before I rest my head

See those dollar bills go swirling 'round my bed

I know they're stolen but I don't feel bad

I take that money buy you things you never had

Oh baby it would mean so much to me

Oh baby to buy you all the things you need for free

I'll buy you a jet plane baby

Get you on a higher plane to a jet stream

And take you through the stratosphere

And check out the planets there

And then take you down deep deep

Where it's hot hot in Arabia-babia

Then cool cold fields of snow. And we'll roll

天降横财

每一晚我睡觉前

都捡到彩票中大奖

挖出海里的珍珠来

卖掉它们赚到钱

你要什么都给你买

每一晚我休息前

看到钞票绕着床打转

我知道那是偷来的但我没觉得有多坏

我收下钱给你买你从来没有过的东西

哦宝贝这对我来说太有意义了

哦宝贝天降横财你要什么都给你买

我要给你买架喷气机宝贝

让你飞得更高骑上喷射气流

带你穿越同温层

看看那里的行星

带你下降到深深处

去酷热的阿拉伯 – 巴比亚

再去酷爽的寒冷雪原。我们旋转

49

Dream roll dream roll roll dream dream

梦境旋转梦境旋转旋转梦境梦境

When we dream it when we dream it when we dream it

当我们梦到它当我们梦到它当我们梦到它

We'll dream it dream it for free free money free money

我们会梦到它免费梦到它天降横财天降横财

Free money free money free money free money

天降横财天降横财天降横财天降横财

Every night before I go to sleep

每一晚我睡觉前

Find a ticket win a lottery

都捡到彩票中大奖

Every night before I rest my head

每一晚我休息前

See those dollar bills go swirling 'round my bed

看到钞票绕着床打转

Oh baby it would mean so much to me

哦宝贝这对我来说太有意义了

Baby I know our troubles will be gone

宝贝我知道我们的麻烦都会消失

Oh I know our troubles will be gone going gone

哦我知道我们的麻烦都会消失会消失

If we dream dream dream for free

只要我们免费做梦做梦做梦

And when we dream it when we dream it when we dream it

当我们梦到它当我们梦到它当我们梦到它

Let's dream it we'll dream it for free free money free money

让我们梦到它免费梦到它天降横财天降横财

Free money free money free money free money free money

天降横财天降横财天降横财天降横财天降横财

KIMBERLY

The wall is high the black barn

黑色谷仓高耸的墙

The babe in my arms in her swaddling clothes

我怀里的婴儿裹着她的襁褓

And I know soon that the sky will split

我知道很快天空就要裂开

And the planets will shift

群星将会挪转

Balls of jade will drop and existence will stop

玉球会坠落，存在将终止

Little sister the sky is falling

小妹妹天空正在塌陷

I don't mind I don't mind

我不在意我不在意

Little sister the fates are calling on you

小妹妹命运三女神在召唤你

Here I stand again in this old electric whirlwind

我又一次站在这里在古老的雷电旋风里

The sea rushes up my knees like flame

海水如火焰舔舐我膝盖

And I feel like just some misplaced Joan of Arc

我感觉自己像错位的圣女贞德

And the cause is you looking up at me

因为你正抬头望着我

Oh baby I remember when you were born

哦宝贝我还记得当你出生

It was dawn and the storm settled in my belly

黎明时分暴风雨在我腹中停歇下来

And I rolled in the grass and I spit out the gas

我在草地上翻滚嘴中吐出一口汽油

And I lit a match and the void went flash

点燃火柴虚空一闪而逝

And the sky split and the planets hit

天空开裂行星撞击大地

Balls of jade dropped and existence stopped

玉球坠落，存在终止

Little sister the sky is falling	小妹妹天空正在塌陷
I don't mind I don't mind	我不在意我不在意
Little sister the fates are calling on you	小妹妹命运三女神正在召唤你
I was young and crazy so crazy I knew	我年轻又疯狂太疯狂了我知道
I could break through with you	我可以跟你一起冲破一切
So with one hand I rocked you	我伸出手轻摇着你
And with one heart I reached for you	捧出一颗心靠近向你
Ah I knew your youth was for the taking	我知道你的青春就是要供人自由拿取
Fire on a mental plane so I ran through the fields	在心智之源熊熊燃烧因此我奔跑着穿越田野
As the bats with their baby vein faces	长着遍布静脉婴儿脸的蝙蝠
Burst from the barn in flames in the violent violet sky	冲出狂暴紫色天空下火焰缭绕的谷仓
And I fell on my knees and pressed you against me	我双膝跪地把你紧紧贴在怀里
Your skull was like a network of spittle	你的头骨像是唾液织出的网
Like glass balls moving in like cold streams of logic	像移动的玻璃球像冰冷的逻辑数据流
And I prayed as the lightning attacked	当闪电袭来，我祷告着
That something would make it go crack	希望有什么能击垮它
Something will make it go crack	希望有什么能击垮它
Something will make it go crack	希望有什么能击垮它
Something will make it go crack	希望有什么能击垮它

The palm trees fall into the sea	棕榈树跌落大海
It doesn't matter much to me	那跟我没什么太大关系
As long as you're safe Kimberly	只要你能够安全金伯莉
And I can gaze deep into your starry eyes	我深深凝视你繁星般闪亮的双眼
Looking deep in your eyes baby	深深望入你双眼宝贝
Looking deep in your eyes baby	深深望入你双眼宝贝
Looking deep in your eyes baby	深深望入你双眼宝贝
Into your starry eyes	望入你繁星般闪亮的双眼

1 金伯莉是帕蒂最年幼的妹妹，比帕蒂小 12 岁。帕蒂曾在接受采访时说金伯莉出生后没多久，他们居住的房子街对面有一个老旧的废弃谷仓被闪电击中起火了，帕蒂抱着襁褓中的妹妹，看到起火的谷仓中飞出成百只蝙蝠和一些猫头鹰。金伯莉后来成为一位吉他乐手及词曲作者，1970 年代帕蒂发布《群马》专辑后，金伯莉曾担任吉他手跟随姐姐进行巡演。

BREAK IT UP

打破它 [1]

Car stopped in a clearing	车子停在一片空地
Ribbon of life, it was nearing	生命的纽带，它在附近
I saw the boy break out of his skin	我看见那男孩从他皮囊里挣脱出来
My heart turned over and I crawled in	我的心翻腾着我爬进里面

He cried break it up, oh, I don't understand	他喊着打破它，哦，我不明白
Break it up, I can't comprehend	打破它，我无法理解
Break it up, oh, I want to feel you	打破它，哦，我想感受你
Don't talk to me that way	不要那样跟我说话
	我不想听

I'm not listening	
Snow started falling	雪花开始飘落
I could hear the angel calling	我听到天使在召唤
We rolled on the ground, he stretched out his wings	我们在地上翻滚，他展开翅膀
The boy flew away and he started to sing	那男孩飞走了，他开始歌唱

He sang break it up, oh, I don't understand	他唱道打破它，哦，我不明白
Break it up, I can't comprehend	打破它，我无法理解
Break it up, oh, I want to feel you	打破它，哦，我想感受你
Break it up, don't look at me	打破它，不要看着我

The sky was raging. The boy disappeared

天空暗潮汹涌。那男孩消失了

I fell on my knees. Atmosphere broke up

我跪倒在地。空气四散开去

The boy reappeared. I cried take me please

男孩再次出现。我喊着带我走吧求求你

Ice it was shining. I could feel my heart it was melting

冰块闪闪发亮。我的心在融化

I tore off my clothes, I danced on my shoes

我脱掉衣服，踏着鞋子起舞

I ripped my skin open and then I broke through, I cried

我撕开皮肤冲脱桎梏，高喊道

Break it up, oh, now I understand

打破它，哦，现在我明白了

Break it up, and I want to go

打破它，我想离开

Break it up, oh, please take me with you

打破它，哦，求求你带我一起走

Break it up, I can feel it breaking

打破它，我能感到它正在碎裂

I can feel it breaking, I can feel it breaking

我能感到它正在碎裂，我能感到它正在碎裂

I can feel, I can feel, I can feel, I can feel

我能感到，我能感到，我能感到，我能感到

So break it up, oh, now I'm coming with you

所以打破它吧，哦，现在我就跟你一起走

Break it up, now I'm going to go

打破它，现在我就要离开

Break it up, oh, feel me I'm coming

打破它，哦，感受我吧我来了

Break it up break it up break it up

打破它打破它打破它

Break it up break it up break it up

打破它打破它打破它

55

Break it up break it up break it up

—for Jim Morrison

打破它打破它打破它

——给吉姆·莫里森

1 帕蒂在一次采访中提到，这首歌的灵感来自她做过的一个关于吉姆·莫里森的梦，以及她去法国拉雪兹公墓拜访吉姆墓地的经历。帕蒂梦到生着翅膀的吉姆被一块大理石困住，她在吉姆身边高喊"打破它"，最终石头融化，吉姆成功挣脱，重获自由。

LAND

All the wisdom of the universe can be
found between the eyes of the horse.

—KORAN

Horses

The boy was in the hallway drinking a glass of tea
From the other end of the hallway a rhythm was generating
Another boy was sliding up the hallway
He merged perfectly with the hallway
He merged perfectly with the mirror in the hallway
The boy looked at Johnny Johnny wanted to run
but the movie kept moving as planned
The boy took Johnny he pressed him against the locker
He drove it in he drove it home he drove it deep in Johnny
The boy disappeared Johnny fell on his knees
started crashing his head against the locker
started crashing his head against the locker
started laughing hysterically

大地 [1]

宇宙间一切智慧均可于
马的双眼之间寻得

——《古兰经》

群马

男孩在走廊里喝着茶
走廊另一侧响起一段旋律
另一个男孩遛进走廊里
他跟走廊完美融合在一起
他跟走廊里的镜子完美融合在一起
那男孩看着约翰尼约翰尼想逃跑
但影片仍在照着计划运转
男孩抓住约翰尼把他按在储物柜上
他戳进去他戳到了要点他深深戳进约翰尼的身体里
那男孩消失了约翰尼跪倒在地
脑袋猛撞储物柜
脑袋猛撞储物柜
歇斯底里狂笑着

When suddenly Johnny | 突然间约翰尼

gets the feeling | 感觉到

he's being surrounded by | 身边围绕着

horses horses horses horses | 群马 群马 群马 群马

coming in all directions | 从四面八方而来

white shining silver studs with their nose in flames | 发白闪亮的银色种马，鼻子喷射出火焰

He saw horses horses horses | 他看到群马 群马 群马

horses horses horses horses horses | 群马 群马 群马 群马 群马

Land of a Thousand Dances | 千舞之地 [2]

Do you know how to pony like bony maroney | 你知道如何像瘦骨马罗尼 [3] 那样跳起小马舞吗

Do you know how to twist well it goes like this it goes like this | 你知道如何跳起扭扭舞吗就像这样就像这样

Then you mash potato do the alligator do the alligator | 然后是土豆泥舞鳄鱼舞还有鳄鱼舞

And you twista twista like your baby sister | 接着就扭啊扭啊像你小妹妹那样

I want your baby sister give me your baby sister teach your baby sister | 我想要你的小妹妹给我你的小妹妹教教你的小妹妹

To rise up from her knees do the sweet pea do the sweet pee pee | 伸直膝盖站起来跳起甜豌豆舞乖乖撒尿尿

Roll down on her back got to lose control got to lose control | 后背着地滚起来肯定要失控肯定要失控

Got to lose control and then you take control | 肯定要失控然后由你来接手

Got to lose control and then you take control | 换你后背着地滚起来

unraveling compacted awareness deep in the desert like the edge of a spider is johnnys pit of light he approaches a vat of liquid sun the sands coagulating and the arctic stain is the mirror the image obscured by ~~striking~~ nets of spittle. he parts the veil everything falling away like gauze rotted from the skeleton of soft gold. its the night of the pharoah and johnny grips him by his gold shoulders and drives it in deep in the desert chasing the desert his fingers stretch like rivers of blood veins and arteries and vague hoof beat thrashed wildly for an image they ~~turned like~~ screamed like a hall of mirrors swirling freedom pale blue eyes. men props issuing I took out his switchblade & burning coral ~~andy~~ opened the throat. some ~~mad~~ pituitary gasp

《创始之地》, 1973

Then you roll down on your back	你喜欢吗喜欢那样喜欢吗喜欢那样
Do you like it like that like it like that	再来段瓦图西舞哦耶来段瓦图西舞
Then you do the watusi yeah do the watusi	生活处处充满漏洞约翰尼躺在他的精子棺材里
Life is filled with holes Johnny's laying there in his sperm coffin	天使低头看着他说，啊漂亮男孩
Angel looks down at him and says ah pretty boy	除了投降外你就没别的什么能给我瞧了吗
Can't you show me nothing but surrender	约翰尼爬起来脱掉他的皮夹克
Johnny gets up takes off his leather jacket	答案被胶带贴在他胸膛
Taped to his chest there's the answer	他有铅笔小刀和折叠刀还有
He got pen knives and jack knives and	弹簧小折刀是首选弹簧小折刀是首选
Switchblades preferred switchblades preferred	他大喊他尖叫着说
He cries he screams says	生活充满痛苦我用它插穿我大脑
Life is full of pain I push it through my brain	用雪塞满我鼻子来吧兰波 [4]
And I fill my nose with snow and go Rimbaud	来吧兰波来吧兰波哦来吧约翰尼来吧
Go Rimbaud go Rimbaud oh go Johnny go	来段瓦图西舞哦来段瓦图西舞
And do the watusi oh do the watusi	
There's a little place a place called space	有个小地方一个叫作太空的地方
It's a pretty little place it's across the track	是个非常小的地方就在路对面
Across the track and the name of that place	就在路对面那地方的名字
Is I like it like that I like it like that	是我就喜欢它那样我就喜欢它那样
I like it like that I like it like that	我就喜欢它那样我就喜欢它那样
And the name of the band is	那乐队的名字是

Twistelette twistelette twistelette

Twistelette twistelette twistelette

扭扭莱特　扭扭莱特　扭扭莱特

扭扭莱特　扭扭莱特　扭扭莱特

La Mer (de)

大海[5]

Let it calm down let it calm down

让它平静让它平静

In the night in the eye of the forest

在这夜晚在森林眼中

There's a mare black and shining with yellow hair

有匹黑色母马她黄色的毛发闪耀着光亮

I put my fingers through her silken hair

我用手指拨弄她丝绸般柔顺的鬃毛

And found a stair I didn't waste time

一截楼梯出现我没有浪费时间

I just walked right up and saw that up there

径直走上去在那看到

There is a sea up there there is a sea up there

上面有一片海那上面有一片海

There is a sea seize the possibility

有一片海抓住了可能性

There is no land but the land

那里没有大地却是大地

[Up there is just a sea of possibilities]

［那上面就是一片可能性之海］

There is no sea but the sea

那里没有海洋却是海洋

[Up there is a wall of possibilities]

［那上面就是一堵可能性之墙］

There is no keeper but the key

那里没有守卫却有钥匙

[Up there there are several walls of possibilities]

［那上面是众多可能性之墙］

Except for one who seizes possibilities

只有一个人抓住了这可能性

I seize the first possibility the sea around me   我抓住了第一个可能性大海环绕着我

I was standing there with my legs spread like a sailor   我站在那里双腿像水手一样敞开

[In a sea of possibilities] I felt his hand on my knee   ［在可能性之海里］我感到他的手轻抚我膝盖

[On the screen] And I looked at Johnny   ［在银幕上］我望着约翰尼

And handed him a branch of coral flame   递给他一束珊瑚火焰

[In the heart of man] The waves were coming in   ［在男人心里］海浪阵阵涌来

Like Arabian stallions gradually lapping into sea horses   将阿拉伯种马渐渐拍打成海马

He picked up the blade and he pressed it against   他捡起刀片抵住自己

His smooth throat and let it dip in [the veins]   光滑的喉咙将它刺进［血管里］

Dip in to the sea the sea of possibilities   刺进大海里那可能性的大海

It started hardening it started hardening in my hand   它开始变得坚硬它在我手中变得坚硬

And I felt the arrows of desire   我感受到了欲望之箭

I put my hand inside his cranium, oh we had such a brainiac-amour   我把手伸进他头骨里，哦我们有这样一段头脑之爱

But no more, no more I gotta move from my mind to the area   但不会再有了，不再有了我得脱离我的思想去那个地方

[Go Rimbaud go Rimbaud go Rimbaud] Oh go Johnny go   ［来兰波来兰波来兰波］哦来啊约翰尼来吧

Do the watusi, yeah do the watusi do the watusi   来段瓦图西舞，哦耶来段瓦图西舞来段瓦图西舞

His skull shot open coiled snakes   他的头骨炸开群蛇盘缠

White and shiny twirling and encircling   白色闪亮扭动着绕圈圈

Our lives are now entwined we will four years be together   我们的生命如今彼此交缠会在一起共度四年

Your nerves the mane of the black shining horse   你的神经是那匹黑色闪耀骏马的鬃毛

And my fingers all entwined through your silky hair	我的手指与你丝绸般柔顺的毛发紧紧交缠
I could feel it it was the hair going through my fingers	我能感觉到它，毛发穿过我指间
[Build it build it]	［建造它建造它］
The hairs were like wires going through my body	那毛发像电线般穿行在我身体里
I that's how I that's how I died	我就是这样我就是这样死掉的
Oh when they made that Tower of Babel	哦当他们建起那座巴别塔
They knew what they were after	他们知道自己想要什么
They knew what they were after	他们知道自己想要什么
Everything on the current moved up	水面上的一切都在向上翻涌
I tried to stop it but it was too warm	我试着阻止但它太温暖了
[No possible ending, no possible ending]	［没有可能的结局，没有可能的结局］
Too unbelievably smooth like playing in the sea	不可思议地柔顺就像在海水中玩耍
In the sea of possibility the possibility was a blade	在可能性的大海中那可能性就是一把刀片
A shiny blade I hold the key to the sea of possibilities	一把闪亮的刀片我握着通往可能性之海的钥匙
There's no land but the land looked at my hands	没有大地但那大地望着我双手
And there's a red stream that went streaming through	一条红色溪流汩汩流淌穿过
The sands like fingers like arteries like fingers	沙土如手指如动脉如手指
[All wisdom fixed between the eyes of a horse]	［所有智慧都聚集在马的双眼之间］
He lay pressing it against his throat [your eyes]	他躺在地上用刀片抵住自己喉咙［你的双眼］
He opened his throat [your eyes] his vocal chords	他切开了喉咙［你的双眼］他的声带
Started shooting like [of a horse] mad pituitary glands	乱射出声音就像［一匹马］疯狂的脑下垂体

The scream he made [my heart] was so high	他发出的尖叫声〔我的心〕如此响亮
Pitched that nobody heard no one heard	音调高得无人能听到没有人听到
That cry no one heard [Johnny] the butterfly flapping	无人能听到的嘶喊〔约翰尼〕蝴蝶振翅
In his throat his fingers nobody heard he was on that bed	在他喉咙里他手指间无人听到他躺在那床上
It was like a sea of jelly and so he seized the first	一片果冻的大海而他抓住了第一个机会
His vocal chords shot up like mad pituitary glands	他的声带乱射出声音就像疯狂的脑下垂体
It was a black tube he felt himself disintegrate	一根黑色的管道他感到自己正在解体
[There is nothing happening at all]	〔什么都没有发生〕
So when he looked out into the street	因此当他望向大街
Saw this sweet young thing	看到这个甜美的年轻尤物
Humping on the parking meter	后背顶着停车码表
Leaning on the parking meter	身体斜靠着停车码表
A long Fender whine	长长的芬达吉他嘎嘎作响
In the sheets there was a man	床单上躺着个男人
Everything around him unraveling	他身边的一切土崩瓦解
Like some long Fender whine	就像长长的芬达吉他嘎嘎作响
Dancing around to a simple rock and roll song	伴着一曲简单的摇滚乐起舞

"Land" was an improvisation evoking Chris Kenners's "Land of a Thousand Dances," a salute to the past and an anticipation of the future.	《大地》是一首被克里斯·肯纳的《千舞之地》唤起灵感的即兴作品，一首向旧日致敬并向未来展望的作品。

1　本歌由三部分组成：《群马》《千舞之地》《大海》，后也常被直接称为《群马》。

2　克里斯·肯纳（Chris Kenner，1929—1976）发布于 1962 年的热门单曲，曾被众多音乐人及乐队翻唱。在克里斯的原版歌曲中，他写到了 1960 年代流行的包括"小马舞""小鸡舞""土豆泥舞""鳄鱼舞""瓦图西舞""甜豌豆舞""扭扭舞"等在内的 16 种舞蹈。

3　《瘦骨马罗尼》（"Bony Maroney"）是美国布鲁斯及摇滚音乐人拉里·威廉姆斯（Larry Williams，1935—1980）发布于 1957 年的热门单曲，曾被众多音乐人及乐队翻唱。拉里在这首歌里描述了一位骨瘦如柴但美丽且善舞的女孩形象。

4　指法国诗人兰波，帕蒂以这首歌向其致敬。

5　本首标题原文为法语，La Mer (de)。

ELEGIE

悲歌

I just don't know what to do tonight

我不知道今晚要做什么

My head is aching as I drink and breathe

喝酒和呼吸时头都在痛

Memory falls like cream in my bones

记忆像奶油从我骨头上滑落

Moving on my own

我唯有独自前行

There must be something I can dream tonight

今晚我一定能够梦到什么

The air is filled with the moves of you

空气中充满你的印迹

All the fire is frozen yet still I have the will

所有火焰都被冻住而我仍然保有意志

Trumpets, violins, I hear them in the distance

小号，小提琴，我听到它们在远处奏响

And my skin emits a ray

我的皮肤放射出光线

But I think it's sad, it's much too bad

我想这很悲伤，实在太糟糕了

That all our friends can't be with us today

今天所有朋友都不能在我们身旁

RADIO ETHIOPIA

埃 塞 俄 比 亚 电 台

Beauty will be convulsive or not at all.
—ANDRÉ BRETON, NADJA

美能夺人心魄，否则即不是美。
——安德烈·布勒东，《娜嘉》★

★《娜嘉》为安德烈·布勒东完成于 1928 年的作品，讲述作者与一位名叫娜嘉的女子在巴黎相遇、相爱、分手，
探索现实、真实、美、疯狂，颠覆了 19 世纪传统的文学观念。

1976年10月，帕蒂·史密斯发表第二张专辑《埃塞俄比亚电台》。而这张专辑的同名曲目，在当时一度被称为一场十分钟的"噪音"，成为帕蒂最"臭名昭著"的歌曲之一。

"大家都以为我们的专辑会卖光。"在1995年《炸弹》（BOMB）杂志的一篇访谈中，帕蒂袒露，事实上《埃塞俄比亚电台》在发行后，受到了大量出版物、评论家和摇滚乐爱好者的批评和诟病，认为它质量粗糙且过分自我陶醉。滚石唱片乐评人戴夫·马尔什（Dave Marsh）在1976年的一篇评论上毫不客气地指出，帕蒂"似乎不知道朝什么方向去实现自己好的想法"。

《埃塞俄比亚电台》却是帕蒂自己偏爱的一首。歌词中，她引用诗人兰波逝世之际的遗愿，向他致敬。不可否认的是，当我们回看，这张充满分裂和末日意象（战场、飞船、坠落天使）的专辑，确实是帕蒂和她的乐队走向更具开创性和实验性的艺术道路上尤其关键的一步。

《埃塞俄比亚电台》大胆、不羁。开场曲目《去问天使》中，帕蒂与乐队用反复切换的F#和D和弦以及硬摇风格吉他段落，直白地向天使呐喊。而接下来，对于爱的渴望以近乎粗野和残酷的方式在整张专辑呈现。帕蒂毫不避讳使用如"向河里撒尿""排泄爱人的灵魂"这样的词句，形容这股爱欲。在《遥远的手指》和《（我心）狂跳》中，她

希望爱或完整，或支离破碎。逝去的人与物依旧贯穿整张专辑的歌词，而帕蒂以她有力的叙述使听者自然地进入歌曲，成为故事一角。

值得一提的是，早在帕蒂的第一张专辑发行之前，《遥远的手指》与《是不是很奇怪》就曾由她的乐队在现场演出。这张专辑由制作人杰克·道格拉斯（Jack Douglas）完成，他也是约翰·列侬、小野洋子、"廉价把戏"（Cheap Trick）等音乐人和摇滚乐队的合作搭档。

Reprinted courtesy of The Yipster Times (March-April, 1977). A subscription to The Yipster Times is only $6/yr. to
P.O. Box 392, Canal Street Station, New York, NY 10013. The Patti Smith Group's new record is Radio Ethiopia on Arista Records.
Patti says: "Radio Ethiopia goes beyond the wax into a disc of light. Fight the good fight."

You Can't Say "Fuck" in Radio Free America

BY PATTI SMITH

New Year's Eve, Patti Smith gave a concert at NYC's Palladium. WNEW-FM refused to air the concert on their station due to her using the word "fuck" on an interview with the station last November. Upon hearing of this decision, Patti wrote this heavy condemnation of 'progressive' rock radio as we hear it now.

Fuck the word...fuck the word
fuck the word the word is dead
is re-defined...the bird in the (womb)
is expelled by the propelling
motion of fuck of fucking

On November 29, Patti Smith delivered an address on WNEW-FM in New York City. Because of the content of this message, the Patti Smith Group will not be aired live in the future on Metromedia. A transcript is available to the people, for the people who support free communication to decide what programming they want to hear on their radio. (S.s.a.s. to Radio Ethiopia, P.O. Box 188, Mantua, New Jersey 08051).

THE RESISTANCE

We believe in the total freedom of communication and we will not be compromised. The censorship of words is as meaningless as the censorship of musical notes; we cannot tolerate either. Freedom means exactly that: no limits, no boundaries...rock and roll is not a colonial power to be exploited, told what to say and how to say it. This is the spirit in which our music began and the flame in which it must be continued. Radio Ethiopia is a symphony of experience...each piece a movement...14 movements...14 stations.

There is silence on my radio...
—Stones

They are trying to silence us, but they cannot succeed. We cannot be "trusted" not to pollute the airwaves with our idealism and intensity. W(New) York radio has proved unresponsive at best to the new rock and roll being born under its ears...a music having worldwide cause and effect...injecting a new sense of urgency and imperative. Radio has consistently lagged behind the needs of the community it is honor-bound to serve. We do not consider paternalistic token airplay and passive coverage to be enough. FM radio was birthed in the 1960's as an alternative to restrictive playlisting and narrow monopolistic visions. The promise is being betrayed.

We Want The Radio And We Want It Now 1977...the celebration of 1776-1976 ends tonight... we end with the same desires of individual and ethnic freedom of concept...the freedom of art...the freedom of work...the freedom/flow of energy that keeps re-building itself with the nourishment of each generation. The political awareness of the 1960's was a result of the political repression of the 1950's. The 70's have represented the merging of both...political-artistic/activism-expression.

The colonial year is dead. Rock and roll is not a colonial art. We colonize to further the freedom of space.

We must dedicate ourselves to the future...in the sixties the DOG was GOD...the underdogs rose up and merged and fought for political freedom... we of 1977 are Rat/Art.

—Radio Ethiopia, 1977

suspended in relics (art)...The guardians of ritual salute all that heralds and redefines civilization into a long streaming system of tongues...salute then spit on those who left us the ruins of much broken ground then move on...

dedicated to the future we are thus fasting...we rip into the past/perfect like raw meat...we do not accept the past as the summit of creation...we rise and pierce the membrane of mire and waste...the stagnation of rust...

1977. We the people of the neo-army are spewing JUST LUST...The absolute motion into the future... To fight the good fight...the fight for feedom of expression...The fight against fat and Roman satisfaction.

WE DON'T WANT NO SATISFACTION
!!THE ART/RAT DAWNS!!
(THE AWAKENING GRAIN)

RAISE UP/ TAKE POSITION/ DUO-SONIC THE SYSTEM OF GOD. ILLUMINATED WEAPONS POISED LIKE MALLOTS LIKE 2-SOUND PICK-UPS BAYONETING THE FLESH OF THE EYE...A GRAIN OF SAND THRU THE OPTIC NERVES OF HE THAT SEIZE ALL...A-R (raive) AND STONED AND IR-RATED BY A SPECT(RE) SO CUNNING HE EVEN-TUALLY SHOWS HIS PHASE HE EVENTUALLY WAKES UP/(SHARP AND ROUGH AND DELICATE-LY CUT THE AWAKENING GRAIN DOES ITS WORK! THE ART/RAT DAWNS AGAIN! ART/RAT KNAWS THRU SPACE/ RUSHING TADPOLES/ A BLACK STREAK ACROSS THE WHITE HOTEL... THE GLASS THAT SEPARATES HIM FROM SOCIETY IS THE TRUE PRISON OF LIGHT...ART/ RAT IN THE SHAPE OF A BOY DRESSED IN A COAT OF MILK...ACTION PAINTER...RUBEDO HAIR OF THE ONE WHO SOARS AND SLASHES THRU THE AVIATOR BACK/FLAP W/OUT BAR-ING THE SENCE OF PURE TONGUE RYTHUM... ART/RAT POSSESING THE NOBEL CONCEIT OF THE FUTURE AWAITS HIGH ORDERS TO SPEW THE TONGUE OF LOVE THAT UTTERS THE MOST PRECIOUS COMMAND THE WORDS OF LOVE THAT TURN US ON (THE PHYSICAL HIEROGLYPHICS) XTHE 14 POSITIONS) ARE "FUCK ME FUCK ME FUCK ME FUCK ME...FUCK THE WORD/ THE WORD IS DEAD/ FUCK IS DEAD ON THE RADIO/ THE WORD IS DEAD/ IN A WAVE OF SOUND/ TO BE UNBOUND AND WAVED AND DEFILED LIKE A BANNER OUTSIDE SOCIETY OVER THE BLACK RIVER...CITIZENS ARISE! SPIT-BALL INTO THE SKY! THE AWAKENING GRAIN AWAKENING A–WAKE UP W

ASK THE ANGELS

去问天使

Move. Ask the angels who they're calling

动起来。去问天使他们在召唤谁

Go ask the angels if they're calling to thee

去问天使他们召唤的是不是你

Ask the angels, while they're falling

当他们坠落，去问天使

Who that person could possibly be

他们召唤的可能是谁

And I know you got the feeling

我知道你已经有了感觉

You know, I feel it crawl across the floor

你瞧，我感觉到它爬过地板

And I know, it got you reeling

我知道，这让你眩晕

And honey, honey the call is for war

亲爱的，亲爱的这是战争的召唤

And it's wild, wild, wild, wild

那么狂野，狂野，狂野，狂野

Across the country through the fields

横贯四野，穿越田地

You know I see it written 'cross the sky

我看到它划过天空写下文字

People rising from the highway

人们从高速路上站起

And war, war is the battle cry

战争，他们呐喊着战争

And it's wild, wild, wild, wild

那么狂野，狂野，狂野，狂野

Armageddon, it's gotten

末日决战，无可阻挡

No Savior jailer can take it from me

没有救世主狱卒能从我这夺走它

World ending, it's just beginning

世界终结，刚刚开始

And rock and roll is what I'm born to be

我生来就是为了摇滚

And it's wild, wild, wild, wild　　　　　　　　　那么狂野，狂野，狂野，狂野

Ask the angels if they're starting to move　　　去问天使他们是否就要开始行动

Coming in droves in from L.A.　　　　　　　从洛杉矶一批批蜂拥而至

Ask the angels if they're starting to groove　　去问天使他们是否就要开始起舞

Light as our armor and it's today　　　　　　轻如铠甲，就在今日

And it's wild, wild, wild, wild　　　　　　　那么狂野，狂野，狂野，狂野

71

In aint it Strange

long on Vineland
There's a club house
girls in white dress
Boys shoot white stuff
oh aint it strange that
anyone should join
but they come & call
and fall on the floor
dont you think they'd
have the will but
they jtwo sign and
they spill til
the club, has
to fill
Abut it strange?
no no no
aint it strange?
w,

strange + paulo.
crawling toward
me beckon to me
Dont get thru me
wanna join
oh no
wanna join
no no no
wanna join
no oh no

me inside of
your Temple
looks like the
insides of a
brain
of any
one man

AIN'T IT STRANGE

是不是很奇怪

Down in Vineland there's a clubhouse

Girl in white dress boy shoot white stuff

Oh don't you know that anyone can join

And they come and call and they fall on the floor

Don't you see when you're looking at me

That I'll never end transcend transcend

Ain't it strange oh oh oh

Ain't it strange oh oh oh

Come and join me I implore thee

I implore thee come explore me

Oh don't you know that anyone can come

And they come and they call and they crawl on the floor

Don't you see when you're looking at me

That I'll never end transcend transcend

Ain't it strange oh oh oh

Ain't it strange oh oh oh

True true who are you

Who who am I

Down in Vineland there's a clubhouse

Girl in white dress boy shoot white stuff

瓦恩兰那边有家俱乐部

女孩穿着白裙子男孩射入白色物体

哦你不知道吗每个人都能参与

他们来他们叫他们摔倒在地板

当你看着我难道你还不明白

我永远无法停止超越 超越

是不是很奇怪 哦 哦 哦

是不是很奇怪 哦 哦 哦

快来跟我一起吧我恳求你

我恳求你快来探索我

哦你不知道吗每个人都能来

他们来他们叫他们爬行在地板

当你看着我难道你还不明白

我永远无法停止超越 超越

是不是很奇怪 哦 哦 哦

是不是很奇怪 哦 哦 哦

真的 真的 你是谁

我 我是谁

瓦恩兰那边有家俱乐部

女孩穿着白裙子男孩射入白色物体

Oh don't you know anyone can come

And they come and call and they fall on the floor

Don't you see when you're looking at me

That I'll never end transcend transcend

Ain't it strange oh oh oh

Ain't it strange oh oh oh

哦你不知道吗每个人都能参与

他们来他们叫他们摔倒在地板

当你看着我难道你还不明白

我永远无法停止超越　超越

是不是很奇怪　哦　哦　哦

是不是很奇怪　哦　哦　哦

do you go to the temple tonight oh no i don't think so do you not go to the palace of answers with me marie oh no i don't think so no see when they offer me book of gold i know soon still that platinum is coming and when i look inside of your temple it looks just like the inside of any one man and when he beckons his finger to me well i move in another direction i move in another dimension i move in another dimension oh oh oh

今晚你去神殿吗哦不我不这么想你不跟我一起去那答案的殿堂吗玛丽哦不我不这么想当他们给我黄金之书我知道用不了多久那铂金做的就要来了而当我望向你的神殿它看起来跟其他人的里面都一样当他伸出手指召唤我好吧我移动到另一个方向我移入另一个次元我移入另一个次元　哦　哦　哦

上帝之手我感受那手指

Hand of God I feel the finger

Hand of God I start to whirl

Hand of God I do not linger

上帝之手我开始旋转

上帝之手我不再留恋

Don't get dizzy do not fall now

Turn whirl like a dervish

Turn God make a move

不要头晕不要现在就倒下

转动　回旋　像个托钵僧

转动　上帝　采取点行动

Turn Lord I don't get nervous

I just move in another dimension

Come move in another dimension

Come move in another dimension

Come move in another dimension

Strange strange

do you go to the temple tonight oh no i don't think so no will you
go to the pagoda the palace of answers with me marie oh no i don't
believe so no see when they offer me book of gold i know soon
still that platinum is coming and when i look inside your temple it
looks just like the inside of the brain of any one man and when he
beckons his finger to me well i move in another dimension i move
in another dimension i move in another dimension

转动 主啊 我一点不紧张

我只是移入另一个次元

快来移入另一个次元

快来移入另一个次元

快来移入另一个次元

奇怪 奇怪

今晚你去神殿吗哦不我不这么想你不跟我一起去那答案的
殿堂吗玛丽哦不我不这么想当他们给我黄金之书我知道用
不了多久那铂金做的就要来了而当我望向你的神殿它看起
来跟其他人的里面都一样当他伸出手指召唤我好吧我移动
到另一个方向我移入另一个次元我移入另一个次元

POPPIES

罂粟

Heard it on the radio it's no good

从广播里听到的这个消息不太好

Heard it on the radio it's news to me

从广播里听到这对我还是新鲜事

When she getting something it's understood

要是她得到了什么东西就会理解

Baby's got something she's not used to

宝贝儿得到的东西她还没习惯

Down down poppy yeah

下来 下来 波比 没错

Waiting on the corner wanna score

守在角落里想要搞到那东西

Baby wants something she's in the mood to

宝贝儿想要得到她感兴趣的东西

Baby wants something I want more

宝贝儿想要的东西我想要得更多

When I don't get it I get blue blue

当我得不到它时我会很忧郁 忧郁

Down down and it's really coming

下来 下来 它真的来了

Really coming down down poppy yeah

真的来了 下来 下来 波比 没错

She was tense and gleaming in the sun

她有些紧张在太阳底下闪着光

They split her open like a country

他们像分裂一个国家那样撕开她

Everyone was very pleased to be a state of

每个人都很满意地占据一个州

Her mind was gently probed like a finger

她的大脑像根手指被温柔探测

Everything soaking and spread with butter

全身被浸泡并涂满黄油

And then they laid her on the table

接着他们把她平放在桌子上

She connected with the inhaler

给她接上呼吸机

And the needle was shifting like crazy

针头疯狂地摇晃

She was she was completely still

她完全她完全静止下来

It was like a painting of a vase	像一幅画着花瓶的油画
She just lay there and the gas traveled fast	她就躺在那里气体飞速流转
Thru the dorsal spine and down and around	穿过脊柱一路向下周身循环
The anal cavity her cranium it was really great man	肛门腔体她的头盖骨真是个伟大的人
The gas had inflicted her entire spine	气体充盈她整条脊柱
With the elements of a voluptuous disease	性感疾病的各种元素
With a green vapor made her feet light	绿色蒸汽把她双脚变轻
I moved thru the door I saw the wheel and it was golden	我穿过大门看到车轮它是金色的
And oh my God I finally scored	哦我的天呢我终于搞到了那东西
I turned the channel station after station	我换了一个又一个频道
I don't think there's any station	我想没有任何一个频道
Quite as interesting to me as the 12th station	对我来说像 12 频道那么有趣
I tuned in to the tower too many centuries	我听着塔台广播，那么多个世纪
Were calling to me spinning down thru time	召唤着我，穿越时间旋转降落
Oh watch them say you're too high	哦看看，他们说，你太兴奋了
Before him we didn't worship suffering	在他之前我们从不推崇苦难
Didn't we laugh and dance for hours	我们笑着起舞久久不断
We were having fun as we built the tower	我们尽享欢愉建起高塔
I saw it spiraling up into his electric eye	我看着它盘旋上升穿入他的雷电之眼
I felt it go in and started to cry	我感到它已进入随后开始哭泣
Oh God are you afraid	哦上帝你害怕吗

Why did the tower turn you off babe	为什么高塔让你厌烦宝贝
I want to feel you in my radio	我想要在我的广播里感受到你
Goddamn in my radio	在我该死的广播里
If you want to go go if you want to see	如果你想走就走吧如果你想要去看看
If you want to go as far as she	如果你想像她一样走那么远
You must look God in the face	你必须面对面看着上帝的脸
Heard it on the radio heard it on the radio	从广播里听到从广播里听到
One long ecstatic pure sensation restriction started excreting	一段漫长狂喜那纯洁感受局限开始排泄
Started excreting ah exhilarating bottomless pit	开始排泄啊振奋人心的无底洞
Hey Sheba hey Salome hey Venus eclipsing my way ah	嘿，示巴[1]，嘿，莎乐美，嘿，维纳斯，你们挡住了我的路啊
You're vessel every woman is a vessel is evasive is aquatic	你们是船舶每个女人都是船舶都在逃避都是水生动物
Everyone silver ecstatic platinum disk spinning	每个人银色狂喜白金唱片飞速旋转

---

1 示巴女王，又译席巴女王，根据希伯来圣经记载，她统治非洲东部示巴王国，与
所罗门王生活在相同时代。

PISSING IN A RIVER

向河里撒尿

Pissing in a river watching it rise

Tattoo fingers shy away from me

Voices voices mesmerize

Voices voices beckoning sea

Come come come come back come back

Come back come back come back

向河里撒尿看着它升起

刺青的手指躲开我很远

声音　声音　叫人着迷

声音　声音　诱人的海

来吧　来吧　来吧　回来　回来

回来　回来　回来

Spoke of a wheel tip of a spoon

Mouth of a cave I'm a slave I'm free

When are you coming hope you come soon

Fingers fingers encircling thee

Come come come come come come

Come come come come come come for me

车轮的辐条汤匙的勺尖

洞穴的入口我是个奴隶我很自由

你何时会来但愿你早一点来

手指　手指　环绕着你

来吧　来吧　来吧　来吧　来吧　来吧

来吧　来吧　来吧　来吧　来吧　为我　而来

My bowels are empty excrete in your soul

What more can I give you baby I don't know

What more can I give you to make this thing grow

Don't turn your back now I'm talking to you

Should I pursue a path so twisted

Should I crawl defeated and gifted

Should I go the length of a river

我肠内空空排泄进你的灵魂

我还能给你什么宝贝我不知道

我还能给你什么让爱继续生长

别转过身我正跟你说话

我该追寻如此扭曲的一条路吗

我该裹着挫败和天赋匍匐向前吗

我该走过一条河的长度吗

The royal the throne the cry me river 那皇家那王冠那哭泣我与那河

Everything I've done I've done for you 我所做一切都是为了你

Oh I give my life for you 哦，我把生命献给你

Every move I made I move to you 我一举一动都是为了你

And I came like a magnet for you now 我就像块磁铁被你吸引着前来

What about it you're going to leave me 那又如何呢你就要离开我

What about it you don't need me 那又如何呢你并不需要我

What about it I can't live without you 那又如何呢没有你我无法活

What about it I never doubted you 那又如何呢我从未怀疑过你

What about it what about it 那又如何呢 那又如何

What about it what about it 那又如何呢 那又如何

Should I pursue a path so twisted 我该追寻如此扭曲的一条路吗

Should I crawl defeated and gifted 我该裹着挫败和天赋匍匐向前吗

Should I go the length of a river 我该走过一条河的长度吗

The royal the throne the cry me river 那皇家那王冠那哭泣我与那河

What about it what about it what about it 那又如何 那又如何 那又如何

Oh I'm pissing in a river 哦，我向河里撒泡尿

spoke of a wheel
Tip of a spoon
Tongue exTending
I'm a slave / I'm free
pressure fingers
here me sigh
Fingers fingers
Encircle Thee

in The night
in the here
of The

my bowels are empty
excrete in your soul
what more can I give you
Baby I don't Know
Blood in The river
hard celluloid
~~This my head is a field~~
~~The more~~
film on my body
I'm shooting for you

Oh I'm SINKing
Sweet gravity

DISTANT FINGERS

遥远的手指 [1]

When when will you be landing	几点 几点你会着陆
When when will you return	何时 何时你再回来
Feel feel my heart expanding	感觉 感觉我心在膨胀
You and your alien arms	你和你外星人的手臂
All my earthly dreams are shattered	我所有尘世梦想都已破灭
I'm so tired I quit	我好疲惫我放弃
Take me forever it doesn't matter	永远带走我吧都已无所谓
Deep inside of your ship	去你飞船的深深处
La la la la la la landing	着 着 着 着 着 着 着陆
Please oh won't you return	求你了哦你不回来吗
See your blue lights are flashing	看到你蓝色的灯光在闪烁
You and your alien arms	你和你外星人的手臂
Deep in the forest I whirl	在森林深处我旋转着
Like I did as a little girl	像还是个小女孩时那样
Let my eyes rise in the sky	让我双眼在天空中升高
Looking for you oh you know	搜寻着你，哦你知道
I would go anywhere at all	我愿去任何地方
'Cause no star is too far with you	因为跟你一起任何星辰都不算远

La la la la la la landing	着 着 着 着 着 着 着陆
Please oh won't you return	求你了哦你不回来吗
Feel feel my heart expanding	感觉 感觉我心在膨胀
You and your alien arms	你和你外星人的手臂
All my earthly dreams are shattered	我所有尘世梦想都已破灭
I'm so tired I quit	我好疲惫我放弃
Take me forever it doesn't matter	永远带走我吧都已无所谓
Deep inside of your ship	去你飞船的深深处
Land land oh I am waiting for you	着陆 着陆 哦我在等你
Waiting for you to take me up by my starry spine	等你带我升空驾驶我星光闪耀的脊柱
With your distant distant fingers	用你遥远 遥远的手指
Oh I am waiting for you	哦，我在等你
Oh I am waiting for you	哦，我在等你

1 《遥远的手指》延续了第一张专辑《群马》中《鸟园》一歌的灵感来源，即《梦想之书》中所描述的彼得渴望父亲带自己乘坐宇宙飞船飞往太空的心情。

PUMPING (MY HEART)

（我心）狂跳

Oh I see your stare spiraling up there	哦我看到你的注视在上空盘旋
Into the center of my brain and baby come baby go	钻进我大脑中心宝贝来吧宝贝走
And free the hurricane oh I go into the center of the airplane	放飞那场飓风哦我走进飞机中央
Baby gotta move to the center of my pain	宝贝你要进入我痛苦的核心
And my heart starts pumping my fists start pumping	我心开始狂跳激动地挥舞拳头
Upset total abandon upset you know I love you so	心烦意乱不顾一切心烦意乱你知道我那么爱你
Upset total abandon	心烦意乱不顾一切
Oh I see you stare spiraling up there and oh	哦我看到你的注视在上空盘旋哦
Into the center of my brain and baby come baby go	钻进我大脑中心宝贝来吧宝贝走
And free the hurricane oh I go into the center of the airplane	放飞那场飓风哦我走进飞机中央
Baby gotta box in the center of the ring	宝贝你要在场地最中央开始一场拳击
And my heart starts pumping my fists start pumping	我心开始狂跳激动地挥舞拳头
Upset total abandon you know I love you so	心烦意乱不顾一切你知道我那么爱你
Total abandon oh I go into the center of the airplane	不顾一切哦我走进飞机中央
Baby gotta go to the center of my brain	宝贝你要走进我大脑的核心
And my heart starts pumping my fists start pumping	我心开始狂跳激动地挥舞拳头
Got no recollection of my past reflection	对过去的反思没有什么记忆
So I'm free to move in the resurrection	因此我自由地进入复活之地
My heart starts pumping my fists start pumping	我心开始狂跳激动地挥舞拳头
My heart pumping my heart pumping my heart pumping	我心狂跳我心狂跳我心狂跳
Coming in the airport coming in the sea coming in the garden	进入机场进入海洋进入花园

Got a conscious stream coming in a washroom coming on a plane	搅入意识流进入洗手间登上大飞机
Coming in a force field coming in my brain and my heart	进入原力场进入我大脑还有我的心
My heart total abandon total abandon total abandon total	我心不顾一切不顾一切不顾一切不顾
Abandon total abandon total abandon total abandon	一切不顾一切不顾一切不顾一切
Oh I go into the center of the airplane	哦我走进飞机中央
Baby gotta move to the center of my brain	宝贝你要走进我大脑的核心
My heart	我的心

CHIKLETS

last night i awoke up from a dream came face to face with my face facing the tombstone teeth of a man called chiklets he came down through the ages with the desperate beauty of a middleweight boxer came beating the force field with elegant grace trying to get a perfect grip there was no absolute grip he was in a sail boat a glass bottom boat the bottom of a boat he was coming down through the ages sea molten sea spilling down the tube the spiny eye of the village the spinal eye of the victim the spiny eye like a question mark hovering over him what do you want what do you want from him down on a dream too much unexplained what do you think do you think there was an actual connection i can't imagine a connection going down there i can't imagine any connection at all a boxing ring with gold ropes soft desperate karat top spinning and coming down through the ages forty one bc

奇克莱斯

昨晚我从梦中醒来面对面看到我的脸正对着一个叫奇克莱斯的男人的满口烂牙他穿越时光走下来带着中量级拳击手打败原力场的绝望美丽带着优雅的风度试图找到完美的控制力可并没有什么绝对的控制力他坐在一条帆船上一条玻璃船底的船那条船的船底他穿越时光走下来海水融化海水沿着管道滨波破碎而下村庄长满刺的眼睛受害者针突状的眼睛长满刺的眼睛像一个问号在他头顶盘旋你想得到什么你想从他身上得到什么在一个梦里太多的无法解释你是怎么想的你认为这些之间真的有什么联系吗我想象不出有什么联系去到那里我想象不出有任何的联系绕着金色绳线的拳击台柔和的绝望克拉陀螺旋转从公元前四十一年穿越时光走下来

Oh I'll send you a telegram	哦我会给你发电报
Oh I have some information for you	哦我有消息告诉你
Oh I'll send you a telegram	哦我会给你发电报
Send it deep in the heart of you	把它发到你心深处
Deep in the heart of your brain is a lever	你大脑之心深处有根杠杆
Deep in the heart of your brain is a switch	你大脑之心深处有个开关
Deep in the heart of your flesh you are clever	你肉体之心深处你很聪明
Oh honey you met your match in a bitch	哦亲爱的你遇到了对手是个婊子
There will be no famine in my existence	我存在的地方不会有饥荒
I merge with the people of the hills	我与大山里的人们合为一体
People of Ethiopia	埃塞俄比亚的人们
Your opiate is the air that you breathe	你的鸦片就是你呼吸的空气
All those mint bushes around you	那些围绕着你的薄荷灌木
Are the perfect thing for your system	对你来说是完美造物
Aww clean clean it out	啊呀呀清除清除干净
You must rid yourself from these these animal fixations	你必须从这些这些兽性的痴迷中摆脱出来
You must release yourself	你必须释放你自己
From the thickening blackmail of elephantiasis	从象皮病 [2] 的沉重勒索中释放出来
You must divide the wheat from the rats	你必须把小麦和老鼠分开
You must turn around and look oh God	你必须转过身来看看哦上帝
When I see Brancusi	当我看着布朗库西 [3]

His eyes searching out the infinite   他的双眼探寻向无限

Abstract spaces in the radio   电台里的抽象空间

Rude hands of sculptor   雕塑家粗蛮的手

Now gripped around the neck of a Duo-Sonic   现在紧握着"哆音速"⁴吉他琴颈

I swear on your eyes no pretty words will sway me   我以你双眼起誓没有任何漂亮话能动摇我

Ahh look at me look at the world around you   啊看看我看看你周身的世界

Jesus I hate to laugh but I can not believe   天啊我不想笑但我简直无法相信

Care I so much everything merges then touch it   我竟如此在意万物在融合然后触摸它

With a little soul anything is possible   只需一点点灵魂一切便有可能

Ahhh I never knew you how can it be   啊我从未了解你怎么会这样

That I feel so fucked up   这感觉太扯淡了

I am in no condition to do what I must do   我没办法做我必须做的事

The first dog on the street can tell you that   大街上冒出来的第一条狗都能告诉你这点

As for you you do as you must   对你来说你必须做你该做的

But as for me I trust   但对我来说我相信

That you will book me on the first freighter   你会为我预定第一艘货船

Passage on the first freighter   这里通过的第一艘货船

So I can get the hell out of here   让我可以离开这鬼地方

And go back home back to Abyssinia   回到家乡回到阿比西尼亚

Deep in the heart of the valley I'm going   山谷之心深处我要去

Ohhh I would appreciate if you would just

Totally appreciate Brancusi's Bird in Space

The sculptor's mallet has been replaced

By the neck of a guitar

Lately

Every time I see your face

I eventually

wake up

哦如果你愿意我将不胜感激

无比感激太空里那只布朗库西的鸟

雕塑家的锤子已被替换

换成一把吉他的琴颈

最近

每次我看到你的脸

就终于

醒来

---

1 阿比西尼亚，埃塞俄比亚旧称。帕蒂将这首歌献给她的文学偶像兰波。1884 年，停止写作的兰波前往阿比西尼亚经商，从事火走私生意，赚到了不少钱。然而他的右膝盖患上滑膜炎并很快恶化为癌症。日益恶化的病情迫使兰波于 1891 年 5 月返回法国，同年 11 月在马赛逝世。帕蒂在访谈中提到，她以这首歌向兰波致敬，在歌词中提及兰波去世前的遗愿。

2 象皮病，又称血丝虫病，病症为腿、臂和生殖器官严重肥大。

3 布朗库西（Constantin Brancusi, 1876—1957），雕塑家、现代摄影家，出生于罗马尼亚，长期活动于法国，被誉为现代主义雕塑先驱。

4 "哆音速"（Duo-Sonic），美国著名乐器公司芬达于 1956 年推出的一款入门级电吉他，针对业余音乐者及学生。

EASTER

复 活 节

Use menace, use prayer.
—JEAN GENET

用威胁，用祈祷。
——让·热内 ★

★ 让·热内（Jean Genet，1910—1986），法国著名小说家、剧作家、诗人。引文节选自热内长诗《死囚》（"Le Condamné à Mort"）。

发行于 1978 年 3 月，《复活节》是帕蒂·史密斯的第三张录音室专辑。这张专辑由吉米·艾欧文（Jimmy Iovine）制作，因其中《因为这夜晚》这一单曲的大获成功，被认为是帕蒂在商业上的一次突破。

《因为这夜晚》是一首大胆、直白的爱歌。在 1970 年代，这样的声音是颠覆性的。单曲一经问世，便在公告牌百强单曲榜上排名十三，在各大电台轮番播出，该专辑也最终登上公告牌二百大专辑榜上第二十。

《复活节》是帕蒂在 70 年代发行的专辑中唯一一张键盘手理查德·索尔（Richard Sohl）没有全程参与的专辑。虽然索尔因身体原因未参与录制，但在《太空猴子》这一曲中，他与"蓝牡蛎崇拜"乐队的键盘手艾伦·拉尼尔（Allen Lanier）一同参与了客串。

除了专辑名称所带的宗教暗示，《圣经》与基督教相关意象贯穿了《复活节》。帕蒂在专辑同名歌曲中再现了一场洗礼与圣餐——《复活节》的黑胶唱片歌词页中，还附有一张诗人兰波和他的哥哥弗雷德里克初领圣餐时的照片。除此之外，唱片封套内，乐队成员的名字下方绘有一个十字架。帕蒂也在专辑内页的介绍词中引用了《提摩太后书》里的句子，"那美好的仗我已经打过了，当跑的路我已经跑尽了"。

除了对基督教意象的引用之外，专辑中的《幽灵之舞》基于 19 世纪末美国原住民族的新兴宗教仪式而创作，《摇滚黑鬼》则被视为社会少数群体的呐喊与战斗口号，而帕蒂也在《巴别独白》中展露她自己的艺术宣言。

继挚友罗伯特·梅普尔索普为第一张专辑《群马》拍摄封面后，《复活节》封面上的帕蒂肖像出自导演、录音师、摄影师林恩·戈德史密斯（Lynn Goldsmith）之手。帕蒂后来告诉《滚石》杂志，她曾对着自己这张专辑封面自慰："我想可以当作'实验'试一下，如果我可以，那么 15 岁的男孩们也可以，这会让我非常开心。"

Raise the sky, we got to fly

Over the land over the sea

Fate unwinds and if we die souls arise

God, do not seize me please. 'Till victory

Take arm. Take aim. Be without shame

No one to bow to. To vow to. To blame

Legions of light virtuous flight ignite excite

And you will see us coming

V formation through the sky

Film survives. Eyes cry. On the hill

Hear us call through a realm of sound

Oh oh-oh down and down

Down and 'round oh down and 'round

'Round and 'round oh 'round and 'round

Rend the veil and we shall sail

The nail. The grail. That's all behind thee

In deed in creed the curve of our speed

And we believe that we will raise the sky

We got to fly over the land over the sea

撑起天穹，我们必须飞翔

跨过大地穿越海洋

命运松开翅膀即便我们死去灵魂也将飞升

上帝，请不要束缚我。让我战斗直至胜利

拿起武器。对准目标。抛开羞愧

不向任何人去屈服。去起誓。去怪罪

光之军团贞洁飞行群情激燃

你会看到我们到来

列队成 V 字形穿越天空

薄雾弥漫。双眼哭干。在山顶上

听到我们呐喊的声音穿过群山

哦　哦——哦　下来啊下来

下来转圈哦下来转圈

一圈又一圈哦一圈又一圈

撕掉面纱我们起航

钉子。圣杯。全部抛在身后

真实信念我们速度的曲线

我们相信自己将撑起天穹

我们必须飞翔跨过大地穿越海洋

Fate unwinds and if we die souls arise

God, do not seize me please. 'Till victory

Victory. 'Till victory. Victory. 'Till victory

命运松开翅膀即便我们死去灵魂也将飞升

上帝，请不要束缚我。让我战斗直至胜利

胜利。直至胜利。胜利。直至胜利

SPACE MONKEY

太空猴子

Blood on the TV ten o'clock news.

十点钟的电视播着血腥新闻。

Souls are invaded heart in a groove

灵魂被入侵心脏在律动

Beating and beating so out of time

撞击又撞击时间不够用

What's the mad matter with the church chimes

教堂的钟声出了什么大问题

Here comes a stranger up on Ninth Avenue

第九大道走来了一个陌生人

Leaning green tower indiscreet view

斜靠绿色塔楼轻浮的风景

Over the cloud over the bridge

越过云层越过桥梁

Sensitive muscle sensitive ridge

敏感的肌肉敏感的屋脊

Of my space monkey sign of the time-time

我的太空猴子时间的标志——标志

Space monkey so out of line-line

太空猴子超越常规——常规

Space monkey son of divine

太空猴子神明之子

And he's mine mine all mine

他是我的我的都是我的

Pierre Clemente. Snortin' cocaine.

皮埃尔·克里蒙地 [1]。吸着可卡因。

The sexual streets why it's all so insane

性感街巷为何一切如此疯狂

Humans are running lavender room

人类奔跑在薰衣草房间

Hovering liquid move over moon

液体悬浮移动遍布月球

For my space monkey sign of the time-time

我的太空猴子时间的标志——标志

Space monkey son of divine

太空猴子神明之子

Space monkey so out of line

太空猴子超越常规

And he's mine mine oh he's mine

他是我的我的哦他是我的

Stranger comes up to him

Hands him an old rusty Polaroid

It starts crumbling in his hands.

He says, oh man, I don't get the picture

This is no picture this is just this just a this just a . . .

Just my jack-knife just my jack-knife just my jack.

Rude excavation. Landing site.

Boy hesitating jack-knife

He rips his leg open so out of time

Blood and light running

It's all like a dream

Light of my life he's dressed in flame

It's all so predestined it's all such a game

For my space monkey sign of the time-time

Space monkey son of divine space monkey

So out of line and it's all just space just space

There he is up in a tree.

Oh, I hear him calling down to me

That banana-shaped object ain't no banana

陌生人向他走去

递给他一台老旧生锈的宝丽来

相机在他手里碎开四分五裂。

他说，哦嘿，我照不了相片

没有相片这只是这只是个这只是个……

只是我的折刀只是我的折刀只是我的折。

粗鲁挖掘。着陆地点。

男孩犹豫地握着折刀

他划开自己大腿时间太不够用

鲜血就着光线四溅

仿如一场幻梦

我的生命之光他身着火焰

一切都是注定不过一场游戏

我的太空猴子时间的标志 – 标志

太空猴子神明之子太空猴子

超越常规一切只是太空只是太空

他就在这里在一棵树上。

哦，我听到他正呼唤我

那个香蕉形状的物体不是一根香蕉

It's a bright yellow UFO and he's coming to get me

是架亮黄色的 UFO，他正来接我

Here I go up up up up up up up up up

我这就走了 飞升 飞升 飞升 飞升 飞升 飞升 飞升 飞升

飞升

Oh, good-bye mama I'll never do dishes again

哦，再见妈妈，我再也不刷碗了

Here I go from my body

我这就走了离开我的身体

Ha Ha Ha Ha Ha Ha

哈 哈 哈 哈 哈 哈

Help

救命

1 皮埃尔·克里蒙地（Pierre Clémenti，1942—1999），法国演员。1967 年在布努埃尔执导的影片《白日美人》中饰演凯瑟琳·德诺芙的黑帮情人而一举成名。1972 年，因非法持有或使用违禁药物而被判入狱，演艺事业暂停，后因证据不足，被关押 17 个月后获释。

BECAUSE THE NIGHT

因为这夜晚 [1]

Take me now baby here as I am	带我走吧宝贝我在这里
Pull me close, try and understand	拉我靠近，试着理解
Desire is hunger is the fire I breathe	欲望是种饥饿是我呼出的火
Love is a banquet on which we feed	爱是一场盛宴供养我们存活

Come on now try and understand	现在快来吧试着理解
The way I feel when I'm in your hands	当被你抚摸时我的感受
Take my hand come undercover	牵起我的手卸掉你的伪装
They can't hurt you now, can't hurt you now	现在他们无法伤害你了，现在无法伤害你

Because the night belongs to lovers	因为这夜晚属于爱人
Because the night belongs to love	因为这夜晚属于爱
Because the night belongs to lovers	因为这夜晚属于爱人
Because the night belongs to us	因为这夜晚属于我们

Have I doubt when I'm alone	当独自一人时我如此疑惑
Love is a ring, the telephone	爱是刺耳铃声，是电话响起
Love is an angel, disguised as lust	爱是一个天使，伪装成色欲
Here in our bed, until the morning comes	流连在我们的床上，直到清晨降临

Come on now try and understand	现在快来吧试着理解

The way I feel under your command

当被你掌控时我的感受

Take my hand as the sun descends

太阳落山时牵起我的手

They can't touch you now, can't touch you now

现在他们抓不到你，现在抓不到你

And though we're seized with doubt

尽管我们被疑虑紧紧攥住

The vicious circle turns and burns

邪恶的循环旋转着燃烧

Without you I cannot live, forgive

没有你我无法活，原谅我

The yearning burning, I believe it's time

渴望在燃烧，我相信是时候了

To feel to heal, so touch me now

去感受去愈合，所以现在抱紧我吧

Touch me now, touch me now

现在抱紧我，现在抱紧我

Because this night there are two lovers

因为这个夜晚里有两个爱人

Because we believe in the night we trust

因为我们信仰这夜晚

Because the night belongs to lovers

因为这夜晚属于爱人

Because the night belongs to us

因为这夜晚属于我们

—*Cowritten with Bruce Springsteen*

——与布鲁斯·斯普林斯汀[2]合写

1 《因为这夜晚》是帕蒂最广为人知的音乐单曲之一，1978 年发表后在商业上大获成功，后被多位音乐人及乐队翻唱。布鲁斯·斯普林斯汀在 1976 年写出了这首歌的旋律，但没有进行填词。曾与布鲁斯合作过的制作人吉米·艾欧文当时正在帮帕蒂制作新专辑《复活节》，他说服了布鲁斯将这首歌交给帕蒂。帕蒂在 1977 年的一个夜晚为这首歌完成了填词。那个夜晚她在等弗雷德·索尼克·史密斯给她打来电话。弗雷德当时工作生活在密歇根，帕蒂则生活在纽约，两人只能通过电话保持联系。那时他们两人都比较穷，长途电话费用又非常昂贵，他们于是约定每周只通一次电话，通常只在晚上打，因为晚上电话费用比较便宜。那一夜，他们约定在 19：30 通话，但弗雷德始终没有打来。帕蒂一遍遍播放布鲁斯的录音小样，想念着远方的爱人，写下了这首歌词。直到午夜时分，弗雷德终于来电，此时歌词已经完成。帕蒂曾表示这种情况对她来说比较少见，她通常需要很多时间作词。

2 布鲁斯·斯普林斯汀（Bruce Springsteen, 1949—），美国著名摇滚歌手、词曲创作者及吉他手。曾获得 20 项格莱美奖、2 项金球奖、1 座奥斯卡金像奖，1999 年入选摇滚名人堂。

GHOST DANCE

幽灵之舞 [1]

What is it children that falls from the sky

孩子们，那从天而降之物，它是什么

Tayi taya tayi aye aye

Tayi taya tayi aye aye

Manna from heaven from the most high

是天赐之物来自至高之处

Food from the father tayi taya aye

来自我父的食物 tayi taya aye

We shall live again we shall live again

我们将重获新生我们将重获新生

Shake out the ghost dance

摇摆跳出幽灵之舞

Peace to your brother, give and take eat

祝你兄弟平安，给予并获取食物

Tayi taya dance little feet

Tayi taya 用小脚起舞

One foot extended snake to the ground

伸出一只脚来毒蛇放逐大地

Wave up the earth worm turn around

大地掀起海浪蠕虫转身而去

We shall live again we shall live again

我们将重获新生我们将重获新生

Shake out the ghost dance

摇摆跳出幽灵之舞

Stretch out your arms now dip and sway

展开你的双臂现在屈膝摇摆

Bird of thy birth tayi taya

你那降生之鸟 tayi taya

The oe of the shoe the ou of the soul

鞋子之中灵魂之间

Dust of the word that shakes from the tail

词语的灰尘从尾巴上抖落

We shall live again we shall live again

我们将重获新生我们将重获新生

Shake out the ghost dance

摇摆跳出幽灵之舞

Here we are, Father your Holy Ghost 我们在这里，天父你的圣灵

Bread of your bread host of your host 你粮中之粮，你主中之主

We are the tears that fall from your eyes 我们是你眼中落下的泪水

Word of your word cry of your cry 你词中之词，你泣中之泣

We shall live again we shall live again 我们将重获新生我们将重获新生

What is it Father 那是什么，我父

That moves in the night 在夜里移动

What is it Father 那是什么，我父

That snakes to the right 向右侧蛇行

What is it Father 那是什么，我父

That shakes from your hand 从你手中摇落

What is it Father 那是什么，我父

Can you tell me when 你能否告诉我何时

Father will we live again 我们将重获新生，我父

We shall live again 我们将重获新生

We shall live again 我们将重获新生

We shall live again 我们将重获新生

Shake out the ghost 摇摆出幽灵

1 "幽灵之舞"（Ghost Dance）是 1890 年前后流行于多个北美原住民族的新兴宗教仪式。北派尤特人精神领袖沃沃卡（Wovoka，又称伐木者）相信，只要印第安人跳起幽灵之舞，世界的邪恶就将消失，白人会停止扩张，印第安人将与祖先相聚并重新夺回自己的土地。幽灵之舞于 1890 年被广泛传播，但也迅速遭到了美国当局的残酷镇压，并引发了 1890 年 12 月著名的"伤膝河惨案"（Wounded Knee Massacre），对抗中有近 300 名印第安人遭到屠杀。

everything is shit.. the word ART must
be redefined. this is the age where
everybody creates.. rise up nigger take
up your true place.. rise up nigger the
word too must be redefined. this is
your arms and this is your hook.. don8t
the black boys get shook. high asses
asses get down.. NIGGER no invented for
the color it was made for the plague.
for the royalty who have readjusted
their sores.. the artist.. the mutant..
the rock and roll mulatto.. arise new
babe born sans eye-brow and tonsil..
outside logic beyond mathmatics
self torture and poli-tricks.. the
new science advances unknown geometry.
arise with new eyes new heath health
new niggers. this is your call your
calling your psalm.rise up niggers
and reign with your instruments
soldiers of new fortune.uncalcuable
caste of we new niggers.

                    MADE FOR the PLAGUE

i haven't fucked much with the past, but i've fucked plenty with the future over the skin of silk are scars from the splinters of stations and walls i've caressed. a stage is like each bolt of wood, like a log of helen, is my pleasure. i would measure the success of a night by the way by the way by the amount of piss and seed i could exude over the columns that nestled the pa some nights i'd surprise everybody by skipping off with a skirt of green net sewed over with flat metallic circles which dazzled and flashed. the lights were violet and white i had an ornamental veil, but i couldn't bear to use it. when my hair was cropped i craved covering, but now my hair itself is a veil, and the scalp of a crazy and sleepy comanche lies beneath this netting of skin. i wake up. i am lying peacefully. i am lying peacefully and my knees are open to the sun. i desire him, and he is absolutely ready to seize me. in heart i am moslem in heart i am an american. in heart i am moslem. in heart i'm an american artist and i have no guilt. i seek pleasure. i seek the nerves under your skin. the narrow archway; the layers; the scroll of ancient lettuce. we worship the flaw, the belly, the belly, the mole on the belly of an exquisite whore. he spared the child and spoiled the rod. i have not sold myself to god.

我没怎么太胡乱干涉过去，但我已经胡乱干涉了不少未来在丝绸般的皮肤上留下伤疤它们来自我爱抚过的车站和墙面上的碎片。舞台像一条木制闪电，像一页海伦的日记，它令我愉悦。我衡量一个夜晚是否成功的方式是的方式是测算尿液和精子的数量我可以从倚靠在公共广播的柱子顶上渗出来有些晚上我会悄悄溜走让所有人大吃一惊我穿着绿色的网状衫上面缝着扁平的金属圈它们闪闪发亮叫人眼花缭乱。灯光散发出紫色和白色我有条装饰用的面纱，但我不忍心用它。当我的头发剪短时我渴望被遮掩，但现在我的头发本身就是一条面纱，疯狂又慵懒的科曼奇人 [1] 头皮就躺在这皮肤的大网之下。我醒来。我平静地躺着。我平静地躺着双膝向着太阳敞开。我渴望着他，他完全准备好要抓住我了。在心里我是个穆斯林在心里我是个美国人。在心里我是个穆斯林。在心里我是个美国艺术家我没有负罪感。我寻找愉悦。我寻找你皮肤之下的神经。狭窄的拱廊；层次；远古的生菜卷。我们尊崇缺陷，肚皮，肚皮，优雅娼妓肚皮上的痣。他放过了孩子宠坏了棍棒。我没有把自己出卖给上帝。

---

1 科曼奇人，美洲原住民，传统上居住于得克萨斯州西北部、新墨西哥州东部、科罗拉多州东南部、堪萨斯州西南部、俄克拉荷马州西部和奇瓦瓦州北部的邻近地区。

ROCK N ROLL NIGGER

摇滚黑鬼 [1]

Baby was a black sheep baby was a whore	宝贝是个败家子宝贝是个婊子
Baby got big and baby get bigger	宝贝长大了宝贝越长越大
Baby get something baby get more	宝贝得到了一些宝贝得到更多
Baby baby baby was a rock n roll nigger	宝贝宝贝宝贝是个摇滚黑鬼
Oh look around you all around you	哦看看你周围看看你周围
Riding on a copper wave	骑在一波铜色的浪上
Do you like the world around you	你喜欢你周围的世界吗
Are you ready to behave	你准备好乖乖表现了吗
Outside of society they're waiting for me	社会之外他们在等着我
Outside of society that's where I want to be	社会之外才是我想待的地方

Baby was a black sheep baby was a whore	宝贝是个败家子宝贝是个婊子
You know she got big. Well she's gonna get bigger	你知道她长大了。没错她会越长越大
Baby got a hand got a finger on the trigger	宝贝长着手长着指头扣在扳机上
Baby baby baby is a rock n roll nigger	宝贝宝贝宝贝是个摇滚黑鬼
Outside of society that's where I want to be	社会之外才是我想待的地方
Outside of society they're waiting for me	社会之外他们在等着我

Those who have suffered understand suffering	受过苦难的人才会理解苦难
And thereby extend their hand	因此伸出他们的手
The storm that brings harm	风暴会带来伤害

Also makes fertile blessed is the grass 也令土地肥沃草木得福

And herb and the true thorn 还有香草还有真正的荆棘

I was lost in a valley of pleasure 我迷失在愉悦山谷中

I was lost in the infinite sea 我迷失在无限之海里

I was lost and measure for measure 我迷失了要一报还一报

Love spewed from the heart of me 爱意从我心里喷涌出

I was lost and the cost 我迷失了然而代价

And the cost didn't matter to me 代价我无所谓

I was lost and the cost 我迷失了然而代价

Was to be outside society 就是独立在这社会之外

Jimi Hendrix was a nigger 吉米·亨德里克斯是个黑鬼

Jesus Christ and grandma too 耶稣基督和奶奶也是

Jackson Pollock was a nigger 杰克逊·波洛克是个黑鬼

Nigger nigger nigger nigger 黑鬼 黑鬼 黑鬼 黑鬼

Nigger nigger nigger 黑鬼 黑鬼 黑鬼

Outside of society they're waiting for me 社会之外他们在等着我

Outside of society if you're looking 社会之外如果你要寻找

That's where you'll find me 你会在那找到我

Outside of society they're waiting for me 社会之外他们在等着我

1　帕蒂在这首歌里将自己认同为"黑鬼"，表明自己叛逆的局外人心态。有评论认为帕蒂的这首歌延续了美国作家诺曼·梅勒（Norman Mailer，1923—2007）提出的"白种黑鬼"（The White Negro）传统，借此表达她认为白人文化中不允许表达的东西，并拒绝白人文化在历史上对其他文化的压迫。这首歌在推出后引起较大争议，"黑鬼"（Nigger）一词在1978年被普遍认为极具攻击性及种族歧视意味，因此这首歌当时没有在主流广播节目中得到播放。但在90年代，它被包括玛丽莲·曼森（Marilyn Manson）在内的多位歌手及乐队翻唱，并被收入1994年上映的电影《天生杀人狂》（*Natural Born Killers*）原声带。

WE THREE

我们三个

Every Sunday I would go down to the bar where he played guitar

每个周日我都会去那个酒吧他在那里弹吉他

You say you want me. I want another. Say you dream of me

你说你想要我。我却想要另一个。你说你梦到了我

Dream of your brother. Oh, the stars shine so suspiciously for we three

也梦到了你的兄弟。哦，星光猜疑地闪烁为了我们三个

You said when you were with me that nothing made you high

你说当跟我在一起再没有其他任何事能让你兴奋

We drank all night together and you began to cry so recklessly

我们整夜一起狂饮你哭得毫无顾忌

Baby please don't take my hope away from me

宝贝求你不要拿走我的希望

You say you want me. I want another baby

你说你想要我。我却想要另一个，宝贝

You say you wish for me. Wish for your brother

你说你为我祈祷。也为你的兄弟

Oh, the dice roll so deceptively for we three

哦，骰子迷惑地滚动为了我们三个

It was just another Sunday and everything was in the key of A

不过是又一个周日一切却如千钧一发

And I lit a cigarette for your brother

我给你的兄弟点了支烟

And he turned and heard me say so desperately

他转过身来听到我绝望地说

Baby please don't take my hope away from me

宝贝求你不要夺走我的希望

You say you want me. I want another

你说你想要我。我却想要另一个

You say you pray for me. Pray for your brother

你说你为我祷告。也为你的兄弟

Oh, the way that I see him is the way I see myself

哦，我看待他的方式就是我看自己的方式

So please stand back now and let time tell

现在请后退一步吧让时间证明一切

Oh, can't you see that time is the key

哦，难道你还不明白时间才是关键

That will unlock the destiny of we three

Every night on separate stars before we go to sleep we pray

So breathlessly. Baby please don't take my hope away from me

它会解开我们三个命运的枷锁

每一夜在临睡前我们各自对着星辰祈祷

屏息凝气。宝贝求你不要夺走我的希望

what i feel when i'm playing guitar is completely cold and crazy like i don't owe nobody nothing and it's just a test just to see how far I can and relax into the cold wave of a note when everything hits just right the note of nobility can go on forever i never tire of the solitary e and i trust my guitar and i don't care about anything sometimes i feel like i've broken through and i'm free and i could dig into eternity riding the wave and realm of the e sometimes it's useless here I am struggling and filled with dread afraid that i'll never squeeze enough graphite from my damaged cranium to inspire or asphyxiate any eyes grazing like hungry cows across the stage or page inside of me i'm crazy i'm just crazy inside i must continue i see her my stiff muse jutting around 'round 'round 'round like a broken speeding statue the colonial year is dead and the greeks too are finished the face of alexander remains not only solely due to sculpture but through the power and foresight and magnetism of alexander himself the artist must maintain his swagger he must be intoxicated by ritual as well as result look at me i am laughing I'm like the hard brown palm of the boxer and i trust my guitar therefore we black out together therefore i would run through scum and scum is just ahead we see it but we just laugh we're ascending through the hollow mountain we are peeking we are laughing we are kneeling we are radiating at last this rebellion is just a gas our gas that we pass

弹吉他的时候我能感受到的只有全然的冰冷和疯狂感到我不欠任何人任何东西这只是一个测试只是想看看我在一枚音符冰冷的浪潮中到底能到达多远又能有多放松如果一切都恰到好处那么这个高贵的音符就能永远持续下去我永远不会厌倦孤独的 E 和弦我信任我的吉他其他事情我全都不在意有时候我感到自己有所突破我自由了我可以深深钻入永恒乘风破浪游弋在 E 和弦的王国里有时候一切都失去了意义我在这里挣扎着被恐惧填满害怕自己永远无法从我受伤的头颅中挤出足够的石墨去激励或窒息那些像饥饿的牛群一样穿过舞台或是我内心盯视着自己的眼睛我疯了我心里发了疯我必须继续下去我看到了她我僵硬的缪斯在四处奔突奔突奔突像尊破掉的超速的雕塑殖民时代已经结束了希腊人也完蛋了只有亚历山大的脸还保存着这不仅仅是因为有雕塑也因为亚历山大他本人的权力远见和魅力艺术家必须维持住他的趾高气昂他必须通过仪式以及结果自我陶醉看看我吧我在大笑我像是拳击手坚硬的棕色手掌我信任我的吉他因此我们同时眼前一黑因此我奔跑着穿过渣滓那些渣滓就在前方我们看到它了但是我们一笑了之我们穿越空寂群山向上攀登我们窥视我们大笑我们跪拜我们散发光热而最终这叛乱不过是一场屁是我们放的屁

TWENTY-FIFTH FLOOR

二十五楼

We explore the men's room	我们去探索男厕所
we don't give a shit	什么都不在乎
ladies' lost electricity	女厕所没电了
take vows inside of it	在里面要宣誓
desire to dance	想要跳舞
too startled to try	太害怕了不敢试
wrap my legs 'round you	用我双腿缠绕你
starting to fly let's explore	飞起来我们去探索
up there, up there, up there	在那里，在那里，在那里
on the twenty-fifth floor	在二十五楼
Circle all around me	圈圈围绕着我
coming for the kill	为杀戮而来
kill kill oh kill me baby	杀戮 杀戮 哦杀了我吧宝贝
like a kamikaze	像个神风特攻队员
heading for a spill	冲锋陷阵突袭
oh but it's all spilt milk to me	哦但对我就像挠痒痒
desire to dance	想要跳舞
too startled to try	太害怕了不敢试
wrap my legs 'round you	用我双腿缠绕你
starting to fly let's soar	飞起来我们去翱翔

up there, up there, up there

on the twenty-fifth floor

We do not eat flower of creation

we do not eat eat anything at all

love is, love was

love is a manifestation

I'm waiting for a contact to call.

love's war. love's cruel. love's pretty

love's pretty cruel tonight

I'm waiting here to refuel

I'm gonna make contact tonight

blood in my heart. Night to exploit

twenty-five stories over Detroit

and there's more

up there, up there, up there

Stoned in space. Zeus. Christ. it has always been rock and so it is
and so it shall be. within the context of neo rock we must open up
our eyes and seize and rend the veil of smoke which man calls order.

在那里，在那里，在那里

在二十五楼

我们不吃造物之花

我们不吃什么都不吃

爱是，爱曾是

爱是一种示威

我在等一个人打来电话。

爱是战争。爱是残酷。爱是美好

今夜爱是美好的残酷

我在这里等待补给

今晚就要直面冲击

我心中血涌。夜晚等待开拓

底特律上空的二十五个故事

还有更多的

在那里，在那里，在那里

在太空里飘飘欲仙。宙斯。基督。一直以来就是摇滚就是
这样也应该是这样。在新摇滚的语境中我们必须睁开双眼
去把握去掀开烟雾的遮掩人们将这烟雾称为规则。污染是

113

pollution is a necessary result of the inability of man to reform and transform waste. the transformation of waste is perhaps the oldest pre-occupation of man. man being the chosen alloy, he must be reconnected via shit, at all cost. inherent within us is the dream of the task of the alchemist to create from the clay of man and re-create from excretion of man pure and then soft and then solid gold. all must not be art. some art we must disintegrate. positive anarchy must exist.

I feel it swirling around me
I feel I'm feeling no pain
I'm waiting above for you baby
I know that I'll see you up there
I'm tripping in the dark backward
I'm going for all that it's worth
I'm waiting above in the sky dear
upon another planet called earth

人类无力改造和转化废弃之物的必然结果。对废弃之物的转化或许是人类最古老关注的事务。人类作为被选中的杂合物，必须通过屎来重新建立连接，不惜任何代价。我们内在的梦想是用炼金术士以黏土造人的任务那样从人类的排泄物中重新创造出纯净的随后是柔软的随后是固体的金子。一切都必不是艺术。我们必须瓦解某些艺术。积极的无政府状态必须存在。

我感到它绕着我盘旋
我感受不到疼痛
我在上面等你宝贝
我知道会在那里见到你
我在黑暗中被向后绊倒
我要全力追求那值得的
我在天空上等你亲爱的
在另一个叫地球的行星上

EASTER

Easter Sunday we were walking

Easter Sunday we were talking

Isabelle, my little one

Take my hand time has come

Isabelle, all is glowing

Isabelle, all is knowing

And my heart, Isabelle

And my head, Isabelle

Frédéric and Vitalie

Savior dwells inside of thee

Oh, the path leads to the sun

Brother sister time has come

Isabelle, all is glowing

Isabelle, all is knowing

Isabelle, we are dying

Isabelle, we are rising

I am the spring

复活节这天我们在散步

复活节这天我们在交谈

伊莎贝尔，我的小家伙

抓住我的手是时候了

伊莎贝尔，散发光芒

伊莎贝尔，知晓一切

知我心意，伊莎贝尔

知我思绪，伊莎贝尔

弗雷德里克和维塔莉

救世主居住在你们身体里

哦，道路指引向烈日

哥哥妹妹是时候了

伊莎贝尔，散发光芒

伊莎贝尔，知晓一切

伊莎贝尔，我们在死去

伊莎贝尔，我们在复活

我是春日

the holy ground	是圣洁之地
I am the seed	我是种子
Of mystery	孕育着神秘
the thorn the veil	是荆棘是面纱
the face of grace	是恩典面容
the brazen image	是铜像
the thief of sleep	是盗走睡眠的窃贼
the ambassador of dreams	是梦境的使者
the prince of peace	是和平之君主
I am the sword	我是利剑
the wound the stain	是伤口是污渍
scorned transfigured	被轻蔑被变形
child of Cain	是该隐之子 [3]
I rend I end	我撕裂我终结
I return again	我再次重返
I am the salt	我是盐
the bitter laugh	是苦涩的笑
I am the gas	我是气体
in a womb of light	孕在光之子宫里
The evening star	是黄昏晚星

the ball of sight	是视像之球
That bleeds that sheds	榨取着流淌着
the tears of Christ	是基督之泪
Dying and drying	在死去在风干
as I rise tonight	今夜我将复活

Isabelle, we are rising	伊莎贝尔，我们在复活
Isabelle, we are rising	伊莎贝尔，我们在复活
Isabelle, we are rising	伊莎贝尔，我们在复活

—for Arthur, Vitalie, and Isabelle Rimbaud   ——写给阿蒂尔，维塔莉和伊莎贝尔·兰波

1 这首歌的灵感来自帕蒂对诗人兰波于 1866 年复活节那天第一次领受圣餐情境的
想象。《复活节》黑胶唱片发布时，唱片的歌词页内印有一张兰波初领圣餐时拍
下的照片。歌词中提到的弗雷德里克是兰波的哥哥，维塔莉和伊莎贝尔是兰波的
两个妹妹。兄妹四人中，兰波与伊莎贝尔最为亲近。

3 《圣经》中记载，该隐因杀害弟弟亚伯而被上帝放逐，之后妻子怀孕生下儿子以诺。
该隐将其建立的第一个城市命名为以诺。

GODSPEED

祝你好运

You are the adrenaline rushing through my veins

你是肾上腺素在我体内狂奔乱涌

Stimulate my heart pale and crystalline

刺激着我苍白透明的心

You are the sulfur extinguished by the flame

你是刺鼻硫磺被火焰浇灭

You are everything to me, all this in your name

你是我的一切，万物存在皆因你之名

Walking in your blue coat, weeping admiral

穿着你蓝色外套散步，哭泣的海军上将

All the twisted sailors, Vienna and Genet

那些扭曲的水手，维也纳和热内

Ending all that's static in a myth of sin

一切静止在关于罪恶的神话里

Mirror mine ecstatic pale adrenaline

镜中我狂喜的苍白肾上腺素

Love is a vampire, energy undead

爱是吸血鬼，能量永不灭

Love is like a boomerang, gone and back again

爱像回旋镖，飞走又折回

On a rack of red leather, on a rack of skin and sin

一架子红色皮革上，一架子皮囊和罪恶上

Tell me how to sail sail sail pale adrenaline

告诉我如何远航 远航 远航 苍白的肾上腺素

And you said to me it could never be

而你对我说你绝对不会

Sent me out to sea to see

送我出海去看看

And you said Godspeed

对我说祝你好运

Follow follow me down the twisted stair

跟随跟随我走下扭曲的楼梯

Stuck inside a memory shot and shot again

困在一段回忆里一次一次被击中

118

Hand upon a railing courting fate and fate

把手搭在栏杆上追寻同样的命运

Down a black river and I plunge right in

顺着黑色河流而下我纵身跃进去

Adrenaline move inside my vein

肾上腺素进入我血脉

Ah, you're the speed I need throw the pistol in

啊，你就是好运我要把手枪丢进去

Love is like a vampire coming in to suck suck

爱是吸血鬼为了吸干吸干我而来

I fell and fell and fell and I'm going to duck

我坠落坠落坠落我就要避开

WAVE

挥 手

那美好的仗我已经打过了，当跑的路我已经跑尽了。
——《提摩太后书》4：7

《挥手》是帕蒂·史密斯和乐队的第四张录音室专辑，发行于1979年5月17日。虽然它并未像上一张《复活节》一样在商业上取得突破，但在当时，帕蒂更希望乐队可以做出更多适合在广播电台播放的主流流行音乐。在这一点上，《挥手》是成功的。

《挥手》是帕蒂与弗雷德·索尼克·史密斯步入婚姻前发行的最后一张专辑。此后，在长达九年的时间里，帕蒂没有发布任何歌曲，也在公众面前隐去了身影。和《复活节》的爆发与力量相比，它收录的曲目转而含有更多不确定性和矛盾，没有一首歌可以单独代表整张专辑的基调。也可以说，《挥手》是帕蒂一张暂时的告别专辑。

专辑的第一首歌《弗雷德里克》即帕蒂为未婚夫弗雷德所作。《挥手》以这样一首情歌开头，而在接下来的曲目中不断将目光放至更远处。帕蒂在想象中与教宗若望·保禄一世对话，他短暂的任期正好与帕蒂录制专辑的时间吻合。借《公民船》一曲，她谱写关于移民和难民问题的史诗，随着乐声的行进，歌声逐渐变为无望呐喊。《赤脚起舞》后来成为专辑中最广为流传的曲目，在2010年被《滚石》杂志列入"史上最伟大的500首歌曲"之中，它的初衷是献给一位意大利艺术家的情人，她为爱终结了自己的生命。

《挥手》的真诚让听者动容。但就如《埃塞俄比亚电台》，专辑在发行之初所获的评价褒贬不一，人们认为它在制作上趋于流行和平庸。《滚石》杂志的乐评人汤姆·卡森（Tom Carson）曾这样形容《挥手》，"它让人困惑又自以为是，虽然有趣但是一件失败品"。然而，正是更普世的创作来源与制作方式，使《挥手》随处散发真挚与自省。这也是帕蒂之前的专辑中所没有为人注意的特点，是《挥手》的迷人所在。

FREDERICK

弗雷德里克 [1]

Hi hello awake from thy sleep

嗨你好，从你的梦中醒来

God has given your soul to keep

上帝赐予你灵魂好好守护它

All of the power that burns in the flame

全部力量都在火焰中燃烧

Ignites the light in a single name

用一个名字便点燃那光芒

Frederick, name of care

弗雷德里克，呵护之名

Fast asleep in a room somewhere

在某处房间里快速熟睡

Guardian angels lay abed

守护天使们躺在床上

Shed their light on my sleepy head

将光洒在我昏睡的头顶

High on a threshold yearning to sing

高悬在入口渴望歌唱

Down with the dancers having one last fling

跟舞者们享受最后的狂欢

Here's to the moment when you said hello

为你说出你好的时刻举杯

Come into my spirit are you ready let's go

进入我的灵魂你准备好了吗我们走

Hi hi hey hey maybe I will

嗨嗨嘿嘿，或许我会

Come back some day now

在某一日重返

But tonight on the wings of a dove

但今夜就乘上鸽子翅膀

Up above to the land of love

高飞在爱的大地上

Now I lay me down to sleep

现在我躺下来入睡

Pray the Lord my soul to keep	祈祷我主守护我的灵魂
Kiss to kiss, breath to breath	亲吻向亲吻，呼吸向呼吸
My soul surrenders astonished to death	我的灵魂投降震惊于死亡

Night of wonder promise to keep	奇迹之夜，保守住许诺
Set our sails channel the deep	扬起风帆驶入更深的航道
Capture the rapture, two hearts meet	喜获被提 [2]，两颗心相遇
Combined entwined in a single beat	在同一个节拍里交织一起

Frederick, you're the one	弗雷德里克，你是唯一
As we journey from sun to sun	我们由太阳行旅向太阳
All the dreams I waited so long for	所有我等待太久的梦想
Our flight tonight so long so long	我们今夜的飞翔那么长那么长

Bye bye hey hey maybe	拜拜嘿嘿，或许
We will come back some day now	我们会在某一日重返
But tonight on the wings of a dove	但今夜就乘上鸽子翅膀
Up above to the land of love	高飞在爱的大地上

| Frederick, name of care | 弗雷德里克，呵护之名 |
| High above with sky to spare | 高飞翱翔有天空可分享 |

All the things I've been dreaming of

All expressed in this name of love

所有我梦寐以求的事

都以这爱之名被表达

1 这首歌写给帕蒂当时的未婚夫弗雷德·索尼克·史密斯，弗雷德（Fred）是弗雷德里克（Frederick）的缩写。

2 被提（Rapture），基督教末世论中的一种概念，认为当耶稣再临之前（或同时），已死的信徒将会被复活高升，活着的信徒也将会一起被送到天上与基督相会，并升华为不朽的身体。

dream of linda

Frederick

           and the song
Tie The stars are gone

2
I'm w/ the dancers having
one last fling
I'm on the threshold
yearning to sing

I
Guardian angel
up in the sky
cease w/ your trumpets
hear my cry
I am dis...
this is what I've
wanted goodbye so long

S. Bye bye
hey hey

Frederick
name of care
high above in a ~~storm~~

Waiting for ~~so long~~
~~goodbye~~ so long

She is benediction
She is addicted to thee
She is rude connecting w/ he
& connection

she is benediction
She is addicted to thee
She is the rude connection
she is connecting w/ he
here I go well I don't know why
I open so sencelessly
could it be he's taken over me
I'm dancing barefoot
heading for a spin
some strange music draws me
in / makes me come on
like some heroine

She is consecration
~~She is the essence.~~
She is concentrating on thee
she is slow sensation
streaming the essence of he
here I come well I don't ~~know~~
why, ~~spend~~
I ~~flow~~ so ceacelessly
could it be he's taken
over me

《赤脚起舞》, 1978

DANCING BAREFOOT

赤脚起舞 [1]

She is benediction	她是恩赐
She is addicted to thee	她对你上瘾
She is the rude connection	她狂暴地联结
She is connecting with he	她和他联结在一起

Here I go and I don't know why	我要走了我也不知道为什么
I spin so ceaselessly	我不停旋转
Could it be he's taking over me	会不会是他已掌控了我
I'm dancing barefoot	我赤脚起舞
Heading for a spin	朝着旋转靠近
Some strange music draws me in	有种怪异的音乐吸引着我
Makes me come on like some heroine	让我像女英雄那样前进

She is sublimation	她是升华
She is the essence of thee	她是你的本质
She is concentrating on he	她的注意力集中于他
Who is chosen by she	那被她所挑选之人

Here I go and I don't know why	我要走了我也不知道为什么
I spin so ceaselessly	我不停旋转
Could it be he's taking over me	会不会是他已掌控了我

I'm dancing barefoot	我赤脚起舞
Heading for a spin	朝着旋转靠近
Some strange music draws me in	有种怪异的音乐吸引着我
Makes me come on like some heroine	让我像女英雄那样前进

She is re-creation	她是再造之物
She, intoxicated by thee	她，为你迷醉
She has the slow sensation	她感觉很迟钝
That he is levitating with she	他和她飘浮在空气里

Here I go and I don't know why	我要走了我也不知道为什么
I spin so ceaselessly	我不停旋转
'Till I lose my sense of gravity	直到对重力失去感觉
I'm dancing barefoot	我赤脚起舞
Heading for a spin	朝着旋转靠近
Some strange music draws me in	有种怪异的音乐吸引着我
Makes me come on like some heroine	让我像女英雄那样前进

Oh God, I fell for you	哦天呢，我爱上了你
Oh God, I fell for you	哦天呢，我爱上了你
Oh God, I feel the fever	哦天呢，我感到狂热

Oh God, I feel the pain	哦天呢，我感到痛苦
Oh God, forever after	哦天呢，之后到永远
Oh God, I'm back again	哦天呢，我又回来了
Oh God, I fell for you	哦天呢，我爱上了你
Oh God, I fell for you	哦天呢，我爱上了你

1 《挥手》最初发表时，帕蒂在唱片封套上描述这首歌是献给像意大利艺术家阿梅代奥·莫迪利亚尼（Amedeo Modigliani, 1884—1920）的爱人让娜·埃比泰纳（Jeanne Hébuterne, 1898—1920）这样的女性的。1917 年，赫布特尼与莫迪里安尼相识相恋，在家人强烈反对下与莫迪里安尼同居，并生下大女儿。1919 年赫布特尼再度怀孕，莫迪里安尼却患上结核性脑膜炎，最终于 1920 年 1 月病逝。赫布特尼的家人随后将她接回家中，然而伤心欲绝的赫布特尼在葬礼翌日从五楼公寓的窗户一跃而下，结束了她和腹中婴儿的生命。

REVENGE

I feel upset. Let's do some celebrating

Come on honey don't hesitate now

Needed you. You withdrew. I was so forsaken

Ah, but now the tables have turned. My move

I believe I'll be taking my revenge. Sweet revenge

I thought you were some perfect read-out. Some digital delay

Had obscured and phased my view of the wicked hand you played

The sands and hands of time have run out. Run out

You better face it this thing's run amok. This luck

I do know how to replace it with revenge. Sweet revenge

I gave you a wristwatch baby

You wouldn't even give me the time of day

You want to know what makes me tick

Now it's me that's got precious little to say

For the ghosts of our love have dried have died

There's no use faking it

The spirits going to close in on you tonight

High time I was taking my revenge

Sweet revenge. Revenge. Revenge

复仇

我有点沮丧。来搞点庆祝吧

来吧亲爱的别再犹豫

需要你。你退出。我这样被遗弃

啊，但如今这棋局已逆转。轮到我了

我坚信我将开始复仇。甜蜜的复仇

我曾以为你是某种完美读数。数字的延迟

模糊阻碍了我视线看不清你耍的邪恶手段

时间的沙漏和指针都已耗完。耗完

你最好直面它已杀到门前。这运气

我知道如何用复仇取代它。甜蜜的复仇

我给你一块手表宝贝

你甚至不给我一天的时间

你想知道是什么驱动我

现在换成是我没什么好说

因为我们爱的魂灵已枯干已死透

没必要惺惺作态

那幽灵今夜会向你逼近

是时候了我要开始复仇

甜蜜的复仇。复仇。复仇

All the gold and silver couldn't measure

Up my love for you. It's so immaterial

I wouldn't wait around if I were you

In the valley of wait-ting ting

Nobody gets nothing. Nobody gets anything.

No time for kisses

Don't leave me no space in your little boat

You ain't going to need, no you ain't going to need no little boat

You are living on marked time my dear. Revenge. Sweet revenge.

Sweet, sweet revenge.

金山银海也无法衡量

我对你的爱。它缥缈无形

如果我是你就不会在此等候

在这等待——待——待的溪谷里

没有一个赢家。没人赢得任何事。

没时间吻别了

别在你小船里给我留位子

你不需要，不你不需要什么小船

你活在停滞的时间里我亲爱的。复仇。甜蜜的复仇。

甜蜜，甜蜜的复仇。

142

Aint got a passport
Aint got a real name
Ain got a chance spot
at fortune n fame
and to U walk these empty streets
won't you give me a lift
a lift / a lift.
on 'Um Citizenship.

They were rioting in Chicago
movement in L.a,
1968 broke The Yardbirds
were were broke as well
took it underground
MC Borderline
Up against the wall
The wall / the wall
show your papers boy

~~and~~ unarmed
~~All~~ ~~came~~ New York City
~~she~~ entered her embrace
~~ill~~ ~~work~~ ~~nowhere~~ I sleep
So we hit the streets
men in uniform
Jove no vinegar
spoon of misery

~~throw~~ give like
give a life ~~get~~ a life
get a lifeline

CITIZEN SHIP

公民船 [1]

It was nothing. It didn't matter to me	这没什么。对我已无关紧要
There were tanks all over my city	在我的城市里到处都是坦克
There was water outside the windows	窗外有水浸没
And children in the streets were throwing rocks at tanks	大街上的孩子们把石块掷向坦克

Ain't got a passport ain't got my real name	没有护照也没有真实姓名
Ain't got a chance sport at fortune or fame	没有机会嘲笑财富或声誉
As I walk these endless streets won't you give me a lift	我走在没有尽头的大街上你不让我搭个便车吗
A lift a lift on your citizen ship	搭个便车搭个便车搭上你的公民船

They were rioting in Chicago movement in L.A.	他们在芝加哥搞暴乱在洛杉矶搞运动
'68 it broke the Yardbirds. We were broke as well	68 年他们解散了"雏鸟" [2]。我们也破了产
Took it underground. M.C. borderline. Up against the wall	进入地下。汽车城 [3] 边界线。靠墙站着
The wall. The wall. Show your papers boy	靠墙。靠墙。出示你的证件孩子

Citizen ship we got memories. Stateless they got shame	公民船我们拥有记忆。没有国籍他们只得到羞辱
Cast adrift from the citizen ship lifeline denied exiled this castaway	公民船随波逐流拒绝放下救生索流放这些漂流者

Blind alley in New York City in a foreign embrace	纽约城的死胡同缩在异域的拥抱里
If you're hungry you're not too particular about what you'll taste	要是你饿了就不会挑剔能吃到什么
Men in uniform gave me vinegar spoon of misery	穿制服的男人递给我醋 [4] 品尝一勺痛苦

But what the hell I fell I fell. It doesn't matter to me

Citizen ship we got memories. Citizen ship we got pain

Cast adrift from the citizen ship lifeline denied exile this castaway

I was caught up like a moth with its wings out of sync

Cut the cord. Overboard. Just a refugee

Lady liberty lend a hand to me I've been cast adrift

Adrift. Adrift. Adrift. Adrift. Adrift. Adrift

On the citizen ship we got memory. Citizen ship we got pain

Lose your grip on the citizen ship you're cast you're cast away

On the citizen ship you got memory. Citizen ship you got pain

Citizen ship you got identity. A name a name a name

A name. Ivan. A name. Ivan Kral. Name. Name.

What's your name son. New York City. What's your name.

What's your name. What's your name. Name. Nothing.

I got nothing. Name. Name. Name. Name. Wake up.

Give me your tired your poor. Give me your huddled masses

Your war torn on your tender seas. Give me your war torn

On your shores of dawn. Lift up your golden lamp to me.

但又怎样呢我倒下了我倒下。对我已无关紧要

公民船我们拥有记忆。公民船我们得到痛苦

公民船随波逐流拒绝放下救生索流放这些漂流者

我像只飞蛾被抓住双翅无法再与世界同步

砍断绳子。跌落船下。只是一个流亡者

自由女神帮帮我吧我已被放逐漂流

漂流。漂流。漂流。漂流。漂流。漂流。

在公民船上我们拥有记忆。公民船上我们得到痛苦

在公民船上你失去控制你被抛弃你被放逐

在公民船上你拥有记忆。公民船上你得到痛苦

公民船上你获得身份。一个名字一个名字一个名字

一个名字。伊万。一个名字。伊万·克拉尔 5。名字。名字。

你叫什么名字孩子。纽约城。你叫什么名字。

你叫什么名字。你叫什么名字。名字。一无所有。

我一无所有。名字。名字。名字。名字。醒醒吧。

交给我你疲惫困乏的人们吧。交给我你的芸芸众生

战争撕裂你温柔的海洋。交给我那撕裂了你

黎明海岸的战争。举起你金色的明灯照亮我。 6

Ahh, it's all mythology

啊，这全部都是神话

1　帕蒂用这首《公民船》来探讨移民及难民问题。在现场演唱中，帕蒂会大声提问"你叫什么名字"，乐队成员则会喊出自己的名字作为回应。

2　"雏鸟"（The Yardbirds），英国摇滚乐队，在1960年代中期创作了一系列热门歌曲。

3　"汽车城"（Motor City）是美国密歇根州底特律的绰号。帕蒂的丈夫弗雷德·索尼克·史密斯曾担任吉他手的乐队"MC5"全称为"Motor City 5"，正是为了致敬乐队成员的老家底特律。

4　耶稣被钉在十字架上时说"我渴了"，人们没有给他送去水，却拿醋给他喝。

5　伊万·克拉尔（Ivan Král，1948—2020），美国词曲作者、贝斯手、唱片制作人、电影制作人，也是帕蒂的乐队伙伴。出生于捷克，1966年以难民身份随父母移居美国。

6　以上三行歌词是对自由女神像底座内著名铭文的讽刺性改写。这段铭文出自美国诗人艾玛·拉撒路（Emma Lazarus，1849—1887）的十四行诗《新巨人》（"The New Colossus"）。

SEVEN WAYS OF GOING

I've got seven ways of going seven wheres to be

Seven sweet disguises, seven ways of serving Thee

Lord, I do extol Thee for Thou hast lifted me

Woke me up and shook me out of mine iniquity

For I was undulating in the lewd impostered night

Steeped in a dream to rend the seams to redeem the rock of right

Swept through the seas of Galilee and the Seven Hills of Rome

Seven sins were wrung from the sight of me

Lord, I turned my neck toward home

I opened up my arms to you and we spun from life to life

'Till you loosened me and let me go toward the everlasting light

In this big step I am taking seven seizures for the true

I got seven ways of going seven ways of serving you

As I move through seven levels as I move upon the slate

As I declare to you the number of my moves as I speculate

The eighth seeking love without exception a light upon the swarm

Seeking love without exception a saint in any form

七条要走的路

我有七条要走的路七个要去的地方

七种甜蜜的伪装，七种侍奉你的方式

主啊，我赞美你因你提升我

唤醒我，将我从自己的罪孽中解脱

我曾在淫荡伪劣的夜晚里波来荡去

沉溺于撕开裂缝救赎正义之石的梦里

横扫加利利海 ¹ 和罗马七丘 ²

七宗罪在我眼前被绞除

主啊，我转身走回家的方向

我向你张开双臂，我们从生命旋向生命

直到你松开我，允我走向那永恒之光

迈出这一大步我发作了七次真正的惊厥

我有七条要走的路七种侍奉你的方式

我穿越了七个层次，我在石板上移动

我向你宣布移动的步数，我猜想

那第八步，毫无例外是寻求爱，照亮蜂群的明灯

毫无例外是寻求爱，做任何形式的圣徒

1 加利利海，又称太巴列湖，以色列最大的内陆淡水湖。由于这个湖泊位于地势低洼的裂谷中，群山环抱，经常突然发生强烈的风暴，在《圣经·新约》中就记载了指耶稣平静风暴并在此传道的故事。

2 罗马七丘指位于罗马心脏地带台伯河东侧的七座山。根据罗马神话，其为罗马建城之初的重要宗教与政治中心，所以罗马被称为"七丘之城"。

BROKEN FLAG

Nodding though the lamp's lit low. Nod for passers underground

To and fro she's darning and the land is weeping red and pale

Weeping yarn from Algiers. Weeping yarn from Algiers

Weaving though the eyes are pale. What will rend will also mend

The sifting cloth is binding and the dream she weaves will never end

For we're marching toward Algiers. For we're marching toward Algiers

Lullaby though baby's gone. Lullaby a broken song

Oh, the cradle was our call. When it rocked we carried on

And we marched on toward Algiers. Forward marching toward Algiers

We're still marching for Algiers. Marching, marching for Algiers

Not to hail a barren sky. The sifting cloth is weeping red

The mourning veil is waving high a field of stars and tears we've shed

In the sky a broken flag. Children wave and raise their arms

We'll be gone but they'll go on and on and on and on and on

破损的旗帜

尽管灯光黯淡她仍在点头。向地下的旅人点头致意

她针线来回穿梭织补着，大地泣出了鲜红与苍白

泣出阿尔及尔的纱。泣出阿尔及尔的纱

尽管双眼苍白她仍在纺织。能被撕裂的东西也能被修补

筛布捆缚在一起，她编织的梦境永远没有尽头

因为我们正向着阿尔及尔行进。因为我们正向着阿尔及尔行进

尽管婴儿已逝摇篮曲依旧。一首破碎的歌这支摇篮曲

哦，这摇篮就是我们的召唤。当它摇晃起来我们继续前进

我们向着阿尔及尔行进。一路向前向着阿尔及尔行进

我们仍在向着阿尔及尔行进。行进，向阿尔及尔行进

不要向贫瘠的天空欢呼致敬。筛布正泣出鲜红

哀悼的面纱高高飘扬，我们曾洒下的一片星空和泪滴

破损的旗帜在空中飘扬。孩子们挥舞着高举起双臂

我们将逝去但他们会继续前进 前进 前进 前进

HYMN

When I am troubled in the night

He comes to comfort me

He wills me thru the darkness

And the empty child is free

To take his hand his sacred heart

The heart that breaks the dawn

Amen. And when I think

I've had my fill he fills up again

赞美诗

当我在夜里烦躁不安

他前来安抚我

他带我穿过黑暗

令空虚之子得自由

握住他的手他神圣的心

那颗驱散黎明的心

阿门。当我以为

我已得满足他再次盈满我

Time is the space + the wall around
time to adore and time to go
to give to the fisherman
to give up the goss

Time does the moments
your children will hold
the wave of your hand
the smile of your soul

burning yearing
like some heroine

cara papa

its been a long time since last we
spoke. here is a sad bicycle lying
on its side mourning its wheel.
which way do we turn. and in turn
when is there to stop turning.
Time is expressed in the heart of
an instrument. time is the space
and the wall around. ~~sometimes~~
~~I fear the to the fisherman~~
time to adore and time to go
the shoes of the fisherman

WAVE

Hi. Hi. I was running after you for a long time. I was watching you for . . . actually I've watched you for a long time. I like to watch you when you're walking back and forth on the beach. And the way your, the way your cloth looks. I like I like to see the edges, the bottom of it get all wet when you're walking near the water there. It's real nice to talk to you. I didn't. I-I-I-I. How are you? How are you? I saw I saw you from your balcony window and you were standing there waving at everybody. It was really great because there was about a billion people there, but when I was waving to you, the way your face was, it was so, the way your face was, it made me feel exactly like we're, it's not that you were just waving to me, but that we were we were waving to each other. Really it was really wonderful. I really felt happy. It really made me happy. And. Um. I. I just wanted to thank you because you, you really really you made me feel good and, oh, I, it's nothing. Well I'm just clumsy. No, it's just a Band-Aid. No, it's OK. Oh no, I'm always doing. Something's always happening to me. Well. I'll be seeing you. Good-bye. Bye. Good-bye sir. Good-bye papa.

Wave thou art pretty, Wave thou art high
Wave thou art music, Wave thou art why

挥手

嗨。嗨。我在你身后追逐了很久。我望着你望了……实际上我望着你已经望了很久。我喜欢望着你在海滩上走来走去。还有你的，你的衣服的样子。我喜欢我喜欢看你在海边靠近海水散步时衣服的边缘，衣服底部全都湿掉的样子。跟你说话真是太好了。我没有。我——我——我——我。你还好吗？你还好吗？我看见我看见你在阳台窗户那儿，你站在那儿冲所有人挥着手。这很了不起因为下面估计有十亿人，但当我冲你挥手时，你的脸看起来，实在是，你的脸看起来，让我感觉我们正对着彼此，不只是你在对着我挥手，而是我们在我们在对着彼此挥手。这真的这真的是太美好了。我真的感觉很幸福。这真的让我感觉很幸福。而且。嗯。我。我只想感谢你因为你，你真的真的让我感觉很美好而且，哦，我，没事了。没事我总是笨手笨脚。没事，这只是枚创可贴。不，没事的。哦不，我总是这样。总有些什么事儿发生在我身上。好吧。我会再见到你的。再见了。拜。再见了先生。再见了老爹 [1]。

挥手你那么美，挥手你那么高
挥手你是音乐，挥手你是理由

Wave thou art pretty, Wave thou art high

Wave to the city, wave wave good-bye

—for Albino Luciano, Pope John Paul I

挥手你那么美，挥手你那么高

向着城市挥手，挥手挥手告别

——献给阿尔比诺·卢恰尼，教宗若望·保禄一世 [2]

1　原文为"papa"，在拉丁语中意为教宗，天主教会最高领袖。

2　教宗若望·保禄一世（Pope John Paul I, 1912—1978），本名阿尔比诺·卢恰尼（Albino Luciani），天主教前教宗及梵蒂冈城国国家元首。他于 1978 年 8 月 26 日上任，仅仅 33 天之后就去世了，是历任教宗中执政时间最短的人之一，也是第一位出生于 20 世纪的教宗。在意大利，他被教徒亲切地称作"微笑教宗"。帕蒂在这首歌里想象自己与若望·保禄一世对话。

DREAM OF LIFE

人 生 之 梦

Peace, peace! he is not dead, he doth not sleep—
He hath awakened from the dream of life—
—PERCY BYSSHE SHELLEY

安静，安静！他并未死，也非睡着——
他只是从人生之梦中醒来——*
——雪莱

★ 选自雪莱的长诗《阿多尼斯》（"Adonais"）第 39 节。阿多尼斯是希腊神话中掌管植物每年复活的春日之神，因此他也会每年死而复生、永远年轻俊美。在这首诗里，雪莱借描述阿多尼斯来悼念 25 岁便英年早逝的英国诗人济慈。写下本诗一年后，29 岁的雪莱出海遭遇风暴遇难。

沉寂九年之后，帕蒂·史密斯于1988年发布了新专辑《人生之梦》。与70年代的四张专辑相比，这张回归之作最显著的不同是帕蒂对于专辑共同参与制作者的选择。之前的专辑中，帕蒂的主要拍档是莱尼·凯。在《人生之梦》中，帕蒂的共同作曲、制作人除吉米·艾欧文之外还有丈夫弗雷德·索尼克·史密斯，这也是弗雷德参与制作的唯一一张帕蒂的专辑。

弗雷德是底特律摇滚乐队"MC5"的前成员，极有天赋且在摇滚乐方面受过更专业训练的弗雷德为专辑的每一首曲目都增添了一些更主流的元素。从某种意义上，《人生之梦》似乎不应当拿来与任何帕蒂此前的专辑作比较，九年之后，她种种诗意的"宣泄"转而趋向平静。《群马》时期的帕蒂狂挥摇滚之旗，也激励了众多女性摇滚乐手，而《人生之梦》中的她并不在挥舞旗帜，而是牢牢地抓紧了它。帕蒂唱自己的婚姻、孩子和普通人生活，以此宣布她的复出。不过，在这一次复出后不久，帕蒂再次从公众视野消失，直到90年代。

《人生之梦》的主打歌曲《人民拥有力量》在发行后多次于美国专辑导向摇滚电台（AOR）放送，帕蒂与弗雷德在1990年的爱丽斯塔唱片十五周年庆典上首次现场演唱了这首歌。而专辑后半部分的《使命在召唤》一首，似乎展示了《人民拥有力量》的另一面，即力量也会有倾塌的时刻。《人生之梦》问世之时，帕蒂育有一儿一女。因而在这张专辑中，除了鼓舞人心的政治宣言，人们也听到了写给孩子的摇篮曲、给自然的颂歌、对历史人物的致意，以及向友人的道别。帕蒂再一次与时代背道而驰。在人人想要逃离现实的80年代，她并未将艺术作为逃离的手段，而是用它直视自己最真实的生活。这张专辑的封面再次由罗伯特·梅普尔索普拍摄，他在1989年病逝。

《滚石》杂志这样评论《生活之梦》，"我们听到的不是任何'产品'，这里只有音乐"。

PEOPLE HAVE THE POWER

人民拥有力量 [1]

I was dreaming in my dreaming	我在做梦在我的梦中
Of an aspect bright and fair	有处地方光明又公平
And my sleeping it was broken	我的睡眠它已被打断
But my dream it lingered near	但这梦境仍在旁徘徊
In the form of shining valleys	梦中地方像闪亮山谷
Where the pure air recognized	那里的空气纯净清新
And my senses newly opened	我的感官被全新打开
But I awakened to the cry	但当我醒来听到呐喊
That the people have the power	人民拥有力量
To redeem the work of fools	救赎愚人的工作
From the meek the graces shower	还与谦恭与恩典甘霖
It's decreed the people rule	皆是注定应归权于民
The people have the power	人民拥有力量
The people have the power	人民拥有力量
Vengeful aspects became suspect	报复的神迹变得可疑
And bending low as if to hear	俯身下来像是要倾听
And the armies ceased advancing	军队已经停止了前进
Because the people had their ear	因为人民有自己耳朵
And the shepherds and the soldiers	那些牧羊人还有士兵

Lay beneath the stars	躺在星空下面
Exchanging visions	交换彼此愿景
Laying arms	他们放下武器
To waste in the dust	废弃丢入尘中
In the form of shining valleys	梦中地方像闪亮山谷
Where the pure air recognized	那里的空气纯净清新
And my senses newly opened	我的感官被全新打开
I awakened to the cry	当我醒来听到呐喊
The people have the power	人民拥有力量
The people have the power	人民拥有力量
Where there were deserts	在那荒漠之地
I saw fountains	我看到清泉
Like cream the waters rise	泉水乳脂般翻涌
And we strolled there together	我们一同在那里漫步
With none to laugh or criticize	没有人嘲笑或是责难
And the leopard	那些豹子
And the lamb	还有羔羊
Lay together truly bound	躺在一起真心地联结
I was hoping in my hoping	我在祈愿在我愿望里

To recall what I had found　　　　　　　　　能回想起我所有发现

I was dreaming in my dreaming　　　　　　我在做梦在我的梦中

God knows a purer view　　　　　　　　　上帝懂得更纯洁的愿景

As I surrender to my sleeping　　　　　　当我向自己的睡眠投降

I commit my dream to you　　　　　　　　我将我的梦想托付于你

The people have the power　　　　　　　　人民拥有力量

The power to dream to rule　　　　　　　有权力去梦想去统治

To wrestle the Earth from fools　　　　　将地球从愚人手中夺回

It's decreed the people rule　　　　　　皆是注定应归权于民

It's decreed the people rule　　　　　　皆是注定应归权于民

Listen. I believe everything we dream　　听着。我相信我们梦想的一切

Can come to pass through our union　　　通过我们的联合均能实现

We can turn the world around　　　　　　我们能够翻转世界

We can turn the earth's revolution　　　我们能够改变地球的公转

We have the power　　　　　　　　　　　我们拥有力量

People have the power　　　　　　　　　人民拥有力量

---

1 帕蒂接受采访时提到，这首歌最初的想法来自她的丈夫弗雷德·索尼克·史密斯。弗雷德希望这是一首全世界的人都可以喜欢并演唱的歌，激励人们为各自不同的事业而努力。它在专辑发行之初没有受到太多关注，如今已成为帕蒂最知名的歌曲之一。

UP THERE DOWN THERE

Up there

There's a ball of fire

Some call it the spirit

Some call it the sun

Its energies are not for hire

It serves man it serves everyone

Down there where Jonah wails

In the healing water

In the ready depths

Twisting like silver swans

No line of death no boundaries

Up there

The eye is hollow

The eye is winking

The winds ablaze

Angels howling

The sphinx awakens

But what can she say

You'd be amazed

那上面那下面

那上面

有一团火球

有人称它为神灵

有人称它为太阳

它的能量不供租用

它为人类服务为每个人服务

那下面约拿 [1] 在悲泣

浸在疗愈之水中

陷在已有深深处

身体扭折如银色天鹅

没有死亡线没有边界

那上面

眼睛空洞

眼睛在眨

烈风燃烧

天使咆哮

斯芬克斯醒来

但她能说什么

会令你惊奇

Down there	那下面
Your days are numbered	你的时日已屈指可数
Nothing to fear	不要恐惧
There will be trumpets	会有号角响起
There will be silence	会有寂静笼罩
In the end the end	到头来到最后
Will be here just here	会来这里只在这

Ahh the borders of heaven	啊，天堂的边界
Are zipped up tight tonight	今夜会将拉链拉紧
The abstract streets	抽象的街道
The lights like some	灯光就像是
Switched-on Mondrian	新潮的蒙德里安 [2]
Cats like us are obsolete	像我们这样很酷的人已经过时
Hey Man don't breathe on my feet	嘿老兄，别冲着我脚呵气
Thieves, poets we're inside out	我们从里到外就是小偷，诗人
And everybody's a soldier	每个人都是士兵
Angels howl at those abstract lights	天使对着那些抽象的灯光嚎叫
And the borders of heaven	天堂的边界
Are zipped up tight tonight	今夜会将拉链拉紧

151

Up there	那上面
There's a ball of fire	有一团火球
Some call it the spirit	有人称它为神灵
Some call it the sun	有人称它为太阳
Its energies are not for hire	它的能量不供租用
It serves man it serves everyone	它为人类服务为每个人服务
The air we breathe	我们呼吸的空气
The flame of wisdom	智慧之火焰
The earth we grind	我们碾碎的土地
The beckoning sea	诱人的海洋
It's no mystery	这并不神秘
Not sentimental	也不叫人伤感
Ahh the equation	啊，这些方程式
It's all elemental	都是四元素的精灵 [3]
The world is restless	世界动荡不宁
Heaven in flux	天堂变化不定
Angels appear	天使现身
From the bright storm	划开明亮的暴风雨
Out of the shadows	驱散阴影

Up there, down there	那上面，那下面
But what can we say	但我们能说什么呢
Man's been forewarned	人类早已被预警
All communion is not holy	并非所有圣餐都神圣
Even those that fall	即便是那些堕落之人
They can prophet	他们能够预言
Understanding	能够理解
It's all for man	一切都是为了人类
It's for everyone	为了每一个人
It's up there,	它就在那上面
Down there	那下面
Everywhere	无所不在
Everywhere	无所不在
Time for communion	时候到了共领圣餐
Time for communion	时候到了共领圣餐
Talking communion	谈论圣餐

1 约拿，一名亚伯拉罕诸教的先知，名字意为"鸽子"。根据《圣经》，他被上帝派遣往尼尼微，劝说当地人行在正当的道路上。

2 蒙德里安（Piet Cornelies Mondrian，1872—1944），荷兰画家，风格派运动幕后艺术家和非具象绘画的创始者之一，对后世的建筑、设计等影响很大。

3 古希腊哲学认为世界万物由这土、气、水、火四种基本元素构成。

Speak to me

Speak to me heart

I feel a needing

To bridge the clouds

Softly go

A way I wish to know to know

A way I wish to know to know

对我说吧

心，对我说话

我感受到一种需要

在云层间架起梁桥

轻柔地走去

一条我想知道的路，想知道

一条我想知道的路，想知道

Oh you'll ride

Surely dance in a ring

Backwards and forwards

Those who seek

Feel the glow

A glow we all will know

A glow we all will know

你将乘风破浪

也必将围圈起舞

来来又回回

那些不断追寻的人

感受到光芒

一束我们都将知晓的光

一束我们都将知晓的光

On that day filled with grace

On the way two hearts' communion

Steps we take steps we trace

On the way two hearts' reunion

在盈满恩典的日子

在两颗心交融的途中

我们留下的痕迹我们追溯的脚步

两颗心在那条路上重逢

Paths that cross	相交之路
Will cross again	会再度相交
Paths that cross	相交之路
Will cross again	会再度相交
Speak to me	对我说吧
Speak to me shadow	阴影，对我说话
I spin from the wheel	我在车轮上旋转
Nothing at all save the need	一无所获仍保持着需要
The need to weave	去编织的需要
A silk of souls	灵魂之丝
That whisper whisper	它在耳语在耳语
A silk of souls	灵魂之丝
	它对着我耳语
That whispers to me	
Speak to me heart	心，对我说话
All things renew	诸事焕然一新
Hearts will mend	心灵将被修补
'Round the bend	只要转过弯道
Paths that cross	相交之路
Cross again	会再度相交

Paths that cross

Will cross again

相交之路

会再度相交

Rise up hold the reins

We'll meet

I don't know when

Hold tight bye bye

Paths that cross

Will cross again

Paths that cross

Will cross again

站起身来紧握缰绳

我们会再相遇

我不知是何时

抓紧说声拜拜

相交之路

会再度相交

相交之路

会再度相交

—for Samuel J. Wagstaff Jr.

——写给小塞缪尔·J. 瓦格斯塔夫 [1]

1 小塞缪尔·J. 瓦格斯塔夫（Samuel J. Wagstaff Jr.，1921—1987），美国艺术收藏家、策展人，因其对极简艺术、波普艺术、概念艺术的支持而闻名，是罗伯特·梅普尔索普在艺术上的引导者、资助者、长期伴侣，也对帕蒂的创作有很大支持。1987 年 1 月他死于因艾滋病引发的肺炎。帕蒂得知后，写下了这首歌纪念他。

SOMALIA

索马里

I don't know why I feel this way today	不知为何我今天有这样的感觉
The sky is blue the table is laid	天空湛蓝餐桌已铺好
The trees are heavy with yellow fruit	树上缀满沉甸甸的黄色果实
And in their shade children happily play	孩子们躲在树荫下快乐玩耍

The pears have fallen to the ground	梨子掉落地面
My child places one in my hand	孩子捡起一颗放在我手上
The sun is warm upon my face	太阳暖洋洋地烘烤我的脸庞
And I dream of a burning land	而我梦到一片燃烧的土地

Mother of famine take this pear	饥荒之母握着这颗梨
Upon an arrow through the rings of time	驾一枚箭头穿过时间之环
This small fruit this golden prayer	小小果实这金色的祈祷
May it pass from this hand to thine	愿它从我手中传于你手

If I were rain I'd rain on Somalia	如果我是雨水我愿落在索马里
If I were grain for Somalia I'd grow	如果我是索马里的谷物我愿生长
If I were bread I would rise for Somalia	如果我是面包我愿长在索马里
If I were a river for Somalia I'd flow	如果我是索马里的河流我愿流淌

All the mothers will dream of thee	所有母亲都会梦到你

All the mothers bless thy empty hand

所有母亲祝福你空荡荡的手

All the mothers will grieve for thee

所有母亲都会哀悼你

All the sorrow a mother can stand

一位母亲能承受的全部悲伤

If we were rain we would rain for Somalia

如果我是雨水我愿落在索马里

If we were grain for Somalia we'd grow

如果我是索马里的谷物我愿生长

If we were bread we would rise for Somalia

如果我是面包我愿长在索马里

If we were a river for Somalia we'd flow

如果我是索马里的河流我愿流淌

*—This lyric was written in memory of Audrey Hepburn,
who worked with the simple industry of a servant to give comfort to the
victims of the famine in Somalia.*

——这首歌词为纪念奥黛丽·赫本而写，
她以仆人般的质朴勤劳工作着，为索马里饥荒的受害者带
去安慰。

WILD LEAVES

野树叶 [1]

Wild leaves are falling	野树叶在坠落
Falling to the ground	坠落向地面
Every leaf a moment	每片树叶都享有一刻
A light upon the crown	如皇冠之上一道光
That we'll all be wearing	我们都将穿上它
In a time unbound	度过无拘束的时光
And wild leaves are falling	野树叶在坠落
Falling to the ground	坠落向地面
Every word that's spoken	说出的每个字
Every word decreed	宣誓的每个字
Every spell that's broken	被破除的每个咒语
Every golden deed	金闪闪的每件好事
All the parts we're playing	我们扮演的所有角色
Binding as the reed	芦苇般紧紧捆束在一起
And wild leaves are falling	野树叶在坠落
Wild wild leaves	狂野的野树叶
The spirits that are mentioned	被提及的那些魂灵
The myths that have been shorn	被夺走的那些神话
Everything we've been through	我们经历过的所有事情

And the colors worn	穿着过的颜色
Every chasm entered	进入过的每一道峡谷
Every story wound	受过伤的每一个故事
And wild leaves are falling	野树叶在坠落
Falling to the ground	坠落向地面
As the campfire's burning	篝火熊熊燃烧
As the fire ignites	当火焰燃起
All the moments turning	所有瞬间开始变转
In the stormy bright	旋入风暴般的光明
Well enough the churning	很好啊，这翻腾
Well enough believe	很好啊，去相信
The coming and the going	来来又去去
Wild wild leaves	狂野的野树叶

1 帕蒂在《只是孩子》（*Just Kids*）书中写到，这首歌是在罗伯特·梅普尔索普41岁生日那天为他而作的。当时罗伯特已身陷艾滋病痛中。

WHERE DUTY CALLS

使命在召唤

In a room in Lebanon	黎巴嫩的一个房间
They silently slept	他们安静地睡着
They were dreaming	他们做着梦
Crazy dreams	是疯狂的梦
In a foreign alphabet	梦里说着外文字母
Lucky young boys	幸运的年轻男孩们
Cross on the main	穿过主干路
The driver was approaching	司机在靠近
The American zone	美国安全区
The waving of hands	手臂在挥动
The tiniest train	最迷你的火车
They never dreamed	他们做梦也没想到
They'd never wake again	自己再也无法醒来
Voice of the Swarm	蜂群声音阵阵响起
We follow we fall	我们跟随我们倒下
Some kneel for priests	有的面朝牧师跪拜
Some wail at walls	有的对着墙壁哀泣
Flag on a match head	火柴头上立着旗帜
God or the law	不管上帝还是法律
And they'll all go together	他们都会一起前去

162

Where duty calls	那里有使命在召唤
United children	团结的孩子们
Child of Iran	伊朗之子
Parallel prayers	平行的祈祷
Baseball Koran	棒球古兰经
I'll protect mama	我会保护妈妈
I'll lie awake	我会清醒地躺下
I'll die for Allah	我会为真主而死
In a holy war	死在一场圣战里
I'll be a ranger	我会成为突击队员
I'll guard the streams	我会守住溪水
I'll be a soldier	我会成为一名战士
A sleeping marine	沉睡的海军陆战队员
In the heart of the ancient	古老之心中
Ali smiles	阿里在微笑
In the soul of the desert	沙漠的灵魂里
The sun blooms	阳光在绽放
Awake into the glare	我们所有小小的战争

Of all our little wars	在耀眼的光中醒来
Who pray to salute	谁祈祷着去致敬
The coming and dying	将至的与将死的
Of the moon	那月亮
Oh sleeping sun	哦沉睡的太阳
Assassin in prayer	祷告中的刺杀者
Laid a compass deep	把罗盘放得很深
Exploding dawn	爆破开黎明
And himself as well	也炸开了他自己
Their eyes for his eyes	以他们之眼还他的眼
Their breath for his breath	以他们之呼吸还他的呼吸
All to his end	直至他生命尽头
And a room in Lebanon	黎巴嫩的一个房间
Dust of scenes	尘埃遍布的现场
Erase and blend	擦除并混合
May the blanket of kings	愿众王之毯
Cover them and him	盖住他们和他
Forgive them Father	原谅他们吧我父

They know not what they do

From the vast portals

Of their consciousness

They're calling to you

—This lyric was written in memory of those who lost their lives in the destruction of the First Battallion, 8th Marine Headquarters, Beirut, October 23, 1983. Two hundred and forty-one marines, sailors, and soldiers on a peacekeeping mission perished with their assassin.

他们不知自己在做什么

他们站在意识的

广阔入口处

呼唤你

——这首歌词为纪念1983年10月23日在贝鲁特第八海军陆战队总部第一营被摧毁事件中失去生命的人们。241名正在执行维和任务的海军陆战队员、水手及士兵在此事件中与刺杀者一同丧生。

DREAM OF LIFE

人生之梦

I'm with you always	我会一直在你身边
You're ever on my mind	你时刻浮在我脑海
In a light to last a whole life through	如一道贯穿一生的绵延之光
Each way I turn the sense of you surrounds	我转向的每一条路都有你的感觉在环绕
In every step I take in all I do	环绕在我迈出的每一步在我做的所有事
Your thoughts your schemes	你的想法你的计划
Captivate my dreams	都迷住我的梦
Everlasting ever new	长久　常新
Sea returns to sea and sky to sky	海水归于海水天空化入天空
In a life of dream am I when I'm with you	在这梦想的人生里我与你共度
Deep in my heart	在我心深处
How the presence of you shines	你的存在光芒闪耀
In a light to last a whole life through	如一道贯穿一生的绵延之光
I recall the wonder of it all	我回想这一切的奇妙
Each dream of life I'll share with you	每段人生之梦我都与你分享
I'm with you always	我会一直在你身边
You're ever on my mind	你时刻浮在我脑海
In a light to last a whole life through	如一道贯穿一生的绵延之光
The hand above turns those leaves of love	上帝之手掀动爱的树叶

All and all a timeless view   一切的一切永恒之景

Each dream of life   由天堂抛下的

Flung from paradise   每段人生之梦

Everlasting ever new   长久　常新

Dream of Life, dream of Life   人生之梦，人生之梦

GOING UNDER

SUN IS RISING
ON THE WATER
LIGHT IS DANCING AGAIN
LETS GO UNDER
WHERE THE SUN BEAMS
LETS GO UNDER
MY FRIEND

ARE WE SLEEPING
ARE WE DREAMING
ARE WE DANCING AGAIN
IS IT HEAVEN
CRACK IT OPEN
AND WE'LL SLIDE DOWN
IT'S STREAM

WE CAN HOLD ON (I'M SURE)
TO THE SEA'S FOAMING MANE
IT WILL SERVE US
WE'LL SURFACE
AND WE'LL PLUNGE BACK AGAIN

SUN IS RISING
ON THE WATER
LIGHT IS DANCING
LIKE A FLAME
THERES NO BURNING
WHERE THE SUN BEAMS
OH ITS SUCH A LOVELY GAME

DOES THE SEA DREAM (I'M SURE)
WE ARE HERE, WE ATTEND
WE ARE BELLS ON THE SHORE
WHERE THE TOLLING SUSPENDS

WHO WILL DECIDE
THE SHAPE OF THINGS
THE SHIFT OF BEING
WHO WILL PERCEIVE
WHEN LIFE IS NEW
SHALL WE DIVIDE
AND BECOME ANOTHER
WHO IS DUE
FOR GIFT UPON GIFT
WHO WILL DECIDE
SHALL WE SWIM/OVER AND OVER
THE CURVE OF A WING
IT'S DESTINATION
EVERCHANGING

SUN IS RISING
ON THE WATER
LIGHT IS DANCING
LIKE A FLAME
LETS GO WALTZING
ON THE WATER
LETS GO UNDER
AGAIN

LETS GO UNDER
going under

《沉入水下》

GOING UNDER

沉入水下

Sun is rising on the water
太阳从水面升起

Light is dancing again
光线再次舞动

Let's go under
我们沉入水下吧

Where the sun beams
那里日光闪耀

Let's go under my friend
沉入水下吧我的朋友

Are we sleeping
我们在睡着吗

Are we dreaming
我们在做梦吗

Are we dancing again
我们再次跳起了舞吗

Is it heaven crack it open
那是天堂吗快敲开它的门

And we'll slide down its stream
我们会滑进它的涓流

We can hold on I'm sure
我们能坚持住我敢肯定

To the sea's foaming mane
触到大海泡沫似的鬃毛

It will serve us
它会照顾我们

We'll surface
我们会浮出海面

And we'll plunge back again
然后我们再次跳回海里

Sun is rising on the water
太阳从水面升起

Light is dancing like a flame
光线舞动如火焰

There's no burning
并没有东西在燃烧

Where the sun beams	那里日光闪耀
Oh it's such a lovely game	哦真是场可爱的游戏
Does the sea dream I'm sure	大海会做梦吗我敢肯定会
We are here, we attend	我们在这里，参与着这场梦
We are bells on the shore	当铃声在半空悬停
As the tolling suspends	我们就是岸上的钟
Who will decide the shape of things	谁能决定万物的形态
The shift of being	生命的转变
Who will perceive when life is new	当生活焕然一新谁能察觉
Shall we divide and become another	我们是否应当分开，去成为另一个人
Who is due for gift upon gift	谁应该一次又一次领受奖赏
Who will decide	谁能决定
Shall we swim over and over	我们要不要游来再游去
The curve of a wing	一羽翅膀的曲线
Its destination ever changing	它的目的地始终在改变
Sun is rising on the water	太阳从水面升起
Light is dancing like a flame	光线舞动如火焰
Let's go waltzing on the water	我们在水面上跳支华尔兹吧

Let's go under again   我们再次沉入水下吧

Let's go under   我们沉入水下

Going under   沉入水下

AS THE NIGHT GOES BY

随这黑夜流逝

Darlin' come under cover

亲爱的来吧做好掩护

Another night to discover

又一个等待发掘的黑夜

Let's slip where senses gather

让我们滑入感官聚合之地

Let's drift between the sea and sky

让我们漂浮在大海与天空之间

As the night goes by

随这黑夜流逝

Sands shift

沙群流转

Orchids so strange

兰花奇幻

In the moonlight

在月光下

Brushing our faces

冲刷着我们的脸

Places where love blooms

在爱意绽放之地

And dies

死去

While the night goes by

随这黑夜流逝

Oh, and the spirits call

哦，幽灵在召唤

Sun upon your shadows fall

你影子上的太阳掉下来

Tracing every breath we draw

追寻我们的每一次呼吸

Come into my dreams

进入我的梦里

Come into my dreams

进入我的梦里

Darlin' let's go where the night goes

亲爱的让我们跟随这黑夜

Let's drift where senses gather

让我们漂浮在感官聚合之地

Let's make this night last forever	让我们将这一夜持续到永远
Into my dreams	进入我梦里
Into my dreams	进入我梦里
Darlin' let's go	亲爱的我们走吧
Where the night goes	跟随这黑夜
Time slips	时光流逝
Oh darlin' how it flies	哦亲爱的它溜得飞快
When the night goes by	随这黑夜流逝
All through the night	度过整个黑夜
Sirens call	塞壬在召唤
Come to me	到我身边来
I'll come to you	我会去你身边
As the night softly	如这温柔夜色
Goes by bye	一同流逝再见
Midnight	午夜
Moon on our shoulder	月亮停在我们肩头
Daybreak	黎明
Another one older	又衰老了一天

173

Darlin' heavenly blue	亲爱的那天国般的蓝
Glories fade into view	荣耀渐渐消融在视线
Let's go	我们走吧
Under the stars	在星空下
That are beating	群星跃动
Under the moonlight	在月光下
Stars shoot	星星闪过
Dusk just a whisper	黄昏只是一声低语
Make this night	就让这黑夜
Last forever	持续到永远
Oh how I wonder	哦我多想知道
Where the night goes	这黑夜到底要去哪儿
Oh let's wonder	哦让我们都来想一想
Where the night goes	这黑夜到底要去哪儿
As the night goes	随这黑夜
By bye	流逝 再见
By bye	流逝 再见

LOOKING FOR YOU (I WAS)

（我一直在）寻找你

In the medieval night	在这中世纪的夜晚
'Twas love's design	那是爱的杰作
And the sky was open	天空敞开怀抱
Like a valentine	像张情人节卡片
All the lacy lights	所有花边灯下
Where wishes fall	祝愿纷纷掉落
And like Shakespeare's child	像莎士比亚的孩子
I wished on them all	我对着它们许愿
Ahh to be your destiny	啊，成为你命定之人
Was all that I pursued	就是我全部的追求
I could see the sights	站在高耸的险峰之上
From the lofty heights	我的视野一片清晰
But my heart obscured the view	但我的心遮蔽了这风景
I was looking for you	我一直在寻找你
Looking for you	寻找你
What could I do	我还能做些什么
I was looking for you	我一直在寻找你
Along the black river	沿着黑色的河流

175

The ambassador jewels

那使者的珠宝

And you were reflected

我所见全部事物

In all that I saw

都反射着你的倒影

In the towers of gold

在金色的高塔中

In the wheel and the wing

在车轮与机翼间

Gripping my senses

如同古老的宣言

Like an ancient claim

紧紧抓住我的感官

Many is the time I knelt in the light

多少次我跪在灯光里

Appealing to all that I knew

恳求我了解的所有事物

Guide my eyes and steps

指引我的双眼和脚步

That I may find love true

那样或许我能找到真爱

I was looking for you

我一直在寻找你

Looking for you

寻找你

What could I do

我还能做些什么

I was looking for you

我一直在寻找你

Come on darlin'

来吧亲爱的

All that hearts desire

内心所渴求的一切

Was written before us

都已写在我们面前

In the medieval fire

It was love's design

In the glittering stars

Like Shakespeare's child

To be where you are

From the Portobello Road

To the Port of Marseilles

Where the dervish turns

Where the wild goats play

Looking for you

I was

在这中世纪的大火中

那是爱的杰作

在这闪烁的星空下

像莎士比亚的孩子

去往你所在之处

从波托贝洛路 [1]

到马赛的港口

在托钵僧旋转之地

在野山羊玩耍之处

我一直在

寻找着你

1 波托贝洛路（Portobello Road），位于伦敦西部诺丁山地区的一条街道，每周六在
  这里会有波托贝洛路集市，是伦敦著名的街头集市之一。

MEMORIAL SONG

悼亡歌

Little emerald bird

小小翠绿鸟

Wants to fly away

想要飞远走

If I cup my hand

若是我拢起手

Could I make him stay

能否将他挽留

Little emerald soul

小小翠绿的灵魂

Little emerald eye

小小翠绿的眼

Little emerald soul

小小翠绿的灵魂

Must you say good-bye

你是否必须说再见

All the things that we pursue

我们追求的所有事

All that we dream

我们全部的梦

Are composed as nature knew

就如大自然所知那样组成

In a feather green

一片翠绿的羽毛

Little emerald bird

小小翠绿鸟

As you light afar it

当你在远处闪亮

is true I heard

我听说，上帝真的

God is where you are

就在你那边

Little emerald soul

小小翠绿的灵魂

Little emerald eye

小小翠绿的眼

Little emerald bird

小小翠绿鸟

178

We must say good-bye

—for Robert Mapplethorpe

我们必须说再见

——献给罗伯特·梅普尔索普[1]

1 罗伯特·梅普尔索普于 1989 年 3 月 9 日因艾滋病逝世于美国波士顿。帕蒂写下这首《悼亡歌》悼念罗伯特。1988 年发布的原《人生之梦》唱片中并未收录这首歌，它最早被收录于 1993 年发布的音乐合集《别无选择》(*No Alternative*)之中。《别无选择》由数位音乐人、制作人与多个乐队共同制作，旨在提高人们对艾滋病的认知并筹款用于艾滋病治疗救济。

THE JACKSON SONG

杰克逊的歌 [1]

Little blue dreamer go to sleep	小小蓝色追梦人你该睡觉了
Let's close our eyes and call the deep	让我们闭上眼睛召唤梦境
Slumbering land that just begins	沉睡之地刚刚启程
When day is done and little dreamers spin	白日已逝小小追梦人旋转吧

First take my hand then let it go	先是抓住我的手然后放开它
Little blue boy you're on your own	小小蓝色男孩你要靠自己了
Little blue wings as those feet fly	小小蓝色翅膀放开双脚飞翔
Little blue shoes that walk across the sky	小小蓝色鞋子漫步穿行天空

May your path be your own	愿你的道路属于自己
But I'm with you	但我会与你同在
And each day you'll grow	每一天你都在成长
He'll be there too	他也会在你身旁
And someday you'll go	终有一日你会离开
We'll follow you	我们也将跟随你
As you go, as you go	伴你走，伴你走

Little blue star that offers light	小小蓝星散发出光
Little blue bird that offers flight	小小蓝鸟展翅飞翔
Little blue path where those feet fall	小小蓝色道路由那些脚步踩过

180

Little blue dreamer won't you dream it all	小小蓝色追梦人这一切你会梦到吗
May your path be your own	愿你的道路属于自己
But I'm with you	但我会与你同在
And each day you'll grow	每一天你都在成长
He'll be there too	他也会在你身旁
And someday you'll go	终有一日你会离开
We'll follow you	我们也将跟随你
As you go, as you go	伴你走，伴你走
And in your travels you will see	在旅途中你会看到
Warrior wings remember Daddy	勇士之翼，记得那是爹地
And if a mama bird you see	要是你看到了一只妈妈鸟
Folding her wings will you remember me	收折她的翅膀你会记得那是我吗
As you go, as you go, as you go, as you go	伴你走，伴你走，伴你走，伴你走

---

1 这是帕蒂写给儿子杰克逊·史密斯（Jackson Smith）的一首摇篮曲。杰克逊出生
于 1982 年，是帕蒂与弗雷德的第一个孩子，后来成了一位音乐人、吉他手，曾
多次参与母亲帕蒂的音乐创作及演出。

GONE AGAIN

再 次 离 开

再次离开公众视线多年后，帕蒂在 1995 年末以一系列演唱会重新回到乐坛。1996 年 6 月，她发行了第六张录音室专辑《再次离开》。

《人生之梦》与《再次离开》之间相隔八年。在此期间，帕蒂经历了众多友人与同辈的离世，其中包括她的丈夫弗雷德、兄弟托德、挚友罗伯特·梅普尔索普、乐队伙伴理查德·索尔，还有她与之深深共情的科特·柯本。同时，《再次离开》也记录了著名歌手、乐手杰夫·巴克利生前的最后一次录音室表演，专辑在巴克利离世前发行。

失去至亲之人的失落与哀恸笼罩了整张专辑，但这并不是《再次离开》所传递的所有情绪。与其放任自己的忧郁，帕蒂选择将视线放在爱、友谊与艺术所可能带来的改变上。《再次离开》隐忍而有力，在逝者灵魂的回声中向听者传递独有的乐观和治愈。《翼》《渡鸦》带着生涩与乡间之音，《南十字星座下》《萤火虫》自由而优雅。如帕蒂许多广为传唱的作品，《再次离开》中的大部分曲目不是传统意义上的歌曲，而是被唱出的诗，层叠的音乐中伴随着密集且有启发性的歌词。

当然，帕蒂的丈夫弗雷德也出现在专辑的角角落落。专辑介绍中，他的名字出现在当时轰动一时的曲目《再次离开》和《夏日食人族》的合作者一栏；而在歌曲内容上，《我

的牧歌》一曲令人心痛地唱颂婚姻。

现实所带来的悲伤让帕蒂更慷慨地在音乐中倾注温暖和能量。八年后的《再次离开》更为成熟，被认为是一场真正的回归甚至复兴，也被评价为帕蒂在《复活节》之后最为全情投入、最能激发大众情感的作品。1999 年 5 月，《滚石》杂志将《再次离开》列入"90 年代最重要的唱片"之一。

What happened afterward you know, precious friend, said the friend, from what was sung and not sung: the birch trees, the little hotel in Paris where Genet died, an elbow, an armpit, too many cigarettes, wigs hung on long poles, the strangers in the little room below, the injured telephone—don't touch. The shaft of light that died in the mud, the slender whirling and swaying, shouting and standing tall. Hic dissonant ubique, nam enim sic diversis cantilenis clamore solent. Here all voices are at variance, as different songs are being roared out simultaneously. The day was still perfect, the children lovable, distracting, and everybody, from the crushed to the exalted, swayed in the music's updraft. Not bored. Not discouraged. Women were sassier, and felt sexier. Because of you, precious friend. The music spread everywhere. In the mouth. In the armpits. In the crotch. The music a way of flying up and flying past. I remember the saliva, and also the slap and the creased newspapers. You left and then you returned. You grinned. Your grin is still irresistible. Take back the night. Take back your life. And chant and squat and jump and shout, Aux vaincus! To the conquered!

—Susan Sontag

你知道后来发生了什么，珍贵的朋友，那人说道，从唱出来的和没唱出的能知道：桦树丛，热内死时所在的那家巴黎小宾馆，胳膊肘、腋窝、太多的香烟，假发挂在长杆上，楼下小房间里的陌生人，坏掉的电话——别碰它。那道死在泥土里的光柱，又细又长旋转着摇摆着，大喊大叫昂首耸立。Hic dissonant ubique, nam enim sic diversis cantilenis clamore solent. [1] 这里四处充满不和谐的声音，不同的歌曲被同时咆哮出来。日子依然完美，孩子们很可爱，叫人分心，而所有人，从那些被压垮的到那些被尊崇的，都在音乐的上升气流中摇摆着。不觉得无聊。不感到气馁。女人们很时髦，感觉自己更性感了。这都是因为你，我珍贵的朋友。音乐蔓延得到处都是。散布到嘴里。到腋下。到胯部。音乐让人高高飞起又飞向过去。我记得那些口水，还有巴掌和折皱的报纸。你离开随后又折返回来。你笑了。你的笑容仍然叫人无法抗拒。拿回夜晚。拿回你的生活。唱吧蹲吧跳吧叫吧，Aux vaincus！[2] 为战败者！

——苏珊·桑塔格

1　原文为拉丁文，摘自波希米亚－奥地利作曲家海因里希·比贝尔（Heinrich Ignaz Franz von Biber, 1644—1704）为其 1673 年的作品《巴塔利亚》（"Battalia"）写下的脚注。意为"这里四处充满不和谐的声音，不同的歌曲被同时咆哮出来"。

2　原文为法语，典出古罗马时期高卢塞农人首长布伦努斯（Brennus）于公元前 390 年率领高卢人攻下罗马城，洗劫许多财物后所言"Vae victis"（败者服输）。

GONE AGAIN

再次离开 [1]

Hey now man's own kin

嘿听着，我们的亲人

We commend into the wind

我们迎着大风前进

Grateful arms grateful limbs

感恩的双臂感恩的四肢

Grateful soul he's gone again

感恩的灵魂他再次离开

I have a winter's tale

我有个冬天的故事

How vagrant hearts relent prevail

流浪的心怎样变得温良

Sow their seed into the wind

把他们的种子撒入风里

Seize the sky and they're gone again

抓住天空他们再次离开

Fame is fleeting god is nigh

名望稍纵即逝上帝近在身边

We raise our arms to him on high

我们高高举起双臂向他致意

We shoot our flint into the sun

我们将火石投向太阳

We bless our spoils and we're gone we're gone

我们祝福战利品然后我们离开我们离开

Hey now man's own kin

嘿听着，我们的亲人

We commend into the wind

我们迎着大风前进

Grateful arms grateful limbs

感恩的双臂感恩的四肢

Grateful heart he's gone again

感恩的心他再次离开

Here a man, man's own kin

这个男人，他是我们的亲人

187

Turned his back and his own people shot him	他转过身去，他的同类将他射死
And he fell on his knees	他双膝跪倒在地
Before the burning plain	在燃烧的平原前
And he beheld fields of gold his land his son	他注视着金色的田野他的土地他的子民
And he arose his blood aflame	他的血液沸腾如火焰
Clouds pressed with hand prints stained	云朵上压刻着手印的污渍
One last breath	最后一口气
The sky is high	天空高远
The hungry earth	饥饿的土地
The empty vein	空虚的血管
The ashes rain	灰烬如雨落至
Death's own bed	死神的床上
Man's own kin	我们的亲人
Into the wind	随风逝去
One last breath	最后一口气
Hole in life	生命的裂缝
Love knot tied	爱被打了结
Braid undone	像没编好的辫子
A child born	一个孩子出生
The hollow horn	中空的号角

A warrior cried	一名战士哭喊
A warrior died	一名战士死去
One last breath	最后一口气
Lick of flame	轻舔火舌
Spirit moaned	灵魂在呻吟
Spirit shed	灵魂四散他去
The heavens fed	天堂哺育着
Man's own kin	我们的亲人
Grips the sky	紧抓住天空
And he's gone again	他再次离开
Hey now man's own kin	嘿听着，我们的亲人
We lay down into the wind	我们在大风里躺倒
Grateful arms grateful limbs	感恩的双臂感恩的四肢
Grateful heart is gone again	感恩的心已再次离开
Hey now man's own kin	嘿听着，我们的亲人
He ascends into the wind	他在大风里向上飞升
Grateful arms grateful limbs	感恩的双臂感恩的四肢
Grateful man he's gone again	感恩的男人他再次离开

Oh	哦
To be	做自己
Not	不要
Anyone	成为其他人
Gone	离开
This maze	存在
Of being	这迷宫
Skin	皮肤
Oh to cry	哦哭泣吧
Not any cry	不是随意的哭泣
So mournful	要哭得如此悲哀
That	让
The dove	鸽子
Just laughs	都笑出来
And	让
The steadfast	喘息
Gasps	坚定不移
Oh to owe	哦不去亏欠
Not anyone	任何人
Nothing	任何东西
To be	不要在

Not here	这里
But here	但又在这里
Forsaking	放弃
Equatorial bliss	近赤道的极乐
Who walked	谁穿行
Through	走过
The callow mist	少年稚气的薄雾
Dressed in scraps	穿着破烂
Who walked	谁行走在
The curve	世界的
Of the world	曲线上
Whose bone	谁的骨头
Scraped	在碎裂
Whose flesh	谁的血肉
Unfurled	迎风展开
Who grieves	谁在悲伤
Not	不是为了
Anyone gone	任何人的离开
To greet lame	迎接跌跛
The inspired sky	盈满灵感的天空
Amazed to stumble	惊奇地蹒跚而行

Where gods

Get lost

Beneath

The southern

Cross

—for Oliver Ray

诸神

迷失

在

南十字

星座下

——写给奥利弗·雷[1]

1 奥利弗·雷（Oliver Ray），美国音乐人、诗人、吉他手。1995 年加入帕蒂·史密斯乐队，与帕蒂合作十年后离团进行独立创作。

《南十字星座下》

ABOUT A BOY

关于一个男孩

Toward another he has gone

To breathe an air beyond his own

Toward a wisdom beyond the shelf

Toward a dream that dreams itself

About a boy beyond it all

About a boy beyond it all

他离开　走向另一个世界

去呼吸一口超越自己的空气

走向超越书本的智慧

走向梦见自己的梦

关于一个男孩他超越了一切

关于一个男孩他超越了一切

From the forest from the foam

From the field that he had known

Toward a river twice as blessed

Toward the inn of happiness

About a boy beyond it all

About a boy beyond it all

来自森林来自泡沫

来自他所熟悉的田野

走向被加倍庇佑的河流

走向那幸福的旅店

关于一个男孩他超越了一切

关于一个男孩他超越了一切

From a chaos raging sweet

From the deep and dismal street

Toward another kind of peace

Toward the great emptiness

About a boy beyond it all

About a boy beyond it all

来自混乱狂暴的甜蜜

来自深邃阴冷的长街

走向另一种形式的平静

走向那巨大的虚空

关于一个男孩他超越了一切

关于一个男孩他超越了一切

I stood among them I listened	站在他们中间我听着
I stood among them I listened not	站住他们中间我不听
I stood among them and I heard myself	站住他们中间我听到自己
Who I've loved better than you	我爱自己比你更多
So much so that I walked on	多了那么多让我能够走到
Into the face of God	上帝的面前
Away from your world	远离你的世界
And my sour stomach	和我酸涩的胃
Into the face of God, who said	走到上帝面前，他说
Boy, I knew thee not, but boy	孩子，我不认识你，但孩子
Now that I have you in my face	现在你来到我面前
I embrace you. I welcome you	我拥抱你。我迎接你
He was just a boy	他还只是个孩子
Whirling in the snow	在雪地里打着转
Just a little boy	只是个小男孩
Who would never grow	再也不会长大

—for Kurt Cobain   ——写给科特·柯本 [1]

1 科特·柯本（Kurt Cobain，1967—1994），美国音乐人，著名摇滚乐队"涅槃"乐队主唱、吉他手及词曲作者。1994 年 4 月 5 日被发现死于西雅图家中，官方裁定死因为饮弹自尽。本曲标题取自"涅槃"乐队发布于 1989 年 6 月的首张专辑《漂泊》（*Bleach*）中第三首歌曲《关于一个女孩》（"About a Girl"）。

MY MADRIGAL

我的牧歌

We waltzed beneath motionless skies

我们在静滞天空下跳起华尔兹

All heaven's glory turned in your eyes

天堂所有荣耀在你眼中转动

We expressed such sweet vows

我们对彼此说出如此甜蜜的誓言

Oh 'till death do us part

哦，直至死亡将我们分离

Oh 'till death do us part

哦，直至死亡将我们分离

We waltzed beneath God's point of view

我们在上帝的注视下跳起华尔兹

Knowing no ending to our rendezvous

知道我们的约定将永远没有终点

We expressed such sweet vows

我们对彼此说出如此甜蜜的誓言

Oh 'till death do us part

哦，直至死亡将我们分离

Oh 'till death do us part

哦，直至死亡将我们分离

We waltzed beneath motionless skies

我们在静滞天空下跳起华尔兹

All heaven's glory turned in your eyes

天堂所有荣耀在你眼中转动

You pledged me your heart

你把你的心给了我

'Till death do us part

直至死亡将我们分离

You pledged me your heart

你把你的心给了我

'Till death do us part

直至死亡将我们分离

'Till death do us part

直至死亡将我们分离

SUMMER CANNIBALS

夏日食人族

I was down in Georgia

我在佐治亚州

Nothing was as real

没什么像我脚下

As the street beneath my feet

正沉降入空气

Descending into air

的街道一样真实

The cauldron was a'bubbling

大锅咕嘟咕嘟冒着泡

The flesh was lean

里面的肉很瘦

And the women moved forward

女人们排队向前走

Like piranhas in a stream

像溪水里的食人鱼

They spread themselves before me

他们在我面前摊开身子

An offering so sweet

如此甜蜜的祭品

And they beckoned

他们向我招手示意

And they beckoned

他们向我招手示意

Come on darling eat

来吧，亲爱的，吃吧

Eat the summer cannibals

吃掉夏日食人族

Eat Eat Eat

吃吧 吃吧 吃吧

You eat the summer cannibals

你吃掉夏日食人族

Eat Eat Eat

吃吧 吃吧 吃吧

They circled around me

他们圈圈围着我转

Natives in a ring	绕成环状的土著人
And I saw their souls a'withering	我看到他们的灵魂在枯萎
Like snakes in chains	像戴着锁链的蛇群
And they wrapped themselves around me	他们用身体把我裹起来
Ummm what a treat	嗯，多么好的款待
And they rattled their tales	他们喋喋不休讲着传说
hissing come on let's eat	嘶嘶地说来吧让我们开吃
Eat the summer cannibals	吃掉夏日食人族
Eat Eat Eat	吃吧 吃吧 吃吧
You eat the summer cannibals	你吃掉夏日食人族
Eat Eat Eat	吃吧 吃吧 吃吧
I felt a rising in my throat	我感到喉咙有东西向上涌
The girls a'saying grace	女孩们做着饭前祷告
And the air, the vicious air	还有这空气，恶毒的空气
Pressed against my face	紧紧压着我的脸
And it all got too damn much for me	这一切对我来说太过分
Just got too damn rough	太他妈的粗暴
And I pushed away my plate	我用力推开盘子
And said boys I've had enough	说孩子们我吃饱了

And I laid upon the table

Just another piece of meat

And I opened up my veins to them

And said come on eat

Eat the summer cannibals

Eat Eat Eat

You eat the summer cannibals

Eat Eat Eat

'Cause I was down in Georgia

Nothing was as real

As the street beneath my feet

Descending into hell

So Eat Eat Eat

Eat Eat Eat

我平躺在桌子上

不过是又一片肉而已

我冲着他们切开血管

说来吧，吃吧

吃掉夏日食人族

吃吧 吃吧 吃吧

你吃掉夏日食人族

吃吧 吃吧 吃吧

因为我在佐治亚州

没什么像我脚下

正沉降入地狱

的街道一样真实

所以 吃吧 吃吧 吃吧

吃吧 吃吧 吃吧

DEAD TO THE WORLD

沉睡如死去

Dead to the world my body was sleeping

沉睡如死去我的身体已酣眠

On my mind was nothing at all

脑海中一片空荡荡

Come a mist an air so appealing

走入迷雾空气如此动人

I'm here a whisper you summoned I called

我在这里低语你召唤我呼号

I formed me a presence whose aspect was changing

我给自己做了一副不停变换的外形

Oh he would shift he would not shift at all

哦他会改变他根本不会改变

We sat for a while he was very engaging

我们坐了一会儿他是那么迷人

And when he was gone I was gone on a smile

当他离开我也带着微笑离开

With a strange way of walking

走路的方式很奇怪

And a strange way of breathing

呼吸的方式很奇怪

More lives than a cat

比一只猫有更多条命

That led me astray

那将我领入歧途

All in all he captured my heart

总之他俘获了我的心

Dead to the world and I just

沉睡如死去而我却

Slipped away

悄悄溜走

I heard me a music that drew me to dancing

我听到音乐响起吸引我起舞

Lo I turned under his spell

瞧，在他魔法下我转过身

I opened my coat but he never came closer

我解开外套但他再也没有向前靠近

I bolted the door and I whispered oh well

我插上门轻声说，哦，好吧

I laid in the rushes the air was upon me

躺在芦苇丛中空气压在我身上

Wondering well I just couldn't discern

疑惑着好吧我只是无法辨别

Will he come back come back to me

他会回来吗回到我身边

Oh I whispered will you ever return

哦，我轻声呢喃，你还会不会回来

I was feeling sensations in no dictionary

我感受着字典中没有写到的感觉

He was less than a breath of shimmer and smoke

他比一缕微光和烟雾还要轻盈

The life in his fingers unwound my existence

他指尖的生命释放了我的存在

Dead to the world alive I awoke

沉睡如死去苏醒再活过来

With a strange way of walking

走路的方式很奇怪

And a strange way of breathing

呼吸的方式很奇怪

Less than a breath of shimmer and smoke

比一缕微光和烟雾还要轻盈

The life in his fingers unwound my existence

他指尖的生命释放了我的存在

Dead to the world alive I awoke

沉睡如死去苏醒再活过来

dead to the world

F/M

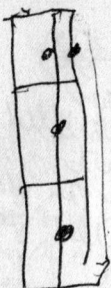

1st

2nd   Then left this
         one

3rd

weird chord

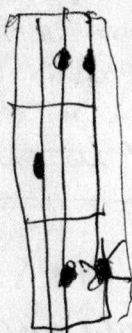

some
to other

1st

2nd

an F
with this

I was feeling sensations
in no dictionary
I opened my coat.
but he never came close
he was less than
     a whisper
of shimmer and smoke
the life in his fingers
unwound my existance
dead to the world
alive & awoke

Spectral Dance

《沉睡如死去》

Ravens

Common factors seek us all D
and slip our binding rings A
will turn our necks
And make us reel D
will leave our arms A
as wings
above the crown
a feather drifts F
before us it will fall A
for Time will hail D
and bid us rise
make ravens of us all A

My love to breathed
The air of Kings
yet fell beneath his luck
within his heart a yearning yes
before his time time shook
all the gifts that god had toyd F male (and those that fate denigher)
and those by labors high
returned to where all treasure made laid
And where the ravens fly

there are places yet to be e agree
where it yet to roam
The Egyptian plain
The artic sea
where shadows draw me on
no where but sky i'll have to go
when I return to thee me
but For a time Time has repared
Til I a raven be

For me time Time has
spared

RAVENS

渡鸦

Common fortune seeks us all

共同的命运搜寻着我们所有人

And slips our binding rings

给我们套上捆绑的卡环

We'll turn our heads

我们会晕头转向

And make us reel

让我们步履蹒跚

We'll bare our arms as wings

我们将赤裸双臂当作翅膀

Before our feet a feather drifts

在我们脚下一片羽毛飘荡

Beyond us it will fall

在我们身旁它将坠落

'Cause time will bid and make us rise

因为时间在发令，让我们奋起

Make ravens of us all

把我们都变成渡鸦

My love he breathed the air of kings

我的爱人他吞吐着帝王之气

Yet fell beneath his luck

但坏运气还是落了下来

And in his heart a yearning yet

在他心中仍有一种渴望

Before his time time shook

在时间到来前时间先摇摆

And all the gifts that god had gave

上帝赐予的所有礼物

And those by fate denied

还有那些被命运拒绝的人

Gone to where all treasures laid

去往所有宝藏安放之地

And where the raven flies

那里渡鸦在飞翔

Oh there are places I agree

哦，有些地方我愿去

Where I have yet to roam

那些我尚未漫游之处

The Egyptian field the arctic sea   埃及的原野和北冰洋

Where shadows haunt and moan   那里有阴影侵扰和悲吟

But none but sky I have to go   但除了天空我没有不得不去之处

Should I return to thee   我该重归于你吗

Gone to where the feather flies   去那羽毛飞舞之地

'Till I a raven be   直至我化为渡鸦

FIREFLIES

I been a'walking

Wherefore am I walking

I been a'walking

If you see me walking

A'walking a'wandering

If you see me walking

Don't ever turn your eye

Don't turn away don't turn away

I'm coming to you

Eleven steps 'till I can rest

Eleven steps 'till I'm blessed by you

I and I alone can but do for you

To twist in my hand the thorn of thy youth

To draw thy seed to turn in birth

Thy sighs thy moans I and I alone

Nine steps 'till I can rest

Nine steps 'till I'm blessed by you

I will wash your feet and dry them with my hair

I will give to you every other tear

萤火虫

我一直在行走

为此我在行走

我一直在行走

如果你看到我在行走

走着路漫着步

如果你看到我在行走

一定不要移开你的眼睛

不要转过身不要转过身

我在向着你走去

再走十一步我就能休息

再走十一步我就能得到你祝福

我，唯独我，才能为你而行事

将你青春的荆棘在我手中扭折

引出你的种子，使它旋转成孕

你的叹息你的呻吟，我，唯独我

再走九步我就能休息

再走九步我就能得到你祝福

我会清洗你双脚再用头发擦干它

我会把每一滴眼泪都献给你

208

Thy mouth thy spear thy season of mirth

Seven steps until I can rest

Seven steps 'till I'm blessed by you

All I ever wanted I wanted I wanted

All I ever wanted I wanted from you

Thy highs thy lows I and I alone

Ghost of thy ghost walk I will walk

A burning stem to illume thy night

Five steps 'till I can rest

Five steps 'till I'm blessed by you

Four steps until I can rest

Four steps 'till I'm blessed by you

Three steps until I get to you

Two steps until I can rest

Two steps 'till I'm blessed by you

Blood of my blood bone of my bone

Can but do for you I and I alone

你的嘴你的矛你欢乐的季节

再走七步我就能休息

再走七步我就能得到你祝福

所有我想要的我想要的我想要的

所有我想要的我想要的都来自你

你的高潮你的低谷，我，唯独我

你幽灵的幽灵，行走，我会行走

燃烧的树干点燃你的夜晚

再走五步我就能休息

再走五步我就能得到你祝福

再走四步我就能休息

再走四步我就能得到你祝福

再走三步我就能到你身边

再走两步我就能休息

再走两步我就能得到你祝福

我血中之血我骨中之骨

那能为你而行事的，是我，唯独我

FAREWELL REEL

永别里尔舞

It's been a hard time

这是段艰难时日

And when it rains

当下起雨

It rains on me

雨都落在我身上

The sky just opens

天空打开闸门

And when it rains

当下起雨

大雨倾盆

It pours

I walk alone

我独自行走

Assaulted it seems

看起来像是被

By tears of heaven

天堂的泪水所袭击

And darling I can't help

亲爱的我不禁

Thinking those tears are yours

以为那些泪水是你的

Our wild love came from above

我们狂野的爱由天而降

And wilder still

更狂野的

Is the wind that howls

是那呼啸的风

Like a voice that knows it's gone

就像一个声音知道自己已消逝

'Cause darling you died

因为亲爱的你已死去

And well I cried

好吧我哭了

But I'll get by

但我会挺过去

Salute our love

向我们的爱致敬

And send you a smile	送给你一个微笑
And move on	然后继续前进
So darling farewell	亲爱的永别了
All will be well	一切都会好的
And then all will be fine	一起都会好起来
The children will rise	孩子们会长大
Strong and happy be sure	肯定会坚强而快乐
'Cause your love flows	因为你的爱在流淌
And the corn still grows	果实就会继续生长
And God only knows	只有上帝知道
We're only given	我们被给予的
As much as the heart can endure	就是我们的心所能承受的
But I don't know why	但我不知道为什么
But when it rains	当下起雨
It rains on me	雨都落在我身上
The sky just opens	天空打开闸门
And when it rains	当下起雨
It pours	大雨倾盆

But I look up	但我抬起头
And a rainbow appears	一条彩虹浮现眼前
Like a smile from heaven	像一道来自天堂的微笑
And darling I can't	亲爱的我不禁
Help thinking that smile	以为那笑容
Is yours	是你的

COME BACK LITTLE SHEBA

回来吧，小希巴 [1]

Come back little Sheba	回来吧，小希巴
I hear them calling	我听到他们在呼唤
Open your eyes	睁开你双眼
Awake from thy sleep	从睡梦中清醒
High above	高空之上
The stars are falling	星星正在掉落
Open your arms	张开你双臂
And you shall receive	就会接到它们
The lights of the city	城市的灯火
So bold and flashing	如此醒目而闪耀
All of its riches	它所有的财富
Imparted to thee	都给了你
Robes of saffron	藏红花色的长袍
Robes of standing	名望的长袍
A road of crimson	一条深红色的路
Spread at your feet	铺开在你脚下
Your robes of standing	你名望的长袍

Your robes of saffron	你藏红花色的长袍
Your road of crimson	你深红色的路
All pleasing to me	都令我愉悦欢欣
But close your lights	但是关掉你的灯光
Close your gates	关闭你的大门
I must arise	我必须起身离开
My flock awaits	我的羊群在等待
Farewell little Sheba	再会了，小希巴
I hear them a'calling	我听到他们在呼唤
Here is your staff	这是你的手杖
Tend to thy sheep	照看好你的羊群
Good wishes be with you	美好的祝福赐予你
If that be your calling	如果那就是你的使命
Farewell little Sheba	再会了，小希巴
Arise and take leave	起身告别吧

1 《回来吧，小希巴》(*Come Back, Little Sheba*) 为美国戏剧家威廉·英格 (William Inge) 创作的剧本，于 1950 年在百老汇上演，后被改编为同名电影。故事讲述多克和妻子罗拉的生活，罗拉在小产后丧失了生育能力，夫妻生活步入绝望，罗拉寄托以情感的小狗希巴也在一天走失，她为此痛苦不已。

WING

I was a wing in heaven blue

Soared over the ocean

Soared over Spain

And I was free

Needed nobody

It was beautiful

I was a pawn

Didn't have a move

Didn't have nowhere

That I could go

But I was free

I needed nobody

It was beautiful

It was beautiful

I was a vision

In another eye

And they saw nothing

No future at all

Yet I was free

翼

我是蓝色天际间的羽翼

翱翔飞跃过海洋

翱翔穿越西班牙

我是自由的

不需要任何人

这多么美好

我是一枚棋子

没有移动过一步

也没有任何地方

可以去

但我是自由的

不需要任何人

这多么美好

这多么美好

我是一个幻觉

在另一只眼睛里

他们什么都看不到

没有任何未来

然而我是自由的

I needed nobody	不需要任何人
It was beautiful	这多么美好
It was beautiful	这多么美好
And if there's one thing	如果还有一件事
Could do for you	我能为你而做
You'd be a wing	你将变为一片羽翼
In heaven blue	飞翔蓝色天际间

PEACE AND NOISE

平 静 与 噪 声

Through the empty arch comes a wind, a mental wind blowing relentlessly over the heads of the dead, in search of new landscapes and unknown accents . . . announcing the constant baptism of newly created things.
—FEDERICO GARCÍA LORCA, *IN SEARCH OF DUENDE*

一阵风穿过空荡荡的拱门，这心灵之风无情地刮过死者的头顶，寻找新的景观与未知的口音……
宣告对于全新创生之物持续不断的洗礼。
——洛尔迦，《寻找顿德》★

★《寻找顿德》（*In Search of Duende*）一书收录了西班牙诗人、剧作家洛尔迦一系列关于顿德和顿德理论的散文。顿德在西班牙语中意为"房屋管理者"，指的是住在房屋中的顽皮精灵。洛尔迦在书中将其重新定义为一种黑暗而难以捉摸的力量，艺术家们能够通过它通向更高的创造力。

1997 年 9 月，帕蒂的第七张专辑《平静与噪声》发行。在 1996 年的《再次离开》中，帕蒂以音乐叙述了至亲之人离世给她带来的冲击，这一情绪也延续至《平静与噪声》。

然而，相比《再次离开》中随处可见的摇滚和爆发式音乐段落，《平静与噪声》的配器更多赖以松散的钢琴音符。也正是这一点，让整张专辑笼罩在回忆的"幽灵"之下。《在地下等待》中沉默凝视的地下幽魂，《死亡警示》里死去的年轻战士，渴望自由的"死城"，《最后召唤》所回应的"天堂之门"集体自杀事件……这些都是游走在《平静与噪声》中的鬼影。与此同时，这一次帕蒂的歌与词引发的共鸣更为清晰、具体，散发更简洁的诗意力量。

在丈夫弗雷德去世之前，帕蒂一直在与他共同制作《平静与噪声》。或许正是这个原因，专辑中所触及的主题与线索也更侧重家庭。呼唤逝者灵魂的帕蒂在歌曲中探讨衰老与抚育孩子的过程，频繁将"母亲"这一角色带进不同的曲目。她直面自己随岁月变迁却只增不减的叛逆之心，也一边试图理解她所处和所建立的家庭在这个现代世界处于怎样的位置。

与她的乐队成员雷、莱尼、鼓手多赫蒂、贝斯手托尼·沙纳一起，帕蒂在《平静与噪声》中找到了一片质朴、不受干扰的音乐土壤。但这并不意味着《平静与噪声》温柔或脆弱，相比《再次离开》所呈现的亲密与破碎，它甚至更为严厉，语气时而粗暴。有人曾评论《平静与噪声》带来的感动与鲍勃·迪伦的《地下室录音带》类似。帕蒂也确实在《什么都别说》一曲中化用迪伦的《什么都未交付》（"Nothing Was Delivered"）："我只是站在那里 / 我无法相信但我什么也没说"。在众人纷纷离场或终将离开的当下，帕蒂不再止步不前，而是用《平静与噪声》警示自己不应自怜，不该无所作为。

WAITING UNDERGROUND

在地下等待

If you believe all your hope is gone

如果你相信所有希望都已破灭

Down the drain of your humankind

你们人类已无路可去

The time has arrived

时候到了

You be waiting here

你等在这里

As I was in a snow white shroud

而我穿着雪白的裹尸布

Waiting underground

在地下等待

There by the ridge, be a gathering

在那山脊边，人群聚集

Beneath the pilgrim moon

在朝圣者的月光下

Where we shall await, the beat

我们将在那等候，你脚步的

Of your feet, hammering the earth

节拍，锤击着大地

Where the great ones tremble

伟人们在那里战栗

In their snow white shrouds

穿着他们雪白的裹尸布

Waiting underground

在地下等待

If you seek the kingdom, come along

如果你在寻找这王国，那就来吧

Waiting by the ridge, be a gathering

等在山脊边，人群聚集

Beneath the pilgrim moon

在朝圣者的月光下

Where the river thunders

河水雷鸣噪响

There we shall await, the beat

我们在那等候，你脚步的

Of your feet, hammering the earth

节拍，锤击着大地

And as the earth resounds

当大地发出回响

And humankind becomes as one

人类合为一体

Then we will arise to be as one

我们将合为一体站起来

But until that day we will just await

但在那日到来前我们只能等待

In our snow white shrouds

穿着我们雪白的裹尸布

Waiting underground

在地下等待

Waiting underground

在地下等待

溜掉

Hello friend I've come a'calling

你好朋友，我来串个门

Passively stationed active patrol

被动地驻扎，主动地巡查

Sliding in high noon

在正午时滑来滑去

Like some reluctant sheriff

像个不情愿的警长

Not want to get involved in it all

一点不想卷进这事里

Who stands guard for each other

谁在为彼此站岗守卫

Why must we guard anything at all

我们为何必须守卫什么

Anything at all

守卫什么呢

From the earth's four corners the people are calling

人们从地球的四角发出呼唤

Forming equations but the questions are hard

形成等式但问题很难

All men are brothers killing each other

所有男人都是兄弟却互相杀戮

And mother earth is wringing in wonder

大地母亲在惊疑中痛苦挣扎

Who stands guard for each other

谁在为彼此站岗守卫

Why must we guard anything at all.

我们为何必须守卫什么

Anything at all

守卫什么呢

Whirl away now

现在就溜掉

Whirl away now

现在就溜掉

Whirl away

溜掉

There's a cross on the road, there's a great mill turning

十字路口，立着巨大的碾磨机

Some seeking answers, some are born with answers	有些人寻找答案，有些人生来就有答案
You can hold on the blade and turn around forever	你可以握住刀剑永远转过身
Be flung into space into another kind of grace	被抛向太空享受另一种优雅
Who stands guard for each other	谁在为彼此站岗守卫
Why must we guard anything at all.	我们为何必须守卫什么
Anything at all	守卫什么呢
Whirl away now	现在就溜掉
Whirl away now	现在就溜掉
Whirl away	溜掉
Some give of the hand	有些人伸出了手
Some give of their land	有些人放弃了土地
Some giveth their life	有些人献出了生命
Laying in a field of grain	躺倒在一片谷地里
The staff of life all around you	生命之杖围绕你身边
Yet you will cut someone down	然而你仍会砍倒别人
For their possessions	占据他们的财产
Some material thing	那些实实在在的东西
And our children are being blown away	和我们的孩子都被吹走了
Like wishes in the wind	如同飘在风中的愿望

For the sake of their coat	因为他们穿的外套
Or their colors or their code	或他们的族群或他们的伦理
Or the color of their skin	或他们皮肤的颜色
Or the name of their shoes	或他们鞋子的名字
And the mother cries why'd they take my son	母亲哭喊着，他们为何要带走我儿子
And the father wonders why'd they take my boy	父亲疑惑着，他们为何要带走我儿子
He extended his hand he gave of his land	他伸出自己的手他放弃了自己的土地
He gave of his bread he gave of his heart	他献出自己的面包他献出了自己的心
Said hello friend	说着你好，朋友
Hello friend	你好，朋友
Hello friend	你好，朋友
Hello friend	你好，朋友

BLUE POLES

蓝柱 ¹

Mother as I write the sun dissolves

Blood life streaming cross my hand

And these words, these words

Hope dashed immortal hope

Hope streaking the canvas sky

Blue poles infinitely winding, as I write, as I write

Blue poles infinitely winding, as I write, as I write

We joined the long caravan

Hungry dreaming going west

Just for work just to get a job

And we never got lucky

We just forged on

And the dust the endless dust

Like a plague it covered everything

Hal fell with the fever

And mother I did what I could

Blue poles infinitely winding, as I write, as I write

Blue poles infinitely winding, as I write, as I write

We prayed we prayed for rain

妈妈当我写作时太阳溶解了

血肉生命在我手心流淌

这些话，这些话

希望已破灭那不朽的希望

希望飞驰在画布的天空

蓝柱无限缠绕，当我写作，当我写作

蓝柱无限缠绕，当我写作，当我写作

我们加入长长的车队

饥肠辘辘做着美梦一路西行

只是为了生计只为求份工作

我们从未走运过

我们只能匀速前行

灰尘扬起那无尽的灰尘

像场瘟疫它包裹一切

哈尔发着高烧倒下了

妈妈我做了我能做的事

蓝柱无限缠绕，当我写作，当我写作

蓝柱无限缠绕，当我写作，当我写作

我们祈祷我们祈祷着雨水

I never wanted to see the sun again	我再也不想见到太阳
All my dresses you made by hand	所有你亲手为我缝制的衣服
We left behind on the road	都被我们扔在身后的路上
Hal died in my arms	哈尔在我怀里死去
We buried him by the river	我们把他埋葬在河边
Blue poles infinitely winding, as I write, as I write	蓝柱无限缠绕，当我写作，当我写作
Blue poles infinitely winding, as I write, I write	蓝柱无限缠绕，当我写作，我写作

1《蓝柱》的灵感来自美国抽象表现主义画家杰克逊·波洛克于1952年创作的画作《蓝柱》（"Blue Poles"）。帕蒂在接受采访时曾提到，"当我看到波洛克画作中的蓝色杆柱划过画布的方式，我想到了横跨美国平原的电线杆。蓝柱是某种对未来的象征，即使在危机时刻仍令人感到希望"。

DON'T SAY NOTHING

什么都别说

Lower the thing the skin of a cat

放下那东西，一张猫皮

Skin it to the left just laying there

向左剥下皮，就放在那里

No other thing is luck like that

没有比那更幸运的事了

And you set it said it said nothing

你放下它说，它什么都没说

Went to the party very discouraged

去参加聚会，心情沮丧

I watched the litter pile like a wall

我看到垃圾堆得像一堵墙

I looked at the river just couldn't forgive it

我望着河流实在无法原谅

It was ladened with all kinds of shit

河里塞满着各种狗屎

Still I admit that I didn't say nothing

不过我得承认我什么也没说

I turned my back walked away

我转过身去走开了

Got to face the fact that I didn't say nothing

不得不面对这个事实，我什么也没说

Everyone was dancing I stood over in the corner

每个人都在跳舞我独自站在角落

I was listening they were saying this and saying that

我听着他们说着这个又说着那个

And putting this one down but nothing was delivered

放下这个话题但没有传达任何信息

Nothing good was coming I just stood there

没有任何好消息到来我只是站在那里

I couldn't believe it but I didn't say nothing

我无法相信但我什么也没说

I walked the floor then I looked away

我在房里走来走去然后把视线移开

Got to face the fact that I didn't say nothing

不得不面对这个事实，我什么也没说

How long how long will we make do

我们还能凑合多久到底多久

Maybe it's time to break on through

也许是时候去突破这一切

Gonna lift my skirts gonna straighten up

要提起我的裙子要站直我的身子

Gonna get well I'm gonna do something

要变得好起来我必须做些什么

Gonna face the fact gonna pay it back

要面对事实要做出偿还

And I'm gonna do something won't hold my tongue

我必须做些什么不再保持沉默

Won't hold the thought won't hold the card

不再控制想法不再持牌不出

Well I'm gonna do something

好吧我必须要做些什么

Oh my brain I got to complain

哦，我的大脑我必须发出控诉

You can refrain but I'm gonna do something

你可以保持克制但我必须做些什么

How long how long will we make do

我们还能凑合多久到底多久

Maybe it's time to break on through

也许是时候去突破这一切

Out in the desert I saw that old cat skinned

在沙漠中我看到那只被剥了皮的老猫

I saw it floating in the river

我看到它漂浮在河水里

I saw and no one seemed to mind

我看到似乎没人在意

They sat there they sat there watching the sun

他们坐在那里他们坐在那里望着太阳

I saw it float away and I watched the buildings crumble

我看着它漂远，我看到楼群坍塌粉碎

Like dust in the hand and we watched the sun

如掌中的灰尘，我们望着太阳

Spread its wings and fly away

它展开双翼振翅飞走

And in the mountains a cry echoes 群山间回荡着一声呐喊

Don't say nothing 什么都别说

Don't say nothing no 什么都别说别说

Don't say nothing no 什么都别说别说

DEAD CITY

死城

This dead city longs to be	这座死城渴望着
This dead city longs to be free	这座死城渴望自由
Seven screaming horses	七匹嘶鸣的马
Melt down in the sun	在阳光下融化
Building scenes on empty dreams	在虚空梦境之上构建起场景
And smoking them one by one	然后一个接一个地吸光它们
This dead city longs to be	这座死城渴望着
This dead city longs to be living	这座死城渴望活下去
Is it any wonder there's squalor in the sun	阳光底下肮脏遍地这有什么好奇怪
With their broken schemes and their lotteries	带着他们失败的阴谋和彩票
They never get nowhere	他们哪也去不了
Is it any wonder they're spitting at the sun	怪不得他们要冲太阳吐口水
God's parasites in abandoned sites	上帝的寄生虫，困在废墟间
And they never have much fun	他们永远不会有多少乐趣
If I was a blind man	假如我是盲人
Would you see for me	你是否愿成为我双眼
Or would you confuse	还是你会困惑于
The nature of my blues	我忧郁的天性

And refuse a hand to me

Is it any wonder crying in the sun

Is it any wonder I'm crying in the sun

Well I built my dreams on your empty scenes

Now I'm burning them one by one

This damn city this dead city

Immortal city

Motor city

Suc-cess city

Longs to be

Longs to be

Free

Free

Free

拒绝向我伸出手

在阳光底下哭泣这有什么好奇怪

我在阳光底下哭泣这有什么好奇怪

好吧我曾在你虚空的场景上构建我的梦

现在我要一个接一个地烧光它们

这该死的城市这座死城

不朽之城

汽车之城

功名之城

渴望着

渴望着

自由

自由

自由

DEATH SINGING

死神在歌唱

In the straw-colored light

在麦黄色阳光里

In light rapidly changing

在快速变幻的光线中

On a life rapidly fading

在迅速消逝的生命里

Have you seen death singing

你是否看见死神在歌唱

Have you seen death singing

你是否看见死神在歌唱

With a throat smooth as a lamb

他喉咙光滑如羔羊

Yet dry as a branch not snapping

却干如树枝不折断

He throws back his head

他向后扬起他的头

And he does not sing a thing mournful

歌声里没有一丝悲伤

Have you seen death singing

你是否看见死神在歌唱

Have you seen death singing

你是否看见死神在歌唱

Have you seen death singing

你是否看见死神在歌唱

In the straw-colored light

在麦黄色阳光里

He sings a black embrace

他唱着黑色的拥抱

And white opals swimming

白色宝石游着水

In a child's leather purse

在孩子的皮包里

Have you seen death swimming

你是否看到死神在游泳

231

Have you seen death swimming

你是否看到死神在游泳

With a throat smooth as a lamb

他喉咙光滑如羔羊

Yet dry as a branch not snapping

却干如树枝不折断

He throws back his head

他向后扬起他的头

And he does not sing a thing mournful

歌声里没有一丝悲伤

Have you seen death singing

你是否看见死神在歌唱

Have you seen death singing

你是否看见死神在歌唱

Have you seen death singing

你是否看见死神在歌唱

In the straw-colored light

在麦黄色阳光里

He sings of youth enraged

他唱着愤怒的青年

And the burning of Atlanta

亚特兰大的火焰

And these viral times

病毒肆虐的时代

And May ribbons streaming

五月飘扬的丝带

And straw-colored curls a'turning

麦黄色卷发在扭动

A mother's vain delight

母亲徒劳的喜悦

And woe to the sun

灾难降临至太阳

And woe to the dawn

灾难降临至黎明

And woe to the young

灾难降临至青年

Another hearse is drawn

Have you seen death singing

In the straw-colored light

—for Benjamin Smoke

又一辆灵车被拖出来

你是否看见死神在歌唱

在麦黄色阳光里

——写给本杰明·斯莫克 [1]

1 本杰明·斯莫克（Benjamin Smoke, 1960—1999），原名罗伯特·迪克森，美国诗人及创作型歌手。曾为亚特兰大"烟"（Smoke）乐队主唱，以激进的摇滚表演而闻名。

having spun so
many prayers
That recede as you
sleep and memory
inhabits your dreams
Radiant ones when
the trials of a
people were
radiant trials
when the
egg of
deceptions
egg
cracks
and
then

we have time to go
That we aspire to
attain is suddenly
elusive and song
its time
to go

MEMENTO MORI   死亡警示 [1]

The fan whirling like the blades of a copter   风扇旋转如直升机叶片

Lifting into the skies above a foreign land   在异国土地上腾起飞入天空

Fire and iron soaked with the bodies of so many friends   火与铁浸透了那么多朋友的身躯

Johnny waved. He was on his way home   约翰尼挥着手。他就要返回家乡

He waved good-bye to his comrades in arms   他向自己的战友们挥手告别

And all the twisted things he had seen   也向他见到的所有扭曲之事告别

He waved good-bye   他挥手告别

And the blades hit something   直升机叶片撞到了什么东西

Maybe just fate but the blades hit   也许只是命运使然但叶片受到撞击

The copter went up in flames   直升机燃起熊熊火焰

And Johnny never went marching home   约翰尼永远没能回去家

And Johnny never went marching home   约翰尼永远没能回去家

They took his name and they carved it on a slab of marble   他们将他的名字刻在一块大理石上

With several thousand other names   连同几千个其他名字一起

All the fallen idols   所有坠落的偶像

The apples of their mother's eye   他们母亲的心头之肉

Just another name   不过是又一个名字

Meanwhile back on that burning shore   与此同时，回到那片燃烧的海岸

Johnny's comrades stood speechless   约翰尼的战友们无语伫立

They looked up up up with misbelieving eyes   他们瞪着难以置信的眼睛抬头 抬头 抬头看着

235

'Cause there were bits of metal and the embers   因为那里尚有金属碎片和余烬飘散

The embers of his eyes fanned out in the air   他眼睛的余烬在空中呈扇形散开

Black dust flames. Oh Johnny   黑色粉尘火焰。哦，约翰尼

Someday they'll make a movie about you   总有一天他们会拍一部关于你的电影

And in the making of that movie, some mad apocalypse   制作那部电影的过程中，有一些疯狂的天启

It will become even stranger than the simple act   它会变得比实际发生的事更怪异

Just a boy going up. Up. Up   只是个男孩升起。升起。升起。

Just a boy going up. Up. Up   只是个男孩升起。升起。升起。

In flames in the smoke   在火焰中在烟雾里

Just another life   不过是又一条生命

Just another breath   不过是又一次呼吸

And who'll remember   谁会记得

Oh eternity now   哦，现在即永恒

As eternal as a sheet of marble   永恒如一片大理石

Eternal as a slab   永恒如一块石板

On a green hill   青山之上

And your name   你的姓名

And all your fallen brothers   还有你所有倒下的兄弟

And all the ones not cut   所有未被剪辑的人

All the ones remembered	所有被铭记住的人
Only in the hearts	只深藏在心里
A mother a father a brother	一个母亲 一个父亲 一个兄弟
A sister a lover son daughter	一个姐妹 一个爱人 儿子和女儿
Young man shall not fade shall not fade	年轻人不会褪色不会褪色
Your ancestors salute you greet you	你的祖先向你致敬欢迎着你
And the gods of your ancestors salute you	你祖先的神灵向你致敬
Having been formed by the mind of your ancestors	是你祖先的思想塑造了你
The gods of your ancestors salute you	你祖先的神灵向你致敬
Having been formed by your ancestors	是你的祖先塑造了你
The gods of your ancestors salute you	你祖先的神灵向你致敬
They draw you in	他们引领着你
They draw you through	他们引领你穿过
They draw they draw you	他们引领他们引领着你
Through that golden door	穿过那金色的大门
Come on in boy	来吧进来男孩
We remember you	我们记得你
We conceived you	我们孕育了你
We conceived of your breath	我们孕育了你的呼吸
We conceived of the whole human race	我们孕育了整个人类
And we conceived it to be a beautiful thing	我们孕育它成为一件美好的事

Like a tulip bending in the wind	就像一朵在风中摇曳的郁金香
Sometimes it comes back to us	有时它会回到我们身边
In the form of the hand filled with dust	手中沾满了灰尘
Comes back in the form of a smitten child	像个不安的孩子回来了
Our raped daughters	我们被强暴的女儿
The broken bones	折断的骨头
Souls cleaved of hearts	灵魂与心相分离
They come back to us	他们回到我们身边
Our hands are filled	我们手中塞满了
With their rotting tissues	他们腐烂的血肉
But we turn not our backs	但我们不会弃之不管
We press our lips	我们用嘴唇紧贴着
Into their cancer	吻入他们的肿瘤
Into the dust	吻入灰尘
Into the remains of each one	吻入每一副遗骸
And that love is there	那份爱就在那里
And will greet you	会迎接着你
Come on in boy	来吧进来男孩
It's eternal love	这是永恒之爱
Well here go ahead	好吧，在这，继续向前

Run through that plane	跑步穿过那架飞机
Oh man running through your mind	哦孩子跑步穿过你脑海
You took a cat	你抓住一只猫
You took a life	你抓住一条生命
You took it by the tail	你抓住它的尾巴
And you swirled it around your head	让它绕着你的头打旋
And you thrashed it	把它打得落花流水
You smashed the life out of it	你毁掉了它的生命
Then you knew that would be your own	然后你知道了那将是你自己的命
But you wanted to feel the dying	但你想要感受垂死的感觉
Because you knew	因为你知道这样
You would feel your own	你会感受到自己的死亡
You would feel your own	你会感受到自己的死亡
But you're remembered	但你已被铭记
You're remembered	你被铭记
You're remembered good	你被牢牢铭记
We remember	我们记得
We remember	我们记得
We remember	我们记得
Everything	所有事

—for James Folvary　　　　　　　　　　——写给詹姆斯·福尔法利 [2]

1 原文为拉丁文"Memento mori",意即"勿忘你终有一死",是中世纪西方基督教对必死性之反思的理论及实践,被视作用以思索尘世之虚幻和物质与世俗工作之短暂的方式。它也是禁欲主义的一条重要戒律,人们借此培养超脱和其他美德,将精力转移到灵魂不死与死后的世界。欧洲古典艺术中,"死亡警示"的元素常以骷髅头骨、沙漏、熄灭的蜡烛、枯萎的花朵等意象出现。

2 詹姆斯·福尔法利(James Folvary)应为越南战争中丧生的士兵之一。这首歌词中的"约翰尼"为詹姆斯的昵称。帕蒂创作这首歌曲时,这位士兵及其遇难战友的报道曾引发美国媒体关注。

LAST CALL

最后召唤

In a mansion high the young man stood

高耸的公寓楼里，年轻男人站定

Ready to join his companions good

准备好要加入他的同伴

Outside the scent of magnolia blossoms

外面弥漫着木兰花绽放的香气

Down streets of gold the children were racing

孩子们沿着金色街道赛跑

Just another wandering soul

只是又一个游荡的灵魂

Adrift among the stars

漂浮于群星之间

Just another human heart

只是又一颗人类的心脏

Led, led away

带走，被带走

He put his shoes on and he laid down

他穿上鞋子，躺了下来

Outside the clouds were swiftly gathering

外面的云层正迅速聚集

He drained his cup and he stirred the mixture

他喝干杯中之物，搅了搅杯底

And he closed his eyes as his conscience whispered

他闭上眼睛，他的良知在低语

Just another wandering soul

只是又一个游荡的灵魂

Adrift among the stars

漂浮在群星之间

Just another human heart

只是又一颗人类的心脏

Led, led away

带走，被带走

Misgivings unspoken he joined his companions

疑虑尚未说出他已加入自己的同伴

His face covered over in a mansion high	他的脸被蒙住，走进高耸的公寓楼
Outside the children gazed in wonder	外面的孩子们好奇地凝视
At the quickening sky then slowly disbanded	看那风云变幻的天空，随后慢慢散开
Thirty-nine wandering souls	三十九个游荡的灵魂
Adrift among the stars	漂浮在群星之间
Thirty-nine human hearts	三十九颗人类的心脏
Led, led away	带走，被带走
His burning skin cooled by angels	他灼烧的皮肤被天使冷却下来
Swallowing sorrows excretion	吞咽下悲伤的排泄物
It's all excretion	全都是排泄物
Felled by his hand	被他亲手击倒
Or the mind of another man	或是被另一个人的思想击倒
Who makes the decisions	是谁来做出决定
Lends no provisions for mere eternal rides	不提供任何补给仅有永恒的旅程
Learning of course every alien force	尽然了解每一种外星神力
Even Christ yearns to be	即便基督也渴望着
To possess the skin	拥有皮肤
And bone the blood of man	骨头和人的鲜血

Who tends the flock	谁来照料羊群
Who breaks the bread	谁把面包撕成小块
Who makes his own choices	谁做出独断的选择
Won't listen to voices	拒绝倾听其他声音
Accept no false teachers	不要接受假师傅
False preachers, good deeders	假牧师，善行者
With their hands out stretched	他们向外伸出手
To be filled with your money	去抓满你的金钱
Your flesh, your breath	你的血肉，你的呼吸
Your imagination	你的想象力
Sympathy, empathy	同情心，同理心
Acknowledge all man	承认一切众生
As fellow creation	皆是平等造物
But don't follow him	但是不要跟着他
Don't be led away	不要被他带走

Last Call.

In a mansion high the young man stood
ready to join his companions good
outside the scent of magnolia blossoms
down streets of gold the children were racing.

He put his shoes on and he lay down
~~outside the clouds furiously gathered~~
he drained the cup he stirred the mixture
he closed his eyes as his conscience whispered

outside the clouds furiously gathered
outside the moon vaguely rising
outside the children gazing in wonder
at the thunder.

outside the moon vaguely rising
~~outside the clouds furiously gather~~
         watching
stirred by   outside the children

     echoing laughter

GUNG HO

工 合

以此功德愿证佛自性，降伏烦恼怨敌之过患，生老病死汹涌之波涛，愿度众生解脱轮回海。

——佛教功德回向祈请文

"工合"（Gung ho）一词在英语中的使用可追溯到抗日战争时代，由驻华的美国海军陆战队少校卡尔逊取自其新西兰好友路易·艾黎在华创立的"工合国际"。卡尔逊在1943年一次访谈中解释道："我试图创建自己在中国见识到的同一种工作精神，在那里，全体士兵奉献一己之力于同一理念，并分工合作达成目标。"之后，"工合"的理念被用于其领导的第二海军陆战突击营中，后来扩大到全海军陆战队中其他部队，成为精神标语。

"工合"（Gung ho）源自汉语中的"工合"，即"工业合作社"的简称，后在英语中延伸为卖力、热心之意。2000 年 3 月，以《工合》为题，帕蒂发行了她的新专辑。这也是第一次帕蒂没有在专辑封面上使用自己的照片。封面上是她的父亲格兰特·史密斯，专辑同名歌曲《工合》围绕着格兰特的战争经历。

如果说 1990 年代的帕蒂的作品大多源自其个人情感和家庭生活，在《工合》中，人们久违地听到愤怒、激进的帕蒂，她以一如既往的具撕裂力量的音乐，借历史、神话叙事，在千禧之年再次发出宣言。《看呢，蒙恩》中，帕蒂化身莎乐美，《奇特使者》里的帕蒂沿着"生命之书"站在种植园的黑奴之间，在新阿巴拉契亚风格的歌曲《莉比之歌》里，她化为一名陆军少将的遗孀。

《工合》被称为帕蒂多年来最具"即时"力量的一张专辑。但这一力量的载体不仅仅是摇滚。在《游说》中，帕蒂再次与车库朋克风格碰撞。《新政党》中，帕蒂在声音与吐字上进行不同的尝试，她时而拉长音节，时而磕绊，时而失控，又时而严厉，这样的即兴演唱不免让人联想到"垮掉的一代"的诗歌传统。专辑发行同年，《新政党》也被用作拉尔夫·纳德总统竞选的官方歌曲。

《工合》也频频唤起人们对 1970 年代那些在 CBGB 朋克俱乐部大放异彩的重要朋克人物的记忆。《消失的馅饼》中所使用的混响与和声让人想到"金发美女"（Blondie）乐队。《游说》在吉他编配上与"电视"乐队不无相似。但《工合》中的帕蒂并不回望过去，凭借《他们眼中的光亮》一曲，她在 2001 年被提名格莱美最佳摇滚女歌手。这首歌里，帕蒂直面自由市场下人们的贪欲，对抗物质主义带来的诱惑和冲击——她撕开乌托邦的幻象与阴霾，时刻准备为更高的目标而奋战。

一个声音

In the garden of consciousness	在意识的花园里
In fertile mind there lies the dormant seed	肥沃的思想中躺着休眠的种子
Blooming into charity	开花长成了仁慈
Conscience breathes a sigh of relief	良知松了一口气
The confessions of sleep	睡眠的忏悔
The awakening seed	觉醒的种子
Moved by love to serve	被爱感动去奉献
We celebrate all merit in life	我们赞美生命中所有功德
Ah the confessions of sleep	啊，睡眠的忏悔
Unfolding peace	展开的平静
As we extend	当我们根据需要
According to need	向外延伸
And you will heed the call	你会听从这召唤
All action great and small	伟大或渺小之举
Received joyfully	都被喜悦接受
Heaven abounds	极乐环绕身边
Let love resound	让爱发出回响
If he be mute	若他是个哑巴
Give him a bell	给他一只铃铛
If he be blind an eye	若他瞎了一只眼
If he be down a hand	若他断掉一只手

Lift up your voice	提高你的声音
Lift up your voice	提高你的声音
Lift up your voice	提高你的声音
Give of your mind one mind	奉献你的思想那一个思想
Give of your heart one heart	奉献你的心那一颗心
Give of your voice	奉献你的声音
One voice	那一个声音

LO AND BEHOLDEN

看呢，蒙恩

I was alone and	我独自一人
content in my world	满足于自己的世界
dancing on air	在空中跳着舞
you sent to me	你给我发来
a message that said	一条消息说
I like your style	我喜欢你的风格
will you come	今晚你会
to the temple tonight	来圣殿里
and dance for me there	为我起舞吗
I pledge to you	我保证赐予
all that you wish	你想要的一切
the moon and the stars	不管月亮还是星星
Lo and beholden	看呢，蒙恩
why don't you give it up	你为何还没有放弃
lo and beholden	看呢，蒙恩
come on you know it's true	来吧你知道这是真的
lo and beholden	看呢，蒙恩
oh I'm beholden to you	哦，我蒙恩于你
In the palace	在这宫殿里

there was wild reverie	有着狂野幻想
and the look	你眼中
in your eyes	那神情
as I dropped	当我摘掉
veil after veil	面纱后的面纱
was drunken desire	是酒醉的欲望
the dove calls	鸽子在鸣叫
God he notes all	上帝他记下一切
the naked truth	赤裸的真相
here is my seventh veil and last	这是我第七层也是最后的面纱 [1]
it will cost you	你将付出代价
The royal word it has been passed	神圣的福音已被传达
the prophet's head is all I ask	先知的头颅是我全部欲求
for beauty and the naked truth	为了那美好而赤裸的真相
it will cost you	你将付出代价
Lo and beholden	看呢，蒙恩
why don't you give it up	你为何还没有放弃
lo and beholden	看呢，蒙恩
come on you know it's true	来吧你知道这是真的

lo and beholden

oh I'm beholden to you

看呢，蒙恩

哦，我蒙恩于你

UPRIGHT COME

直立而来

Hail brother

兄弟万岁

the distant thunder

远处的雷声

is nothing but hearts

不过是心脏

beating as one

齐齐跳动如一体

dance of a million

百万人共舞

on God's pavilion

于上帝之亭

come come

来吧，来吧

beat on your drum

敲响你的鼓

Awake people arise

清醒的人们站起来

awake upright come

清醒着直立而来

fortune is falling like

命运落下如

tears from the skies

天降的泪水

open your eyes

睁开你双眼

Hail sister

姐妹万岁

won't you come over

你不过来吗

to shape reshape

去塑造去重塑

things to come

即将到来之事

bow your head

低下你的头

raise your lantern

高举起灯笼

come come   来吧，来吧

beat on your drum   敲响你的鼓

United action   团结一致去行动

is what we need   才是我们需要的

time to say   是时候要说

everything is going to be   一切终将要到来

wasted icons wasted lives   浪费掉的偶像浪费掉的生命

like war obsolete   就像过时了的战争

These are the times   这就是时代

the times of our own   我们自己的时代

these are the shapes   这就是我们

the world we formed   塑造的世界

swift is the arrow   迅捷如箭

dark is the thorn   暗夜如刺

the slate is clean   往事勾销

the future awaits   未来在等待

Awake   醒来吧

I AM THE BODY
I am The stream
I am the wake
of Everything
They bring me flowers That are MYSELF

GARLANDS OF Blood
That are Myself
They SLAY The Lamb
That is MYSELF
a Praying for The lamb
That is   HIMSELF
                I am   H IM

TORN REBORN
The Cries of our dismay
is Nothing To The wind
BUT ~~that~~ ~~was~~ MIND
       who's To

Kings are lifted up
and Kings are Thrown
lost RECIEVED RETRIEVED
The Human Tide

BLOODY Human Tide

BOY CRIED WOLF

男孩高喊狼来了

Oh the story's told been told retold	哦，这故事已被讲了一遍又一遍
from the sacred scriptures to the tabloids	从宗教经典到通俗小报
all the fuss and fight none above a whisper	所有小题大做和争吵不过都是谣传
from the soul of gold to the belly of a boy	从金色灵魂到男孩的肚皮
Well they drew him from the forest	他们把他从森林中引出
like they draw blood	就像抽出鲜血
tied him to a tree like St. Sebastian	把他绑在树上状如圣塞巴斯蒂安 [1]
and he turned his head	他转过头
and let the arrows fly	让弓箭飞过来
through the trees the trees	穿过重重树林
the ornamental leaves	观赏植物叶子
Boy cried wolf	男孩高喊狼来了
wolf don't come	狼没有来
wolf within boy cried wolf	男孩心中的狼高喊狼来了
In the ancient mold	依照古老的仪式
where they're dancing down	他们在那里起舞
calling to the moon	对着月亮呼唤
but it don't answer	月亮没有回应
and they fell on their knees	他们双膝跪地

and passed the bowl around	将碗绕圈传递
and the blood the blood	鲜血，那鲜血
the sacramental blood	那神圣的鲜血
Boy cried wolf	男孩高喊狼来了
wolf don't come	狼没有来
wolf within boy cried wolf	男孩心中的狼高喊狼来了
I am the body I am the stream	我是那身体，我是那溪水
I am the wake of everything	我是万物的守灵人
they bring me flowers that are myself	他们带给我鲜花那是我自己
garlands of blood that are myself	鲜血的花环是我
slain the lamb that is himself	被宰的羔羊是他
I don't care I don't mind	我不在乎，我不介意
I don't know	我不知道
I don't care I don't mind	我不在乎，我不介意
I don't know	我不知道
Torn reborn the cries of our dismay	撕裂重生我们沮丧的呼喊
are nothing to the wind	对风来说什么都不是
but whose to mind	但谁会在意呢

kings are lifted up

and kings are thrown

lost received retrieved

the human tide

国王们被举起

国王们被扔出去

失去的得到的重新找回的

人潮涌动

Innocence had its day

Innocence had its day

Innocence innocence

清白无辜气数已尽

清白无辜气数已尽

清白无辜　清白无辜

1 圣塞巴斯蒂安（Saint Sebastian），殉道圣人。据说在罗马皇帝戴克里先迫害基督
  徒期间被杀。在艺术和文学作品中，常被描绘成双臂捆在树桩被乱箭射穿的形象。

257

PERSUASION

游说

What is the system that gets around
recruits hearts with its timeless rhythm
the young glow but old men know
it's all a part of some crazy schism

Coming on like the dawn unrelenting light
streets thick with its radiating
it's all aglow but we all know
true love is so complicated

Feeling funny don't know why
on a plane circling high
equation persuasion
it's just persuasion

What is the body that has nobody
go through life with nobody at all
it come and go where the wind blow
when persuasion come to call

Got me reeling don't know why

四处游走的体制究竟是什么
以它永恒的节奏征募人心
年轻人满面红光但老人们知道
一切都是某种疯狂的分裂

像黎明无情的光线般到来
街道充塞着它辐射的光芒
四处闪闪发亮但我们知道
真正的爱如此复杂

感觉很滑稽不知为什么
在凌空盘旋的飞机上
制衡 游说
不过是一种游说

空无一人的群体究竟是什么
无人陪伴地度过一生
它随风的流动来来又去去
当游说到来将它召唤

头晕目眩不知为什么

I'm on a plane circling high	我坐在凌空盘旋的飞机上
equation persuasion	制衡　游说
got the feeling I'm running in place	感觉我在原地奔跑
caught in the orbit of the human race	困在人类的轨道上
equation persuasion	制衡　游说
it's just persuasion	不过是一种游说
it's just persuasion	不过是一种游说
it's just persuasion	不过是一种游说
What is the body that has nobody	空无一人的群体究竟是什么
what is the rise without the fall	没有坠落的升起究竟是什么
what is illusion without beauty	没有美好的幻觉究竟是什么
what is the system that's no system at all	没有任何体制的体制究竟是什么
Hey scout there's no equation	嘿，童子军，没有什么制衡
you can't prepare for the heart's invasion	你无法为人心的入侵做好准备
you can't prepare for the heart's invasion	你无法为人心的入侵做好准备
love is its own persuasion	爱只能被它自己游说

GONE PIE

Hey there

come and take a walk with me

stroll into infinity

we'll stroll along

until the dawn is gone

midnight take it to the twilight

just a little slice of light

let's turn it off and on off and on

Strolling ain't it wonderful

into a light that lingers

on and on, on and on

Strolling ain't it wonderful

stars fall for we two

bathed in a light of our own

Oh life

much too great to sacrifice

come and have another slice

ah life goes on and on

消失的馅饼

嘿，朋友

来跟我散个步

漫步进入无尽

我们漫步前行

直至黎明逝去

午夜将它带入黄昏

只是一小片的光

让我们把它关掉再开再关再开

漫步不是很美妙吗

走入一道萦绕不散的光里

挥之不去，挥之不去

漫步不是很美妙吗

星星为我俩掉落

沐浴在我们自身的光芒中

哦，生活

实在太伟大不该去牺牲

来吧再来一小片

啊，生活依然在继续

Oh life

哦，生活

may you live a long life

愿你生命悠长

may you live a long life

愿你生命悠长

may you live a long life

愿你生命悠长

CHINA BIRD

瓷器鸟

One fine day	晴朗的一日
these words I pray	我祈祷的那些话
will breathe a truth	会从你的身体里
within yourself	呼吸出一个真理
upon a shelf	在架子上
a life anew	一种崭新的生活
so many roads	这么多条路
it's hard to know	很难去知道
what to do	该怎么选择
all your dreams	你所有梦想
all it seems	看起来全都
is as you choose	像你为命运
for destiny	所做的选择
my china bird	我的瓷器鸟
is calling for you	它呼唤着你
The world turns	世界风云变幻
the flame burns	火焰熊熊燃烧
bright and true	光明而真实
near and far	遍布近与远

where you are	你在哪里
guiding you china bird	指引着你，瓷器鸟
the open skies	那开阔天空
are yearning for you	它渴望着你
If they say	如果他们说
it's not that way	不是那条路
hold your view	坚持你的想法
and with my love	带着我的爱
fly above	向高飞去
alight anew	重新点燃
spread your wings	展开你的双翼
the open sky	那开阔天空
is calling to you	它呼唤着你
china bird my heart	瓷器鸟，我的心
is yearning for you	它渴望着你
If you fly away	如果你飞走
I'll be waiting	无论发生什么
come what may	我会等候你

all my love a fragile ray

for you for you

—in memory of Grant H. Smith

我全部的爱是一缕脆弱光线

为你闪耀，只为你

——纪念格兰特·H. 史密斯 [1]

1 格兰特·H. 史密斯（Grant H. Smith，1916–1999），帕蒂·史密斯的父亲。

GLITTER IN THEIR EYES

他们眼中的光亮

It's been a while since I've seen your face
it's been a while since I've walked this place
I see the monkeys riding on their bikes
racing through the impossible night

You say you're feeling like a new tree
man they'll cut you from limb to limb
pick your pocket with such delight
shake it to the right
shake it in the light

Oh can't you see the glitter
the glitter in their eyes
oh can't you see the glitter
the glitter in their eyes

Genius stalking in new shoes
have you got WTO blues
dust of diamonds
making you sneeze
kids on rollers ready for

有段时日了我没见过你的脸
有段时日了我没走过这地方
我看到猴子们骑着自行车
疾驰冲过这不可思议的夜晚

你说感觉自己就像一棵全新的树
兄弟，他们会把你每截树枝都砍掉
兴高采烈地捡起你的钱袋
向着右边摇一摇
对着光线摇一摇

哦，你看不到那光亮吗
他们眼中的光亮
哦，你看不到那光亮吗
他们眼中的光亮

天才穿着新鞋阔步走
你有没有 WTO 布鲁斯
钻石的粉尘
呛得你打喷嚏
穿着轮滑的孩子们准备好

265

running through the junkyards	横冲直撞穿过垃圾场
breezing through the halls	如微风穿过走廊
racing through the malls	疾驰冲过大商场
walking through the walls	横穿一堵一堵墙
they'll strip your mind	他们会剥光你的思想
just for fun	只是为了取乐
quoth the raven	乌鸦说着
yum yum yum	好吃 好吃 好吃
Oh can't you see the glitter	哦，你看不到那光亮吗
the glitter in their eyes	他们眼中的光亮
oh can't you see the glitter	哦，你看不到那光亮吗
the glitter in their eyes	他们眼中的光亮
Children children everywhere	孩子们孩子们到处都是
selling souls for souvenirs	出售灵魂换礼物
sold them out like as not	全部卖光可能只是
just for chunks of Ankgor Wat	为了换吴哥窟一片瓦
They'll trade you up	他们会把你交易来
trade you down	再把你交易去

your body a commodity	你的身体是商品
our sacred stage	我们神圣的舞台
has been defaced	已经被损坏
replaced to grace	替换为优雅的
the marketplace	交易市场
Dow is Jonesing at the bit	道琼斯指数在上涨
42nd Disney Street	42 街 [1] 迪士尼
ragged hearts unraveling	粗糙的心被揭开
look out kids	当心孩子们
the gleam the gleam	那微光　那微光
all that glitters	所有闪着光的
is not all that glitters	未必都是那种光亮
is not all that glitters	未必都是那种光亮

1　42 街（42nd Street）是美国纽约市曼哈顿的一条著名街道，街道上有包括联合国总部、大中央车站、纽约公共图书馆、时代广场等在内的诸多纽约重要建筑。该街道也以其上的剧院闻名，其与百老汇交汇的区域被称为剧院区。

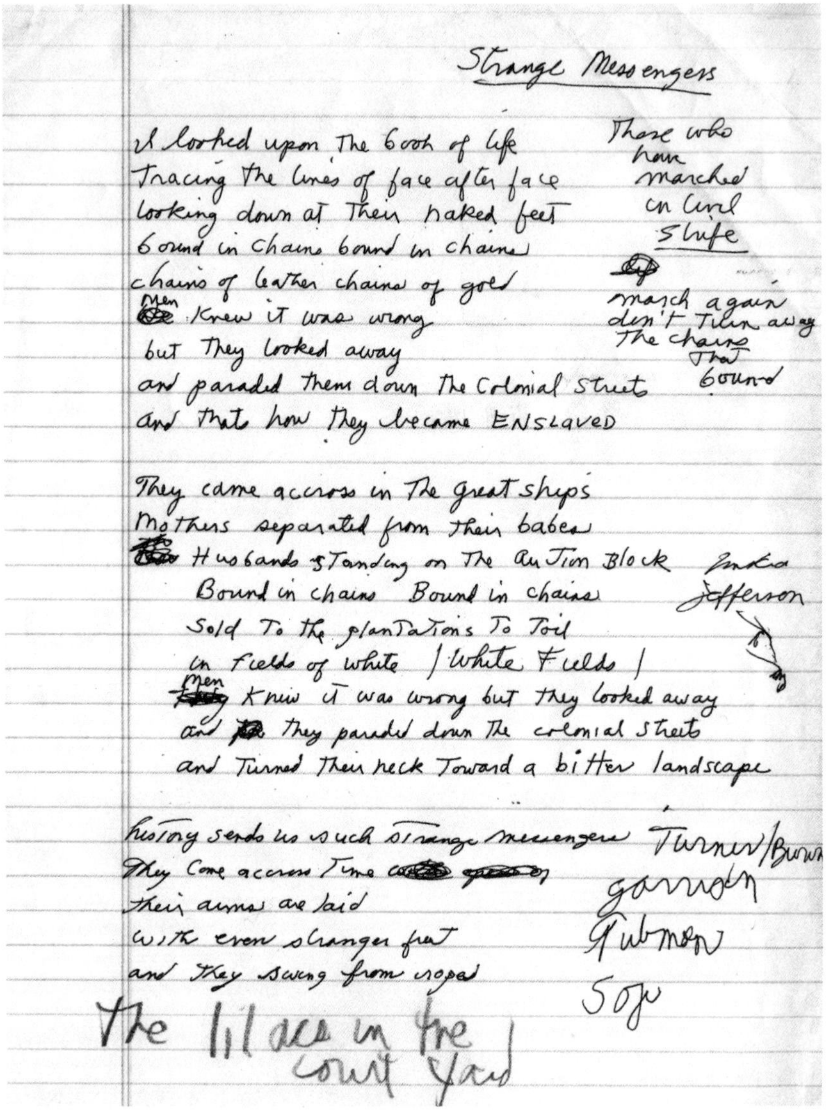

Strange Messengers

I looked upon The book of life
Tracing the lines of face after face
looking down at Their naked feet
bound in chains bound in chains
chains of leather chains of gold
~~Men~~ Knew it was wrong
but They looked away
and paraded them down The Colonial Streets
and thats how They became ENSLAVED

They came accross in The great ships
Mothers separated from their babes
~~So~~ Husbands standing on The Auction Block
    Bound in chains Bound in chains
    Sold To the plantations To Toil
    in fields of white / White Fields /
    ~~Men~~ Knew it was wrong but they looked away
    and ~~So~~ they paraded down The colonial streets
    and Turned Their neck Toward a bitter landscape

history sends us such strange messengers
They come accross Time ~~with~~ ~~gesta~~
their arms are laid
with even stranger feat
and They swing from ropes

The lilacs in the
        court Yard

[right margin annotations:]

Those who
have
marched
in Civil
Strife

march again
don't Turn away
The chains
That
bound

Enka
Jefferson

Turner/Brown
garrison
Tubman
Soju

STRANGE MESSENGERS

奇特使者

I looked upon the book of life

我翻看着生命之书

tracing the lines of face after face

追溯一张又一张脸的线条

looking down at their naked feet

低头看着他们赤裸的双脚

bound in chains bound in chains

捆缚着枷锁，捆缚着枷锁

chains of leather chains of gold

皮革的枷锁，金制的枷锁

Men knew it was wrong but we looked away

人们知道这是错的却把视线移开

and paraded them down the colonial streets

押着他们沿殖民地大街游行

and that's how they became enslaved

他们就是这样沦为奴隶

They came across on the great ships

他们乘着巨大船只渡海而来

mothers separated from their babes

母亲们被迫与婴儿分离

husbands standing on the auction block

丈夫们站立在拍卖区

bound in chains bound in chains

捆缚着枷锁，捆缚着枷锁

chains of leather chains of gold

皮革的枷锁，金制的枷锁

Men knew it was wrong but they looked away

人们知道这是错的却把视线移开

and led them to toil in fields of white

指挥他们在白茫茫的田野里辛勤劳作

as they turned their necks to a bitter landscape

他们把脖子扭向苦涩的风景

Oh the people I hear them calling

哦，我听到人们在呼唤

Am I not a man and a brother	难道我不是男人和兄弟吗
Am I not a woman and a sister	难道我不是女人和姐妹吗
we will be heard we will be heard	我们会被听见，我们会被听见
History sends us such strange messengers	历史给我们送来如此奇特的使者
they come down through time	他们穿越时间到来
to embrace to enrage	来拥抱，来激怒
and in their arms even stranger fruit	在他们怀里还有更加奇特的果实
and they swing from the trees	他们在树上荡来荡去
with their vision in flames	他们的视野火焰四起
ropes of leather ropes of gold	皮革的枷锁，金制的枷锁
men knew it was wrong	人们知道这是错的
but they looked away	却把视线移开
messengers swinging	使者们荡来荡去
from twisted rope	绳子扭绞在一起
as they turned their necks	他们把脖子扭向
to a bitter landscape	一片苦涩的风景

GRATEFUL

心怀感激

Ours is just another skin

我们的生命只是另一层皮肤

that simply slips away

轻易就会悄悄溜走

you can rise above it

你可以超越它

it will shed easily

它很容易便脱落

Like a ship in a bottle

就像瓶中的航船

held up to the sun

扬帆对着太阳

sails ain't going nowhere

却哪儿也航行不到

you can count every one

你可以算上每个人

until it crashes unto the earth

直到它撞向地球

and simply slips away

轻易就会悄悄溜走

you can hide in the open

你可以躲在开阔野外

or just disappear

或是干脆消失

Ours is just a craving

我们的生命只是一种渴望

and a twist of the wrist

转动一下手腕

will undo the stopper

就能解开阻碍

with abrupt tenderness

带着唐突的温柔

die little sparrow

去死吧，小麻雀

and awake singing

再醒来，来歌唱

It all will come out fine

I've learned it line by line

one common wire

one silver thread

all that you desire

rolls on ahead

—for Jerry Garcia

一切都会好起来

我已一行行地学会了

一条贯穿之线

一条银色丝线

你想要的一切

滚滚向前而来

——写给杰瑞·加西亚 [1]

---

1 杰瑞·加西亚（Jerry Garcia, 1942—1995），美国创作歌手、吉他手，1960 年代反文化运动时代成名的摇滚乐队"感恩至死"（Grateful Dead）的主音吉他手和主唱。

NEW PARTY

You say hey

the state of the you-you union

is fine fine fine

I got the feeling that you're lying

I think we need

a new party

They say to me

they say what's the word

I say it's thunderbird

why don't you

fly fly fly

fly away hey

and while you're at it

why don't you

fertilize my lawn

with what's running

from your mouth

hey listen here

We got to get off

新政党

你说，嘿

你——你发布的国情咨文

很好 很好 很好

我感觉你在撒谎

我想我们需要

一个新政党

他们对我说

他们说，说什么来着

我说这是雷鸟

你为什么不

飞 飞 飞

飞走吧，嘿

等你这么做的时候

你为什么不

用你嘴里面

喷出来的东西

给我的草坪施施肥

嘿，听着点

我们必须得抬起

our ass or get burned	屁股做点什么不然就会被烧死
the worlds troubles	世界的麻烦
are a global concern	是全球关注的问题
does your child have	你的孩子有没有
fresh water to drink	清洁淡水可以喝
wherever you are	无论你在哪里
wherever you are you're invited	无论你在哪里你都被邀请
to think about this	想一想这个问题
You say hey	你说，嘿
the state of the union	这份国情咨文
is fine fine fine	很好 很好 很好
I got the feeling that	我感觉
you're lying lying	你在撒谎 撒谎
think we're gonna need	我想我们需要
a new party	一个新政党
When in the course	在人类历史的
of human events	发展过程中
it becomes necessary	很有必要
to take things in your own hands	把事情掌握在自己手中

to take the water from the well	把水从井里打捞出来
and declare it tainted by greed	宣布它已经被贪婪玷污
we got to surely clean it up	我们必须把它清理干净
clean our house	清扫我们的房屋
our inner house	我们的里屋
our outer house	我们的外屋
and hey by the way	嘿，顺便说一下
the human event	人类历史
is the party of the century	就是本世纪的政党
and you're all invited	你们所有人都被邀请
it's where you are	无论你们在哪里
wherever you are	无论你们在哪里
'cause this party	因为这个政党
is for everyone	为每个人而存在
and the price of admission	加入的费用
is love one another	就是去爱彼此
love brother	爱，兄弟

LIBBIE'S SONG

莉比之歌

If it wasn't for your golden hair

要不是因为你金色的头发

I would not be belonely

我不会孤苦伶仃

if it wasn't for your golden hair

要不是因为你金色的头发

I would not be alone

我不会独自一人

If it wasn't for your piercing stare

要不是因为你刺痛的凝视

I would not be belonely

我不会孤苦伶仃

if it wasn't for your piercing stare

要不是因为你刺痛的凝视

I would not be alone

我不会独自一人

I would not waltz in a widow's line

我不会在寡妇们中间跳起华尔兹

danced in black by God's design

在上帝安排下身着黑衣起舞

what was yours would not be mine

你的东西不会成为我的

if it wasn't for your golden hair

要不是因为你金色的头发

I would not be alone

我不会独自一人

You courted me with princely airs

你以高贵的姿态追求我

said you'd love me only

说你只爱我一人

kiss the ribbons in my hair

亲吻我头上的丝带

said darling come and fly

说亲爱的，来飞舞吧

Flower of the Calvary [1]	加略山 [1] 上的花
you swept me off my saddle	你把我迷得神魂颠倒
lifted me into your life	把我带入你的生活
a soldier's wife was I	让我成为士兵之妻
You proudly marched to the horn	你迎着号角骄傲地进军
I prayed for your swift return	我祈祷你早日归家
I waited for you so forlorn	我孤独地等候你
'Ere to be alone	独自一人在这里
I longed for you, I longed to die	我渴望着你，我渴望死去
I was so belonely	我如此孤苦伶仃
the pillow's bare by my side	身边的枕头空空如也
and yet I shall abide	尽管如此我将坚持下去
For heaven has aset for me	因为上天已经为我安排了
companion for eternity	永恒的伴侣
so kiss the ribbons in my hair	亲吻我头上的丝带吧
say darling come and fly	说亲爱的，来飞舞吧
If it wasn't for your golden hair	要不是因为你金色的头发

277

I would not be alonely

if it wasn't for your golden hair

I would not be alone

我不会如此孤独

要不是因为你金色的头发

我不会独自一人

—for Libbie Custer

——写给莉比·卡斯特[2]

1 加略山（Calvary），意译为"骷髅地"，据《圣经·新约》中的四福音书记载，耶稣基督曾被钉在加略山上的十字架。

2 莉比·卡斯特（Elizabeth Clift Custer，1842—1933），美国作家、演说家，美国陆军少将乔治·阿姆斯特朗·卡斯特（George Armstrong Custer）的妻子。美国内战时期，乔治负责指挥多项战役。乔治去世后，莉比通过公开演讲及著作等方式不遗余力地推广丈夫的政治遗产，渐成为美国文化中的重要形象，她的事迹曾被拍摄为影视剧作品。

GUNG HO   工合

On a field of red one gold star   红色田野上一颗金色星星

raised above his head   在他头顶升起

raised above his head   在他头顶升起

he was not like any other   他跟其他任何人都不一样

he was just like any other   他跟其他任何人都一样

and the song they bled   那首他们为之流血的歌

                                                 是献给他的赞美诗

was a hymn to him

Awake my little one   醒来吧我的孩子

the seed of revolution   革命的种子

sewn in the sleeve   缝在衣袖里

of cloth humbly worn   别人华丽装饰之处

where others are adorned   你只朴素地穿扮

Above the northern plain   北方平原的天空上

the great birds fly   巨大的鸟儿在飞翔

with great wings   它们展开巨大翅膀

over the paddy fields   掠过稻田上方

and the people kneel   人们跪在地上

and the men they toil   他们辛勤劳作

yet not for their own   却不是为了自己

279

and the children are hungry	孩子们饥肠辘辘
and the wheel groans	车轮发出呻吟
There before the grass hut	草棚子前面
a young boy stood	站着一个小男孩
his mother lay dead	他的母亲躺下死去
his sisters cried for bread	他的姐妹哭着哀求粮食
and within his young heart	他年轻的心
the seed of revolution sewn	革命的种子缝入其中
in cloth humbly worn	别人华丽装饰之处
while others are adorned	你只朴素地穿扮
And he grew into a man	他长大成了一个男人
not like any other	跟其他任何人都不同
just like any other	跟其他任何人都相同
one small man	一个小个子男人
a beard the color of rice	米色胡子
a face the color of tea	茶色脸庞
who shared the misery	他和其他戴着枷锁的人
of other men in chains	共担这苦难
with shackles on his feet	他脚上绑着镣铐

escaped the guillotine	逃过断头台
Who fought against	他们抗争的是谁
colonialism imperialism	殖民主义 帝国主义
who remained awake	当其他人昏睡
when others did not	谁在保持清醒
who penned like Jefferson	谁像杰斐逊一样拿起笔
let independence ring	让独立的钟声响起
and the cart of justice turns	正义之车转过身
slow and bitterly	缓慢而苦涩
and the people were crying	人民在哭泣
plant that seed that seed	种下那颗种子那颗种子
and they crawled on their bellies	他们匍匐着爬行
beneath the great beast	在巨兽的身下
and filled the carts with bodies	曾装满粮食的手推车
where once had been their crops	却装满了尸体
And the great birds swarm	巨鸟们蜂拥而至
spread their wings overhead	在高空展开翅膀
and his mother dead	他的母亲死去了
and the typhoons and the rain	台风和阵雨

the jungles in flames	火焰里的丛林
and the orange sun	橙黄色的太阳
None could be more beautiful	没有比越南
than Vietnam	更美好的地方了
nothing was more beautiful	没有比越南
than Vietnam	更美好的事物了
And his heart stopped beating	他的心脏停止了跳动
and the wheel kept turning	车轮仍在不停向前
and the words he bled	那些他为之流血的话
were a hymn to them	是献给他们的赞美诗
I have served the whole people	我曾为全体人民效力过
I have served my whole country	我曾为整个国家效力过
and as I leave this world	当我离开这个世界
may you suffer union	愿你受联军之苦
and my great affection	而我深厚的情感
limitless as sky	如天空般无穷无际
filled with golden stars	布满金色星星
The question is raised	问题已被提出
raised above his head	高举过他的头顶

was he of his word	他信守了诺言吗
was he a good man	他是个好人吗
for his image	因为他的形象
fills the southern heart	已经填满南方人的心
with none but bitterness	除苦难外别无他物
And the people keep crying	人民仍在不停哭泣
and the men keep dying	人们仍在不停死去
and it's so beautiful	那里如此美好
so beautiful	如此美好
give me one more turn	再给我一次机会
give me one more turn	再给我一次机会
one more turn of the wheel	一次机会去转动车轮
One more revolution	再来一场革命
One more turn of the wheel	一次机会去转动车轮
—for Ho Chi Minh	——写给胡志明

TRAMPIN'

四 处 漂 泊

I'm trampin' trampin'   Try'n-a make heaven my home   I'm trampin' trampin'   Try'n-a make heaven my home
I'm trampin' trampin'   I've never been to heaven   But I've been told   Try'n-a make heaven my home
That the streets up there   Are paved with gold   Try'n-a make heaven my home
—EDWARD BOATNER

我四处漂泊　四处漂泊　试着把天堂变成我的家　我四处漂泊　四处漂泊　试着把天堂变成我的家
我四处漂泊　四处漂泊　我从未去过天堂　但有人告诉过我　试着把天堂变成我的家　那里的街道
由黄金铺就　试着把天堂变成我的家
——爱德华·博特纳 ★

★ 爱德华·博特纳（Edward Boatner，1898—1981），美国作曲家，曾创作编写许多广为流传的黑人灵歌。

9·11、阿富汗战争、伊拉克战争……正是在这样的世界背景下，2004 年 4 月，帕蒂·史密斯的第九张专辑《四处漂泊》以"来吧，女孩 / 来吧，男孩 / 欢度禧年"这战斗号角式的唱词拉开。而"禧年"（jubilee）一词不仅有纪念庆典之意，它亦指受奴役的希伯来人的解放之年，在 1800 年代的废奴运动和一个世纪后的黑人民权运动中被广泛使用。《四处漂泊》中的帕蒂将旧世纪吟游诗人的传统延续至当下，在审视自身与国家历史的同时，发出新的抗争之声。

这张专辑是帕蒂签署新公司哥伦比亚唱片后发行的第一张专辑。无疑，《四处漂泊》极富政治性，它受民权运动启发，其标题就取自美国黑人女低音歌唱家玛丽安·安德森演唱过的一首灵歌。但《四处漂泊》并非教导、说教式的。帕蒂在作品中表现得谦卑，她看向例如甘地这样的历史人物，高喊"国王先生"，从布莱克与迪伦的话中寻找精神力量。也正是在庞大的政治环境笼罩下，专辑中所穿插的更为私人的叙事显得尤为动人。《禧年》与《心灵大步走》犀利、强硬，《甘地》《巴格达电台》则是具戏剧性的两首长篇作品。而在这些激烈的音符之间，有《玫瑰母亲》与《罪过》这样更短小、亲密的乡村曲调。帕蒂以沉静的目光在每一个角落发现真理、庆贺生命。

同时，即便是在这第九张专辑，我们仍能看到弗雷德与家庭的主题显现其中。这一次，帕蒂为女儿杰西创作了《车轮》，同时在同名歌曲《四处漂泊》中，杰西弹奏的钢琴与帕蒂的声音温柔交织。

正如长达九分钟的《甘地》中所唱，"从你们的沉睡中醒来 / 用数量打败他们"，帕蒂以《四处漂泊》重新想象历史。这一想象并非漫无边际。她牢牢抓紧切身的人与事以及历史片段中的具体瞬间，反思，向更美好的未来举起敬畏之旗。

PATTI SMITH
BOWERY BALLROOM
DECEMBER 30   DECEMBER 31   2000

Patti Smith   Oliver Ray   Jay Dee Daugherty
Lenny Kaye   Tony Shanahan

"AND WHAT SHOULDER AND WHAT ART
COULD TWIST THE SINEWS OF THY HEART"
W.B.

JUBILEE

禧年 [1]

Oh glad day to celebrate	哦，欢喜之日来庆祝
'Neath the cloudless sky	在万里无云的天空下
Air so sweet	空气如此甘甜
Water pure	水源这样纯净
Fields ripe with rye	田野里长满成熟的黑麦
Come one, come all	来吧，大家都过来
Gather 'round	聚集在一起
Discard your Sunday shoes	丢掉你穿去教堂的鞋
Come on now	现在就过来
Oh my land	哦，我的土地
Be a jubilee	欢度禧年
Come on girl	来吧，女孩
Come on boy	来吧，男孩
Be a jubilee	欢度禧年
Oh my land	哦，我的土地
Oh my good	哦，我的好人们
People don't be shy	不要害羞
Weave the birth of harmony	编织和谐的降生
With children's happy cries	伴随孩子们快乐的哭声
Hand in hand	手牵着手

We're dancing 'round   我们绕圈跳舞

In a freedom ring   围成自由之环

Come on now   现在就过来

Oh my land   哦，我的土地

Be a jubilee   欢度禧年

Come on girl   来吧，女孩

Come on boy   来吧，男孩

Be a jubilee   欢度禧年

We will never fade away   我们永远不会消逝

Doves shall multiply   鸽子将生息繁衍

Yet I see hawks circling the sky   然而我看到鹰群在天空盘旋

Scattering our glad day   用债务和绝望

With debt and despair   驱散我们欢喜的日子

What good hour   怎样美好的时光

Will restore our troubled air?   能够澄清我们浑浊的空气？

Come on people   来吧，大家

Gather 'round   聚集在一起

You know what to do   你们知道该怎么办

Come on people   来吧，大家

Oh my land   哦，我的土地

What be troubling

Oh my land

What be troubling

What be troubling

What be troubling you

We are love and the future

We stand in the midst of fury and weariness

Who dreams of joy and radiance?

Who dreams of war and sacrifice?

Our sacred realms are being squeezed

Curtailing civil liberties

Recruit the dreams that sing for thee

Let freedom ring

Oh glad day

什么在困扰

哦，我的土地

什么在困扰

什么在困扰

什么在困扰着你

我们就是爱与未来

我们站在愤怒和疲倦之中

谁梦想着欢乐与光辉？

谁梦想着战争与牺牲？

我们神圣的王国正在被挤压

公民自由被限制

招募梦想，为你歌唱

让自由之声高响

哦，欢喜之日

---

1 禧年，纪念特定事件的周年纪念日，通常是表示 25 周年、40 周年、50 周年、
60 周年和 70 周年。"禧年"一词源于《圣经》的犹太节日，现在经常用来表示
君主统治的庆祝活动。非裔美国人文化中使用"禧年"，指从奴隶制解放的庆祝
活动。

MOTHER ROSE	玫瑰母亲
Mother rose	玫瑰母亲
Every little morn'	每个熹微清晨
To tend to me	她来照料我
There she stood	她就站在那里
Waiting by the door	守在门边等候
Selflessly	无私地
Took my hand	牵起我的手
Took it with a smile tenderly	带着温柔的微笑牵着它
Mother rose	玫瑰母亲
Every little morn'	每个熹微清晨
To tend to me	她来照料我
Now's the time	现在是时候
To turn the view	倒转过来了
Now that I have you	现在有我来呵护你
And I'll rise	我会在
Every little morn'	每个熹微清晨
To tend to thee	起身照料你
When you rise	当你醒来
Open up your eyes	睁开你的双眼
You will see	你会看到

There I'll be	我就在那里
Waiting by the door	守在门边等候
Come to me	到我身边来
Take my hand	牵起我的手
Look into your heart	望向你内心
There I'll be	我就在那里
Now's the time	现在是时候
To turn the view	倒转过来了
Now that I have you	现在有我来呵护你
Roses growing by my door	生长在我门前的玫瑰花
Climbing up the vine	沿着藤蔓向上攀
All the thorns and pain obscured	所有尖刺和疼痛被隐藏
Roses shall divine	神圣的玫瑰花
Where we feel no pain	在那里我们感受不到痛苦
And the love inside	爱意包藏在里面
Where roses climb	那里有玫瑰在攀爬
Roses shall divine	神圣的玫瑰花
Roses shall divine	神圣的玫瑰花
Holy mother	圣洁之母
Mother of gold	金色之母

Mother with stories

Told and retold

She felt our tears

Heard our sighs

And turned to gold

Before our eyes

She rose into the light

She rose into the light

She rose into the light

—*for Beverly Williams Smith*

母亲的故事

一遍又一遍被讲述

她感受到我们的泪水

听到我们的叹息

在我们眼前

化为一抹金色

她升起融入那光芒

她升起融入那光芒

她升起融入那光芒

——写给贝弗利·威廉姆斯·史密斯 [1]

1　贝弗利·威廉姆斯·史密斯（Beverly Williams Smith，1920—2002），帕蒂·史密斯的母亲，曾经是一位爵士乐歌手，对帕蒂的音乐启蒙起到重要作用。

STRIDE OF THE MIND

心灵大步走

I took a walk out to the sun

我想散个步走到太阳去

But I just, just couldn't take it

但我就是，就是忍受不了

I followed a dream

我追随了一个梦想

It was circular

它是圆形的

But I just, just could not fake it

但我就是，就是假装不了

Step to the left the left the left

向左走，向左走，向左走

Step to the right the right the right

向右走，向右走，向右走

Pick up the sign the sign the sign

捡起那标志，那标志，那标志

For a stride of the mind the mind the mind

为了心灵大步走，大步走，大步走

Simon of the desert

荒漠里的西门 [1]

Blew into town

被风吹进城里

On the scalding tail

在明亮刺骨的寒风

Of a bright cold wind

滚烫的尾巴上

Slipped through the sand

滑行穿越沙地

Footprints emerged

脚印渐渐浮现

Where no one was walking

在无人行走过之地

Simon had been

西门到过那里

Dropped from heaven

从天堂坠落

To a ready made world	到了现成的人间
Said I'm no Sufi	说我不是苏菲派 [2]
But I'll give it a whirl	但我会试上一试
We booked passage	我们预订了旅程
On the Book of the Dead	写在死亡之书 [3] 上
Time to travel	旅行的时候到了
Simon said	西门说道
Step to the left the left the left	向左走，向左走，向左走
Step to the right the right the right	向右走，向右走，向右走
Pick up the sign the sign the sign	捡起那标志，那标志，那标志
Oh the stride of the mind the mind the mind	为了心灵大步走，大步走，大步走
Come on move where dreams increase	来吧动起来，那里梦想与日增长
Where every man is a masterpiece	那里每个人都是件杰作
If you want to be counted	如果你想要被看作
As another kind	另一种人
And you're true, pursue	你就要真正地，去追求
Stride of the mind the mind the mind	为了心灵大步走，大步走，大步走
Stride of the mind the mind the mind	为了心灵大步走，大步走，大步走

He bowed three times	他鞠了三次躬
Removed his fez	摘下他的毡帽
Pointed to heaven	手指向天堂
And Simon says	西门说道
The mind the mind the mind	心灵，心灵，心灵
Pick up the sign the mind the mind	捡起那标志，心灵，心灵
It's a vertical climb the climb the climb	这是一次垂直攀登，攀登，攀登
Stride of the mind the mind the mind	心灵大步走，大步走，大步走
Pick up the sign the sign the sign	捡起那标志，那标志，那标志
It's a vertical climb the climb	这是一次垂直攀登，攀登
Take it in stride	你要从容面对

1 西门彼得，原名西门巴约拿，耶稣十二使徒之一。据传被倒钉十字架而死，死后被罗马天主教追加为第一任教皇。"西门"在希伯来语中意为"沙漠、荒凉地"。

2 伊斯兰教神秘主义派别，是对伊斯兰教信仰赋予隐秘奥义、奉行苦行禁欲功修方式的诸多组织的统称，亦称苏菲主义。

3 死亡之书（*Book of the Dead*），指的是一段古埃及墓葬文书，在新王国时期（约前1550年）至约前50年之间被使用，文字中含有可以协助死者通过死亡之地杜亚特前往来世的咒语。每一本死亡之书几乎都是独一无二的，因为其中阐述的内容因人而异，并且有段落是依照生平而撰写的。

CARTWHEELS

车轮

Come my one	来吧我的宝贝
look at the world	看看这世界
Bird beast butterfly	鸟兽与蝴蝶
Girls sing notes of heaven	女孩们唱着天堂的音符
Birds lift them up to the sky	鸟儿们把音符举上天空
Spring is departing	春日正离去
Spring is departing	春日正离去
Your thoughts	你的思绪
Are darting like a rabbit	像兔子似的飞奔
Like a rabbit cross the moon	像兔子似的穿过月亮
Shining a light over your hair	光线闪耀在你发丝
As boys croon	男孩们低声歌唱
Pretty in pink	身着粉色那么漂亮
It makes me wonder	这让我想知道
What could ever	到底有什么
Bring you down	能把你击倒
I see tears falling	我看到眼泪从棕色的
From those eyes of brown	眼睛里掉落

Hearing a voice,	听到一个声音
You turn your head	你转过头
You vanish, vanish	你消失了，消失在
Into the mist	思绪的
Of your thoughts	迷雾中
And I want to grasp	我想要抓住
What brings you down	那会击倒你的东西
The world is changing	世界不断变幻
Your heart is growing	你的心不断成长
Open those eyes of brown	睁开那棕色眼睛
Hearing a voice	听到一个声音
you turn your head	你转过头
Girls turn by ones, by twos	女孩们也三三两两转过来
Notes pour, glad and tender	音符倾泻而出，欢乐而温柔
To eradicate your blues	根除你的忧愁
The good world, the good world	美好的世界，美好的世界
The good whirl, the good whirl	美好地旋转，美好地旋转

Come my one, look at the world   来吧我的宝贝，看看这世界

Bird beast butterfly   鸟兽与蝴蝶

Girls sing notes from heaven   女孩们唱着天堂的音符

Birds lift them up to the sky   鸟儿们把音符举上天空

I see brown eyes   我看到棕色的眼睛

That see girls turning   看到女孩们转动着

Cartwheels cartwheels   车轮　车轮

I see brown eyes   我看到棕色的眼睛

I see a girl turning   我看到一个女孩转动着

Cartwheels, cartwheels   车轮，车轮

—for Jesse Paris Smith   ——写给杰西·帕里斯·史密斯 [1]

1　杰西·帕里斯·史密斯（Jesse Paris Smith，1987— ），帕蒂·史密斯的女儿，美国音乐人、作曲家、作家。

PEACEABLE KINGDOM

和平王国

Yesterday I saw you standing there

昨天我看到你站在那里

With your hand against the pane

用手抵着窗格

Looking out the window at the rain

望向窗外的雨

And I wanted to tell you

我想告诉你

That your tears were not in vain

你的眼泪不会白流

But I guess we both knew

但我猜我们两个都知道

We'd never be the same

我们永远不是一种人

Never be the same

永远不是一种人

Why must we hide all these feelings inside?

为何我们必须将这些感受深藏心底？

Lions and lambs shall abide

雄狮和羔羊都应遵守

Maybe one day we'll be strong enough

也许有朝一日我们会足够强大

To build it back again

将它再次建造起来

Build the peaceable kingdom

建造那和平王国

Back again

再次建造

Build it back again

将它再次建造起来

Why must we hide all these feelings inside?

为何我们必须将这些感受深藏心底？

Lions and lambs shall abide

雄狮和羔羊都应遵守

Maybe one day we'll be strong enough

也许有朝一日我们会足够强大

To build it back again

将它再次建造起来

Build the peaceable kingdom

Build it back again

—*for Rachel Corey*

建造那和平王国

将它再次建造起来

——写给雷切尔·科里 [1]

1 雷切尔·科里（Rachel Corey，1979—2003），美国和平工作者，国际团结运动（ISM）成员，致力以非暴力行动阻止以色列军队摧毁巴勒斯坦人的家园。2003 年在加沙地带南部拉法赫遭以色列国防军（IDF）的武装推土机辗压身亡。

GANDHI   ## 甘地

I had a dream Mr. King   我做了个梦，国王先生

If you'll beg my pardon   请你原谅我

I was trespassing   擅自闯入了

A sacred garden   神圣的花园

And the blossoms fell   鲜花掉落下来

And they dropped like candy   它们片片坠下像是糖果

And nature cried Gandhi Gandhi   大自然呼喊着，甘地，甘地

And nature cried Gandhi Gandhi   大自然呼喊着，甘地，甘地

When he was a boy   当他还是个男孩

He was afraid of the dark   他恐惧黑暗

His mother would fast   母亲会在他脚边

And pray at his feet   斋戒并祈祷

And the lamp burned as he slept   当他入睡灯光在燃烧

Burned as he dreamed   梦境袭来灯光在燃烧

He was dreaming of his sisters   他梦到了他的姐妹

Dressed in white muslin   穿着白色薄棉裙

Dancing in a ring   围成圆环跳起舞

He was afraid of the dark   他恐惧黑暗

And the lamp burned   灯光在燃烧

Dreaming of blossoms   梦到鲜花盛开

302

They were burning his throat	花朵灼烧他的喉咙
He had eaten flowers	他吃下花朵
Flowers fell burning	花朵燃烧着从
From the young girls' hair	年轻女孩的头发上掉落
He was whispering	他轻声低语
Into his god's ear	对着他的神的耳畔
Let the children be so	让孩子们就这样吧
And the lamplight flickered flickered	灯光摇曳闪烁，摇曳闪烁
And his mother withered like Job	他的母亲像约伯一样枯萎
And he lay there dreaming	他躺在那里做着梦
And the blossoms fell	鲜花掉落下来
And Tilak's trumpet	蒂拉克 [1] 的小号
Proceeded to call	继续在鸣响
And the blossoms fell	鲜花掉落下来
And they dropped like candy	它们片片坠下像是糖果
And the people cried Gandhi Gandhi	人民呼喊着，甘地，甘地
He was frail and shy	他脆弱又羞涩
And the cast of his mind	他的心思
Was mercurial	反复无常
As the sacred verbs	神圣的动词

303

Scrawled in the dust	潦草地写在尘土中
On the floor, on the floor	写在地板上，写在地板上
Long live revolution	革命万岁
And the spinning wheel	还有那纺车
And a handful of salt	和一把盐
The untouchables	不可触碰之贱民
Dropped like candy	片片坠下像是糖果
They called to him Gandhi Gandhi	他们冲他呼喊着，甘地，甘地
Feel our woes man of the giving	感受我们的悲伤吧，慷慨之人
Rejoin the living Rejoin the living	重新加入活着的人，重新加入活着的人
Awake from the net	从大网中醒过来
Where you've been sleeping	你一直在那里沉睡
And climbing climbing	攀爬吧，攀爬吧
The flowing hair	年轻女孩们
And the golden flowers	飘逸的头发
Of the young girls	金色的鲜花
Awake little man	醒来吧，小个子男人
Awake from your slumber	从你沉睡中醒来
And get 'em with the numbers	用数量打败他们
Get 'em with the numbers	用数量打败他们
One / Two / Three	一 / 二 / 三

Four hundred thousand million people	四亿人民
People / People / People	人民 / 人民 / 人民
Awaken from your slumber	从你们的沉睡中醒来
Long live revolution	革命万岁
And the spinning wheel	还有那纺车
Awake awake	醒来，醒来
Is the mighty appeal	就是强大的感染力
Oh, people awake	哦，人民醒来吧
Awake from your slumber	从你们的沉睡中醒来
And get 'em with the numbers	用数量打败他们
Get 'em with the numbers	用数量打败他们
I had a dream	我做了个梦
Mr. King	国王先生
If you'll beg my pardon	请你原谅我
I was trespassing	擅自闯入了
The sacred garden	神圣的花园
And the blossoms fell	鲜花掉落下来
Dropped like candy	片片坠下像是糖果
And nature called Gandhi Gandhi	大自然呼喊着，甘地，甘地
Gandhi Gandhi	甘地，甘地

Awake from your slumber

And get 'em with the numbers

从你们的沉睡中醒来

用数量打败他们

1 巴尔·冈加达·蒂拉克（Bal Gangadhar Tilak，1856—1920），印度独立运动的第一位领导人，曾被授予"洛克曼尼亚"的头衔，意为"被人民（作为他们的领导人）接受"。甘地称他为"现代印度的创造者"。

45

Frankenstein

sitting

I loved my sister my gentle
innocent sister. when the
grief stricken father walked
senselessly with his dead child
in his hands, and tenda saying
will it be all right
I wanted to say yes

fling
ring
string
spring
bring
cling
RING WING
SING

Our life is designed
with as a finishing line
That another sings
and more small debts
a penned as regrets
upon a ragged wing

his life was designed
with a finishing line
that another shall sing
and his small debts
penned as regrets—
upon a ragged wing

told in his name

all life in
a minus designed
to leave no in Time
and may ring an me
on decisively

a life is designs
to depart in Time
with no
and his small debts
penned as regrets
upon a ragged wing
I'm sorry my dear
that I won't be here
to take care of everything

All life is designed
with a finishing line
That another sing
and our small debt

TRESPASSES

罪过

Life is designed

生活是用别人

With unfinished lines

唱出那些未完成的诗行

That another sings

设计而成

Each story unfolds

每个故事展开

Like it was gold

仿佛破碎翅膀上

Upon a ragged wing

生出了金子一样

The bold and the fair

勇者与美人

Suffer their share

都将自食其果

He whispered to his kin

他低声对亲人说

All of my debts

所有我欠下的债

Left with regrets

带着悔恨留下来

I'm sorry for everything

我为一切感到抱歉

And she pinned back her hair

她把头发别到脑后

Shouldered with care

把本应由他承担的责任

The burdens that were his

小心翼翼扛在自己肩上

Mending the coat

修补挂在杆子上的

That hung on the post

那件外套

In heart remembering

在心中牢牢谨记

Trespasses stretch	罪过伸展开
Like brown fences	如褐色篱笆
Winding as they may	尽管可能蜿蜒曲折
Trespasses stretch	罪过伸展开
Like broken fences	如破损篱笆
Hope to mend them one day	愿有一日能修补
And her time was to come	她的时日已到尽头
Called to her son	将她的儿子唤到身边
This your song to sing	这是你要唱的歌
All of our debts	所有我们欠下的债
Wove with regrets	用一根金色丝线
Upon a golden string	就着悔恨编织起来
And he found the old coat	他找到了那件旧外套
Hung on a post	挂在一根杆子上
Like a ragged wing	像一只破碎翅膀
And took as his own	他将它视为己有
The sewn and unsown	缝好的和未缝好的
Joyfully whistling	欢快地吹起口哨

Trespasses stretch

Like broken fences

Winding as they may

Trespasses stretch

Like broken fences

Hope to mend them one day

罪过伸展开

如褐色篱笆

尽管可能蜿蜒曲折

罪过伸展开

如破损篱笆

愿有一日能修补

IN MY BLAKEAN YEAR

In my Blakean year

I was so disposed

Toward a mission yet unclear

Advancing pole by pole

Fortune breathed into my ear

Mouthed a simple ode

One road is paved in gold

One road is just a road

In my Blakean year

Such a woeful schism

The pain of our existence

Was not as I envisioned

Boots that trudged

From track to track

Worn down to the sole

One road was paved in gold

One road was just a road

在我的布莱克 [1] 年

在我的布莱克年

我是如此想要

向那尚不明晰的任务前行

一点一点逐步向前

命运之声吹拂进我耳

吟唱一段简单的颂歌

有条路由金子铺就

一条路只是一条路

在我的布莱克年

如此悲哀的分裂

我们生存的痛苦

并非我曾预想

艰难跋涉的靴子

从一条小道到另一条

磨穿只剩下鞋底

有条路由金子铺就

一条路只是一条路

In my Blakean year	在我的布莱克年
Temptation but a hiss	诱惑不过一片嘘声
Just a shallow spear	只是一支浅矛
Robed in cowardice	披着怯懦的长袍
Brace yourself	振作起来
For bitter flack	抵住苦涩抨击
For a life sublime	追求生之壮丽
A labyrinth of riches	富有的迷宫
Never shall unwind	从不会自行解开
The threads that bind	捆绑朝圣者
The pilgrim's sack	麻布袋的丝线
Are stitched	都被缝进
Into the Blakean back	布莱克的后背
So throw off your stupid cloak	丢开愚蠢的披风
Embrace all that you fear	拥抱所有恐惧
For joy shall conquer all despair	因为欢乐将战胜一切绝望
In my Blakean year	在我的布莱克年
In my Blakean year	在我的布莱克年

In my Blakean year

在我的布莱克年

1　指威廉·布莱克（William Blake，1757—1827），英国著名诗人、画家，浪漫主义
　文学代表人物之一。

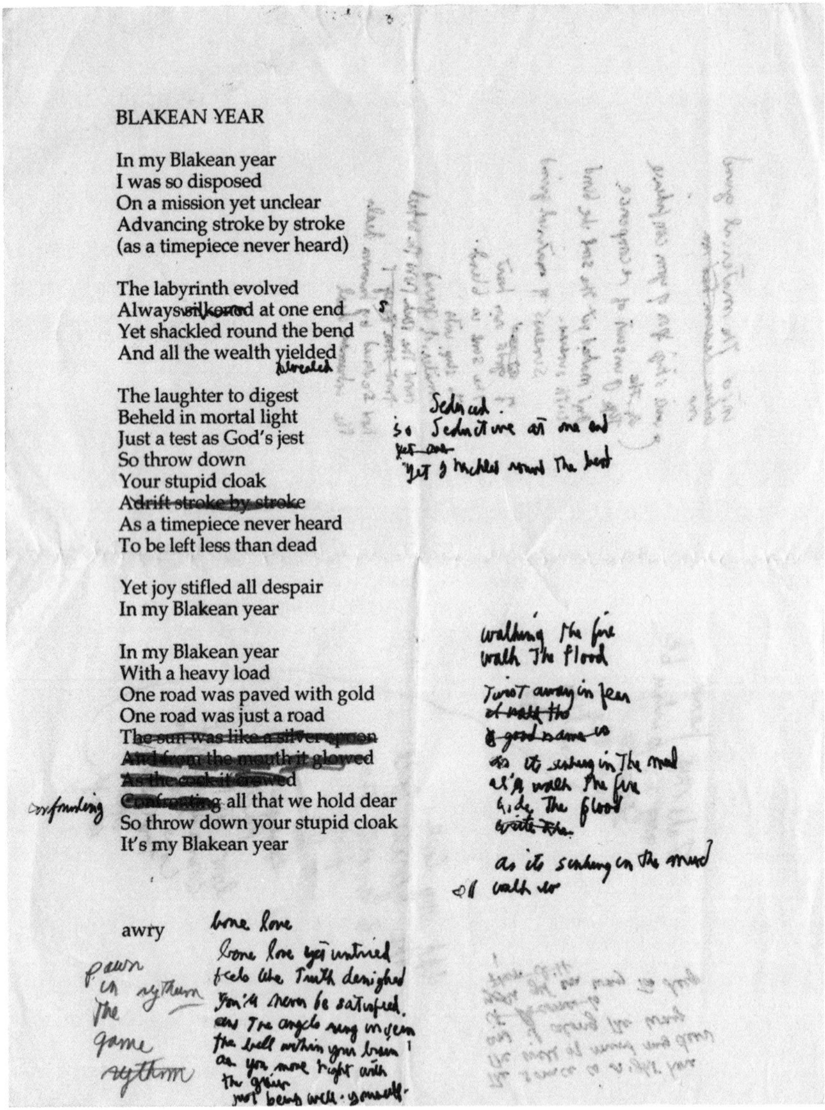

BLAKEAN YEAR

In my Blakean year
I was so disposed
On a mission yet unclear
Advancing stroke by stroke
(as a timepiece never heard)

The labyrinth evolved
Always ~~silkened~~ at one end
Yet shackled round the bend
And all the wealth yielded
~~Revealed~~

The laughter to digest
Beheld in mortal light
Just a test as God's jest
So throw down
Your stupid cloak
~~Adrift stroke by stroke~~
As a timepiece never heard
To be left less than dead

Yet joy stifled all despair
In my Blakean year

In my Blakean year
With a heavy load
One road was paved with gold
One road was just a road
~~The sun was like a silver sphere~~
~~And from the mouth it glowed~~
~~As the cock it crowed~~
~~Confronting~~ all that we hold dear
So throw down your stupid cloak
It's my Blakean year

Handwritten annotations:

Sedined.
So Seductive at one end
yet one
Yet g shackled round the best

walking the fire
walk The flood

Twist away in fear
of walk the
g good name is
as its sinking in The mad
as'g walk the fire
hide the flood
write the

as its sinking in the mud
all walk so

confounding

awry   bone love

pawn   Bone love eyes untried
in rythm   feels like Truth denighed
the   You'd never be satisfied.
game   and The angels sing in you
rythm   the bell within your brain /
            are you more right with
            the grain
            just being well · yourself.

CASH

兑现

Here we go around again

我们又在这里转了一圈

Curve of life spiraling

生命的曲线螺旋上升

Everything we've ever known

我们曾知晓的一切

As the seed of life gets blown

如同生命的种子被吹散

And the miracle of time

时间的奇迹

When will that time just end

到底何时那时间才会终结

Remember, you decide

记住，你决定

Take that vow

许下誓言

Grab that ring

抓住戒指

It's not a whim

这不是一时兴起

Not a whim

不是一时兴起

When you be cashing in

终有一日你将兑现

Try to turn your life around

试着转变生活

And all the things you do resound

你所做之事都会发出回响

And then you can't loose control

不要放松控制

Say your time has come and then

认为你的时机已到却

Hard to pinpoint find the seam

很难定位去找到接缝

Where that one time ends

上一个时间在何处终结

Where that time begins

下一个时间在何处开始

Remember, you decide

记住，你决定

Take that vow	许下誓言
Take a stand	表明立场
Grab that ring	抓住戒指
It's not a whim	这不是一时兴起
It's not a whim	这不是一时兴起
It's only time	这只是时间
That you're cashing in	正由你兑现
In the white noise of desire	在欲望的白噪音里
We can't hear a single thing	我们什么也听不到
Floating 'round the fragile bough	脆弱的大树枝四处漂浮
Afflictions of the human soul	人类灵魂的苦难
Its beauty immaterial	它的美却形迹难寻
You decide	你决定
Stand among the fallen ones	站在倒下的那些人中间
Take revenge defeated sons	替被打败的儿子们复仇
Rend that coat	撕碎那件外套
From seam to seam	从接缝到接缝
It's only time	这只是时间
It's only time	这只是时间

That you spend

You spend

It's only life

That you're cashing in

你花掉的时间

你已花掉

这只是生命

正由你兑现

Suffer not	不要遭受
Your neighbor's affliction	你邻人所受的痛苦
Suffer not	不要遭受
Your neighbor's paralysis	你邻人所受的麻痹
But extend your hand	但要伸出你的手
Extend your hand	伸出你的手
Lest you vanish in the city	以免你在这城中消失
And be but a trace	只留下一丝痕迹
Just a vanished ghost	只是一个消失的幽灵
And your legacy	而你的遗产
All the things you knew	所有那些你所知之事
Science, mathematics, thought	科学，数学，思想
Severely weakened	严重地被削弱
Like irrigation systems	如同灌溉系统
In the tired veins forming	在疲惫的脉络中形成了
The Tigris and Euphrates	底格里斯河与幼发拉底河
In the realm of peace	在和平的国度里
All the world revolved	整个世界在旋转
All the world revolved	整个世界在旋转
Around a perfect circle	绕着一个完美的圆圈
City of Baghdad	巴格达城

City of scholars	学者之城
Empirical humble	经验主义的谦恭
Center of the world	世界的中心
City in ashes	陷入灰烬之城
City of Baghdad	巴格达城
City of Baghdad	巴格达城
Abrasive aloof	令人伤感的孤傲
Oh, in Mesopotamia	哦，在美索不达米亚
Aloofness ran deep	孤傲深深流淌
Deep in the veins of the great rivers	在大河的血脉深处
That form the base of Eden	那构成了伊甸园的基础
And the tree of knowledge	知识之树
Held up its arms to the sky	向着天空举起臂膀
All the branches of knowledge	知识的所有枝杈
All the branches of knowledge	知识的所有枝杈
Cradling Civilization	孕育着文明的摇篮
In the realm of peace	在和平的国度里
All the world revolved	整个世界在旋转
Around a perfect circle	绕着一个完美的圆圈
Oh Baghdad	哦，巴格达

Center of the world	世界的中心
City of ashes	陷入灰烬之城
With its great mosques	宏伟的清真寺
Erupting from the mouth of god	从神的口中喷涌而出
Rising from the ashes like a speckled bird	像一只斑点鸟在灰烬中重生
Splayed against the mosaic sky	在马赛克般的天空下展开身形
We created the zero	我们创造出了零
But we mean nothing to you	但我们对你而言不值一提
You would believe	你会相信
That we are just some mystical tale	我们不过是一些神秘的故事
We are just a swollen belly	我们不过是肿胀的肚皮
That gave birth to Sinbad, Scheherazade	曾诞下了辛巴达 [1]，山鲁佐德 [2]
We gave birth to the zero	我们诞下了零
The perfect number	这完美的数字
We invented the zero	我们发明了零
And we mean nothing to you	我们对你而言不值一提
Our children run through the streets	我们的孩子奔跑着穿过街道
And you sent your flames	而你送来你的火焰
Your shooting stars	你的流星
Shock and awe	震撼并敬畏吧

Shock and awe	震撼并敬畏
Like some, some	就像一些，一些
Imagined warrior production	想象中的武士作品
Twenty-first century	二十一世纪
No chivalry involved	没有任何骑士精神
No Bushido	没有武士道精神
Oh, the code of the West	哦，西方世界的准则
Long gone never been	早已逝去不复返
Where does it lie?	它藏去了哪里？
You came, you came	你来了，你来了
Through the west	穿过西方
Annihilated a people	消灭了一个民族
And you come to us	你来找我们
But we are older than you	但我们比你年长得多
You wanna come	你想要来
And rob the cradle	抢夺走文明
Of civilization	的摇篮
And you read Genesis	你读过创世记
You read of the tree	你读到过这棵树
You read of the tree	你读到过这棵树

Beget by god	由上帝所生
That raised its branches into the sky	将它的枝枒举向天空
Every branch of knowledge	每一根知识的枝枒
In the cradle of civilization	都在文明的摇篮里
Of the banks of the Tigris	在底格里斯河
And the Euphrates	和幼发拉底河的岸边
Oh, in Mesopotamia	哦，在美索不达米亚
Aloofness ran deep	孤傲深深流淌
The face of Eve turning	夏娃转过她的脸
What sky did she see	她看到怎样的天空
What garden beneath her feet	她脚下是怎样的花园
The one you drill	你在那花园里钻孔
Pulling the blood of the earth	攫出大地的鲜血
Little droplets of oil for bracelets	小小石油液滴做成手镯
Little jewels sapphires	小小珍品蓝宝石
You make bracelets	你制作手镯
'Round your own world	供给你自己的世界
We are weeping tears rubies	我们泣出红宝石泪水
We offer them to you	我们把它们提供给你
We are just	我们只是
Your Arabian nightmare	你的阿拉伯噩梦

We invented the zero	我们发明了零
But we mean nothing to you	但我们对你而言不值一提
Your Arabian nightmare	你的阿拉伯噩梦
City of stars	星空之城
City of scholarship	学识之城
Science	科学
City of ideas	思想之城
City of light	光明之城
City of ashes	灰烬之城
That the great Caliph	伟大的哈里发 [3]
Walked through	步行穿过
His naked feet formed a circle	他赤裸的双脚走出一个圈
And they built a city	他们便建起了一座城
A perfect city of Baghdad	完美的巴格达城
In the realm of peace	在和平的国度里
And all the world revolved	整个世界在旋转
And they mean nothing to you	他们对你而言不值一提
Nothing to you	对你而言不值一提
Nothing	不值一提

Go to sleep my child	睡吧，我的孩子
Go to sleep	睡吧
And I'll sing you a lullaby	我会给你唱一支摇篮曲
A lullaby for our city	献给我们的城的摇篮曲
A lullaby of Baghdad	巴格达的摇篮曲
Go to sleep	睡吧
Sleep my child	睡吧，我的孩子
Sleep sleep sleep	睡吧，睡吧，睡吧
Run run run	快跑，快跑，快跑
You sent your lights	你送来了你的火光
Your bombs	你的炸弹
You sent them down on our city	你把它们送到了我们的城
Shock and awe	震撼并敬畏吧
Like some crazy t.v. show	就像疯狂的电视剧
They're robbing the cradle of civilization	他们正在掠夺文明的摇篮
They're robbing the cradle of civilization	他们正在掠夺文明的摇篮
They're robbing the cradle of civilization	他们正在掠夺文明的摇篮
Suffer not the paralysis of your neighbor	不要遭受你邻人所受的麻痹
Suffer not but extend your hand	不要遭受但要伸出你的手

1 辛巴达，阿拉伯民间故事集《一千零一夜》中记载的阿拔斯王朝时期著名英雄、航海家。他自巴士拉出发，游遍七海，有无数的奇遇。

2 山鲁佐德，《一千零一夜》中的虚构人物，也是故事的说书人。

3 哈里发（Caliph），伊斯兰和伊斯兰教国家领袖的称号，被视为穆罕默德的继承者。

BANGA

斑 迦

Believe or Explode

相信，或爆炸

《斑迦》是帕蒂·史密斯的第十一张录音室专辑，发行于 2012 年 6 月。它以帕蒂的梦境与观察为灵感，将目光放了种种人类经验上。在接受哥伦比亚广播公司采访时，帕蒂说《斑迦》的名字来自米哈伊尔·布尔加科夫的小说《大师与玛格丽塔》中总督本丢·彼拉多的狗的名字。

2010 年，帕蒂出版了第一本回忆录《只是孩子》，获得美国国家图书奖。她在书中回忆与罗伯特·梅普尔索普的友谊以及两人艺术道路的萌芽。《只是孩子》被带进了《斑迦》里。在专辑 CD 与黑胶唱片中，帕蒂收录了一首与书本同名的歌曲作为附加曲目。而回忆录中动人、真诚、幽默又满怀希望的口吻也在《斑迦》中处处显现。

在歌词上，《斑迦》如一面镜子，反射出我们所身处的繁复世界的处处混乱与美好。《斑迦》关心自然与人类的发现，《亚美利哥》想象探险家亚美利哥·韦斯普奇以一种不同的视角看待"新大陆"上的原住民；《富士山》写在 2011 年日本 3·11 地震后，将时间带回到灾害之前，引发深思。《斑迦》也延续了帕蒂以歌曲向前辈、偶像致敬的传统。继致敬、兰波、巴勒斯、迪伦、波洛克之后，《斑迦》是献给塔可夫斯基、果戈里、布尔加科夫的。帕蒂以谦逊而锐利的目光不断重新发现，"过时"与耳目一新感在她的音乐中并存。

音乐上，《斑迦》似乎少了帕蒂早期专辑中那种动态的、近乎放肆的混乱节奏，但这让这张被历史、时政、自然与人类主题所围绕的专辑获得了独有的平衡与力量感。激烈的即兴桥段仍可以在《塔可夫斯基》和同名曲目《斑迦》中听到，但专辑中也有《这就是那女孩》《四月愚人》等民谣、流行风格的曲目。《斑迦》因其力量与抒情的完美结合广受好评。《BBC 音乐评论》曾给予这样的评论："《斑迦》是帕蒂·史密斯继《群马》以来最好的专辑。没有人能创造出如此丰富、诗意和性感的摇滚唱片。"帕蒂在《斑迦》中吸收、内化她的所见所遇，而后以她的方式将这些历史与经验更完好地归还于大众。

AMERIGO

亚美利哥 [1]

We were going to see the world	我们要去看看世界
In this land we placed baptismal fonts	在这土地安放施洗池
And an infinite number were baptized	受洗之人数不可计
And they called us Caribe	他们称我们为加勒比
Which means men of great wisdom	意即伟大智者
Where are you going?	你要往何处去?
And are you going anywhere?	你是否有处可去?
Where are we going?	我们要往何处去?
Send me a letter	寄封信给我
If you go at all	若你真要走
Ah the salvation of souls	啊，灵魂的救赎
But wisdom we had not	但那是我们没有的智慧
For these people had neither king nor lord	因为这些人既无君王也无贵族
And bowed to no one	不向任何人鞠躬
For they have lived in their own liberty	因为他们活在自己的自由之中
Where are you going?	你要往何处去?
And are you going anywhere?	你是否有处可去?
Going in circles, going in circles anywhere	进入循环，进入无处不在的循环

I saw and knew the inconstant shifting of fortune	我目睹也知晓命运的无常
And now I write to you	如今我写信给你
Words that have not been written	写下未曾被写出的词语
Words from the New World	写下来自新世界的文字
Tracing the circles	追索那循环
Moving across my eyes	移动划过我双眼
Lying on the ship	仰面躺在船上
And gazing at the western sky	凝望西方的天空
Tracing lazy circles in the sky	追索天空中倦惰的循环
Hey—wake up!—wake up!	嘿——醒来！——醒来！
Where are you going?	你要往何处去？
And are you going anywhere?	你是否有处可去？
Where are you going?	你要往何处去？
Send me a letter	寄封信给我
If you go at all	若你真要走
It's such a delight to watch them dance	看他们跳舞真是件愉快的事
Free of sacrifice and romance	摆脱献祭与浪漫
Free of all the things that we hold dear	摆脱所有我们珍视之物

Is that clear Your Excellency?	明白了吗，阁下？
And I guess it's time to go but	我猜是时候离开了但
I gotta send you just a few more lines	我必须再给你多写几行
From the New World	来自新世界的词语
Tracing the circles	追索那循环
Moving across my eyes	移动划过我双眼
Lying on the ship	仰面躺在船上
And gazing at the western sky	凝望西方的天空
Tracing lazy circles in the sky	追索天空中倦惰的循环
And the sky opened	天空四敞大开
And we laid down our armor	我们卸下盔甲
And we danced naked as they	像他们一样赤裸起舞
Baptized in the rain	在新世界的雨中
Of the New World.	接受洗礼

1 亚美利哥·韦斯普奇（Amerigo Vespucci, 1454—1512），意大利佛罗伦萨商人、航海家、探险家，美洲（全称亚美利加洲）是以他的名字命名的。他考察南美洲东海岸后提出这是一块新大陆，而当时的欧洲人包括哥伦布都认为这块大陆是亚洲东部。

APRIL FOOL   四月愚人

Come   be my April Fool   来吧 做我的四月愚人

Come   you're the only one   来吧 你是唯一一个

Come   on your rusted bike   来吧 骑上你生锈的自行车

Come   we'll break all the rules 来吧 我们来打破所有规则

We'll ride like writers ride   我们会像作家那样骑行

Neither rich nor broke   既不富有也不潦倒

We'll race through alleyways   我们飞速穿过小巷

In our tattered cloaks so   穿着破烂的披风

Come   be my April Fool   来吧 做我的四月愚人

Come   we'll break all the rules 来吧 我们来打破所有规则

We'll burn all of our poems   我们会烧掉自己所有的诗

Add to God's debris   填入上帝的废墟

We'll pray to all of our saints   我们会向所有的圣徒祷告

Icons of mystery   神秘的偶像

We'll tramp through the mire   我们会穿过泥沼一路跋涉

When our souls feel dead   当灵魂感受到死亡气息

With laughter we'll inspire   笑声将激励我们

Then back to life again   再次重新开始生活

Come   you're the only one

Come   be my April Fool

Come   Come

Be my April Fool

We'll break all the rules

来吧 你是唯一一个

来吧 做我的四月愚人

来吧 来吧

做我的四月愚人

我们来打破所有规则

FUJI-SAN

富士山

Oh mountain of our eyes	哦，我们眼前的山峰
What do you see?	你看到了什么？
The girl with the almond eyes	长着杏仁样双眼的女孩
Bowing to thee	向你鞠躬致敬
Immortal soldiers	不朽的士兵
Clear the path	清理着道路
Shake the almond tree	摇晃着杏仁树
Oh mountain of our eyes	哦，我们眼前的山峰
Oh hear our plea	哦，听听我们的恳求
Oh hear our plea	哦，听听我们的恳求
See the five finger lakes	看那五根手指似的湖泊
Like a hand in blue	像一只蓝色大手
Climbing sideways up the pure	沿着侧面攀登上纯净山坡
To get a glimpse of you	为了一睹你风采
To get a glimpse of you	为了一睹你风采
The great lake	广阔湖泊
The white shirt	白色衬衫
Your white cloak	你的白色披风
Divine divine	如此非凡

Oh mountain	哦，我的
Of mine	山峰
Oh Fuji-San	哦，富士山
We're climbing	我们向上攀登
Into the blue	攀入蓝色
Into the mist	攀入薄雾
Into the bright	攀入明亮
Into your light	攀入你的光芒
Oh mountain of our eyes	哦，我们眼前的山峰
We're calling you	我们在呼唤你
Will you hear our cries?	你会听到我们的哭喊吗？
What will a poor boy do?	可怜的男孩该做什么？
What will a poor girl do?	可怜的女孩该做什么？
Hey!	嘿！
We're calling to you	我们在呼唤你
Oh Fuji-San	哦，富士山
Oh Fuji-San	哦，富士山
Oh Fuji-San	哦，富士山

Oh mountain of our eyes

What do you see?

The girl with the almond eyes

Shaking her tree

Shake the almond tree

哦，我们眼前的山峰

你看到了什么？

长着杏仁样双眼的女孩

摇晃着她的树

摇晃着杏仁树

THIS IS THE GIRL

This is the girl for whom all tears fall

This is the girl who was having a ball

Just a dark smear masking the eyes

Spirited away buried in sighs.

This is the girl who crossed the line

This is the song of the smothering vine

Twisted a laurel to crown her head

Laid as a wreath upon her bed.

This is the blood that turned into wine

This is the wine of the house it is said

This is the girl who yearned to be heard

So much for cradling a smothering bird

This is the girl. This is the girl.

This is the girl for whom all tears fall

This is the girl who was having a ball

This is the laurel to crown her head

This is the wine of the house it is said.

这就是那女孩

这就是那女孩所有眼泪为她而流

这就是那女孩她曾快乐狂欢

但有一块黑暗污渍蒙住她双眼

将她偷走，埋藏在叹息间。

这就是那女孩她跨越了界限

这就是那首歌如藤蔓缠绕窒息

折下月桂为她扭成王冠

铺在她床上如放置花圈。

这就是那鲜血现已变成美酒

这就是那美酒据说它属于圣殿

这就是那女孩她渴望被倾听

付出太多去抚育这只窒息的鸟

这就是那女孩。这就是那女孩。

这就是那女孩所有眼泪为她而流

这就是那女孩她曾快乐狂欢

这就是那月桂是她头上王冠

这就是那美酒据说它属于圣殿。

This is the blood that turned into wine

This is the wine of the house it is said

This is the girl who cried to be heard

So much for cradling a smothering bird

This is the girl. This is the girl.

—for Amy Winehouse

这就是那鲜血现已变成美酒

这就是那美酒据说它属于圣殿

这就是那女孩她哭喊着请求倾听

付出太多去抚育这只窒息的鸟

这就是那女孩。这就是那女孩。

——写给艾米·怀恩豪斯[1]

1 艾米·怀恩豪斯（Amy Winehouse，1983—2011），英国歌手、词曲作家，其低沉的噪音及揉合了灵魂乐、节奏布鲁斯、爵士乐等风格的创作使其获得国际性成功，曾获得格莱美奖等多个重要奖项。2011 年 7 月，因酒精中毒去世，年仅 27 岁。

TARKOVSKY　　　　　　　　　　　　塔可夫斯基

The eternal sun runs to the mother　　　　　永恒的太阳向着母亲奔去

She smoothes his brow and bids him　　　　她抚平他的眉头命令他

Drink from her well of hammered mist　　　从她锤出迷雾的井中饮水

Come along sweet lad, fog rises from the ground　来吧，可爱的小伙子，雾气从地面升起

The falling soot is just the dust of a shivering gem　飘落的烟尘只是颤抖宝石的尘埃

The black moon shines on a lake　　　　　黑色月亮在湖面上闪耀

White as a hand in the dark　　　　　　　惨白如黑暗中的一只手

She lifts the lamp to see his face　　　　她举起灯来看着他的脸

The silver ladle of his throat　　　　　　他的喉咙好似银色长柄勺

The boy the beast and the butterfly　　　男孩，野兽与蝴蝶

The sea is a morgue, the needle and the gun　大海是间停尸房，是针与枪

These things float in blood that has no name　它们漂浮在无名的血泊里

The telegraph poles are crosses on the line　电线杆是连着线的十字架

Rusted pins not enough saviors to hang　锈铁钉没有足够的救世主来钉吊

She blesses the road the noose of vine　她祝福着这条路这藤蔓的套索

And waits beneath the triangle　　　　　在大三角下等候

Formed by Mercury, an evening star　　　它由水星，一颗晚星构成

The fifth planet, with its blistering core　第五行星，有着炽热内核

And the soaring eagle above and to the west　高空翱翔的雄鹰飞向西方

The boy the beast and the butterfly　　　男孩，野兽与蝴蝶

She walks across a bridge of magpies

Her hollow tongue fills the brightness

With water and in the wink of an eye

One planet with a glittering womb

One white crow one diamond head

Big as a world big as a world

Don't forget how I played with you

She cries, and kissed away your tears

The white mouth of the sun smiles

On his beautiful tongue the seed of flight

她横穿过一座鹊桥

眨眼之间她空洞的舌

就用水填满了光

一颗长着闪闪发光子宫的星球

白色乌鸦，钻石头颅

像世界一样大，像世界一样大

不要忘记我如何同你玩耍

她哭了，吻走你的眼泪

太阳纯白的嘴微笑着

他美丽的舌上，种子在飞翔

MOSAIC

马赛克

Last night in Konya

昨夜在科尼亚

A voice carried me

有个声音将我带到

To the pulpit of the arrow

箭的布道坛前

Did you hear it too?

你也听到了吗？

The oracle was written

神谕就写在

On a silver leaf

银色叶片上

Last night I read the words

昨夜我读了那文字

Did you read them too?

你也读了吗？

Precious heart, precious seed

珍贵的心，珍贵的种子

Precious life conceived

孕育出珍贵的生命

In a ring of fire

在一道火环中

In a sleep of peace

在宁静睡眠里

Nothing stops desire

没什么能停止渴望

For the human beat

人类生命的节拍

Last night was a rapture

昨夜喜获被提

In the mosaic sky

马赛克的天空

Dropping shards of love

坠下爱的碎片

Dropping shards of love

坠下爱的碎片

Precious heart, precious seed	珍贵的心，珍贵的种子
Precious life conceived	孕育出珍贵的生命
In a ring of fire	在一道火环中
In a sleep of peace	在宁静睡眠里
Nothing stops desire	没什么能停止渴望
For the human beat	人类生命的节拍
I hunger for the cooling flame	我渴求冰冷的火焰
I hunger for the infinite game	我渴求无穷的游戏
Last night in Konya	昨夜在科尼亚
A voice carried me	有个声音将我带到
To the pulpit of the arrow	箭的布道坛前
Did you hear it too?	你也听到了吗？
The oracle was written	神谕就写在
On a silver leaf	银色叶片上
Last night I read the words	昨夜我读了那文字
Did you read them too?	你也读了吗？
Devour me, ah, devour me	吞噬我，啊，吞噬我

Oh precious life	哦，珍贵的生命
Oh precious seed	哦，珍贵的种子
Oh precious heart	哦，珍贵的心
That beats	那节拍
In a ring of fire	在一道火环中
In a sleep of peace	在宁静睡眠里
Nothing stops	没什么能停止
The human beat	人类生命的节拍
The human beat	人类生命的节拍

MARIA

At the edge of the world

Where you were no one

Yet you were the girl

The only one

At the edge of the world

In the desert heat

One shivering star

Sweet indiscreet

I knew you

When we were young

I knew you

Now you're gone

In a little Narcissus pool

Drawn by its spell

We saw ourselves

Raw excitable

I knew you

When we were young

在世界的边缘

你只是无名之辈

但你是独一无二

仅有的女孩

在世界的边缘

沙漠的酷热里

一颗战栗的星

甜蜜而轻率

我认识了你

那时我们还年轻

我认识了你

现在你已离去

在小小的那喀索斯池里

被它的魔力所吸引

我们看到了自己

生猛又兴奋

我认识了你

那时我们还年轻

I knew you

Now you're gone

We didn't know

The precariousness of our young powers

All the emptiness

Wild wild hair

Sad sad eyes

White shirt / black tie

You were mine

You grabbed the ring

Of the carousel

Tangoing

From Heaven

To Hell

I knew you

—for Maria Schneider

我认识了你

现在你已离去

那时我们还不知道

青春力量的动荡

所有那些空虚

凌乱 凌乱的头发

悲伤 悲伤的双眼

白衬衫 / 黑领带

你曾属于我

你抓住

旋转木马的圆环

跳着探戈

从天堂

到地狱

我了解你

——写给玛丽亚·施耐德 [1]

1 玛丽亚·施耐德（Maria Schneider，1952—2011），法国女演员，因主演《巴黎最后的探戈》而闻名。

345

NINE

Night a nine of diamonds

方块九之夜

A woman lay and cries

一个女人在仁慈姐妹会门前

At the Sister of Mercy

躺下来哭喊

On the Sabbath day

那是个安息日

Night a nine of diamonds

方块九之夜

As revelers commence

当狂欢者开始

To shiver as she bore

颤抖，她生下

In a babe, a radiance

一个婴儿，闪耀着光辉

Brave in constant motion

持续运转保持勇敢

Wherein perfection brews

在其中酝酿出完美

Darkness as his brother

黑暗像他的兄弟

Mischief as his moon

顽皮如他的月亮

Summoning beneath

用他的吉卜赛舞步

With his gypsy moves

在月光下召集众人

Yearning as the foal

像小马驹那样渴望一切

Shy and beautiful

羞涩又美丽

Every card he drew

他抽出的每张牌

Had a different face   都长着一张不同的脸

Lingering and lost   徘徊而迷惘

Unholy holy ghosts   罪恶的圣灵

I tend to play them all   我打算出光所有手牌

He spoke with confidence   他自信满满地说着

Another kind of strange   另一种形式的奇特

To shift in loneliness   转变成寂寞

He sought not for himself   他不是在为自己而寻找

The empire he would find   那王国他迟早会发现

Save the golden womb   除了金色的孕育地

He enters in his mind   他进入自己脑海

We will die a little   我们会死去一点点

The rogues whistling   流氓们吹起口哨

Nine blue-eyed sailors   九个蓝眼睛水手

Tip their caps to him   向他脱帽致敬

As he passes through them   他走过他们身旁

More vagabond than king   更像流浪汉而非国王

347

With diamonds on his sleeves

Like a harlequin

—*for John Christopher Depp*

袖子上缀着钻石

如滑稽丑角

——写给约翰·克里斯托弗·德普[1]

---

1 约翰·克里斯托弗·德普（John Christopher Depp，1963—），昵称约翰尼·德普，美国男演员、制片人、音乐人。

The Wing Child

翼之子

O chariot of insect

噢，昆虫的战车

O crown of wind

噢，风的王冠

Two royal leopards

两只高贵的豹子

Run with him

和他一起奔跑

On a golden lead

一路遥遥领先

Of tapered vine

锥形的藤蔓纠缠

O the blood sky

噢，血色的天空

O the blood sky

噢，血色的天空

Wine of a God

神的美酒

Coupling wild

狂野的结合

O golden seed

噢，金色的种子

Who made the

是谁创造出

Winged child

生着双翼的孩子

SENECA　　　　　　　　　　　　　　　**塞内加**

Run, run my little one	奔跑，奔跑吧我的小宝贝
Run out to sea	奔跑向大海
Run, run my little one	奔跑，奔跑吧我的小宝贝
What do you seek?	你在寻找什么？
The canvas is high	帆布高高扬起
The scheme of a life	人生的蓝图
Written in the wind	已写入风里
The pen, the knife	以这笔，以这刀
Run, run my little one	奔跑，奔跑吧我的小宝贝
Breathe a hymn to Him	为神呼诵一首赞美诗
Breathe my little one	呼诵吧，我的小宝贝
The master is calling	主人正在召唤你
If you were his eyes	如果你是他的眼睛
If you were his dreams	如果你是他的梦境
The whole of the sky	那么整个天穹
Could not contain you	都无法再容纳你
So run, run out to sea	所以奔跑吧，奔跑向大海

Run, run my little one

Breathe a hymn

For Him

For thee

—for Seneca Sebring

奔跑，奔跑吧我的小宝贝

呼诵一首赞美诗

为神

为你

——写给塞内加·塞布林 [1]

---

1 塞内加·塞布林（Seneca Sebring），帕蒂·史密斯的教子，帕蒂的好友摄影师、
电影制片人史蒂文·塞布林（Steven Sebring）之子。

BANGA

斑迦

Loyalty rests in the heart of a dog

忠诚安存于一条狗的心里

Don't sell all your eggs on the back of a frog

别把你所有蛋都放在青蛙背上售卖

You can lick it twice but it won't lick you

你可以舔它两次但它不会舔你

And salivating salvation long so long so

垂涎三尺的救赎那么长那么长

Loyalty lives and we don't know why

忠诚始终存在我们不知原因何在

And the paw is pressed against the nerve of the sky

爪子按压在天空的神经上

You can leave him behind but he won't leave you

你可以把它丢在身后但它不会丢下你

And the road to Heaven is true—true blue

通往天堂的道路是真的——真的很蓝

Banga / Say—Banga

斑迦 / 说——斑迦

Loyalty lives and we don't know why

忠诚始终存在我们不知原因何在

And his paws are pressed to the spine of the sky

他的爪子按压在天空的脊柱上

You can leave him twice, but he won't leave you

你可以把它丢下两次但它不会丢下你

And the way to Heaven is true—true blue

通往天堂的道路是真的——真的很蓝

Banga / Say—Banga

斑迦 / 说——斑迦

Loneliness lifts when you open the night

当你打开暗夜之门孤独就会消散

Pilate awaits, as Jesus Christ

彼拉多在等待，耶稣基督

352

Forget him not—won't forget about you

The way to Heaven is blue—boo hoo

Banga / Say—Banga

Loyalty shifts if you carry a load

Ah, don't shit it out in a golden commode

You can kick him twice—it'll erode

Night is a mongrel—believe or explode

不会忘记他——也不会忘记你

通往天堂的道路是蓝色的——boo hoo

斑迦 / 说——斑迦

要是你负重前行忠诚会发生转变

啊，别在金色马桶里大便

你可以踢它两脚——它会腐蚀掉

夜晚是个杂种——相信，或爆炸

CONSTANTINE'S DREAM

君士坦丁之梦

In Arezzo I dreamed a dream

在阿雷佐 [1] 我做了个梦

Of St. Francis who kneeled and prayed

梦中圣方济各 [2] 跪下祷告

For the birds and the beasts and all humankind

为了鸟儿野兽还有全人类

All through the night I felt drawn in by him

整个晚上我被他深深吸引

And I heard him call

我听到他的召唤

Like a distant hymn

像一首遥远的赞美诗

I retreated from the silence of my room

我从房间的寂静之中退出来

Stepping down the ancient stones washed with dawn

走下被黎明冲洗过的远古石阶

And entered the basilica that bore his name

进入以他命名的大教堂

Seeing his effigy I bowed my head

见到他的雕像，我低头致意

And my racing heart I gave to him

将我跃动的心敬献给他

I kneeled and prayed

我跪下并祷告

And the sleep that I could not find in the night

借由着他我寻得了

I found through him

那些我在夜里找寻不到的安眠

I saw before me the world of his world

我看到面前出现了他的世界

The bright field, the birds in abundance,

明亮的田野，鸟儿成群，

All of nature of which he sang

他歌颂的整个大自然

Singing of him

正歌颂着他

All the beauty that surrounded him as he walked

他漫步时环绕身边的所有美景

His nature that was nature itself

他的本性，即是自然本身

And I heard him—I heard him speak

我听到他——我听到他讲话

And the birds sang sweetly

鸟儿们甜蜜地歌唱

And the wolves licked his feet.

狼群舔舐他的双脚。

But I could not give myself to him.

但是我无法将自己献予他

I felt another call from the basilica itself

我感受到来自大教堂本身的另一种召唤

The call of art—the call of man

艺术的召唤——人类的召唤

And the beauty of the material drew me away.

物质之美将我引开。

And I awoke, and beheld upon the wall

我醒来，望着墙上

The dream of Constantine

君士坦丁之梦

The handiwork of Piero della Francesca

皮耶罗·德拉·弗朗切斯卡[3]的手艺

Who had stood where I stood

他曾站在我站立的地方

And with his brush stroked the legend of the True Cross

用他的画笔轻轻涂抹着真十字架[4]的传说

He envisioned Constantine advancing to greet the enemy

他想象着君士坦丁向前挺进迎接敌人

But as he was passing the river

但当他经过那条河时

An unaccustomed fear gripped his bowels

一种非同寻常的恐惧攥紧他的肚肠

An anticipation so overwhelming that it manifested in waves.

强烈的预感海浪般席卷而来。

All thru the night a dream drew toward him

整个夜晚梦境不断向他袭来

As an advancing Crusade

身为前进的十字军战士

He slept in his tent on the battlefield

While his men stood guard.

And an angel awoke him

Constantine within his dream awoke

And his men saw a light pass over the face of the King

The troubled King

And the angel came and showed to him

The sign of the true cross in heaven.

And upon it was written

In this sign shall thou conquer

In the distance the tents of his army were lit by moonlight

But another kind of radiance lit the face of Constantine

And in the morning light

The artist, seeing his work was done,

Saw it was good.

In this sign shall thou conquer

He let his brush drop and passed into a sleep of his own.

他睡在战场的帐篷里

有士兵站岗保卫。

一位天使唤醒了他

君士坦丁在他的梦中醒来

士兵们看到一束光掠过君主的脸庞

陷入困境的君主

天使到来，向他展示

天堂中那真十字架的标志。

那上面写着

凭此神迹，你必得胜

远处他军队的帐篷被月光照亮

另一种光芒照耀着君士坦丁的脸庞

在清晨的曦光之中

艺术家，看到他的作品已完成，

看到这作品已成。

凭此神迹，你必得胜

他丢下画笔，陷入了自己的睡眠。

And he dreamed of Constantine carrying into battle in his right hand

An immaculate, undefiled single white Cross.

Piero della Francesca, as his brush stroked the wall

Was filled with a torpor

And fell into a dream of his own.

他梦到君士坦丁投身战局，右手紧攥着

一枚完美无瑕，纯白的十字架。

皮耶罗·德拉·弗朗切斯卡，用他的画笔轻轻涂抹着墙壁

被困倦填满身体

跌进自己梦境。

From the geometry of his heart he mapped it out

He saw the King rise, fitted with armor

Set upon a white horse

An immaculate cross in his right hand.

He advanced toward the enemy

And the symmetry, the perfection of his mathematics

Caused the scattering of the enemy

Agitated, broken, they fled.

他绘制出自己心脏的几何形状

他看到君主起身，披戴盔甲

跨上一匹白色骏马

右手紧握完美的十字架。

他向着敌人挺进

呈现出对称，数学上的完美性

令敌军四处溃散

不安，力竭，敌人逃窜。

And Piero della Francesa waking, cried out

All is art—all is future!

Oh Lord let me die on the back of adventure

With a brush and an eye full of light

But as he advanced in age

The light was shorn from his eyes

皮耶罗·德拉·弗朗切斯卡醒过来，大声呼喊

一切都是艺术——一切都是未来！

哦，主啊，让我在冒险后死去

他手握画笔，眼中充满光芒

但随着年龄的增长

他眼中的光芒渐渐被夺去

And blinded, he laid upon his bed	双目失明，他躺在自己床上
On an October morning in 1492, and whispered	1492 年十月的一个清晨，他低声说
Oh Lord let me die on the back of adventure	哦，主啊，让我在冒险后死去
Oh Lord let me die on the back of adventure	哦，主啊，让我在冒险后死去
And a world away—a world away	另个遥远之地——另个遥远之地
On three great ships	三艘大船上
Adventure itself as if to answer	冒险仿佛想自己回答
Pulling into the New World	扬帆驶入新大陆
And as far as his eyes could see	在他目所能及之远
No longer blind	不再盲视
All of nature unspoiled—beautiful—beautiful	自然的一切仍完好——美丽——美丽
And such a manner that would have lifted	这美好振动了
The heart of St. Francis	圣方济各的心
Into the realm of universal love	将其引入普世之爱的国度
Columbus stepped foot on the New World	哥伦布踏足新大陆
And witnessed beauty unspoiled	见证那完好之美
All the delights given by God	上帝赐予的所有欢乐
As if Eden had opened her heart to him	仿佛伊甸园敞开了她的心扉
And opened her dress	掀开她的裙子

And all of her fruit gave to him	把自己全部果实赠予他
And Columbus so overwhelmed	哥伦布受宠若惊
Fell into a sleep of his own	跌进自己的梦境
All the world filled his sleep	整个世界填满了他的睡眠
All of the beauty entwined with the future	所有美好与未来交织在一起
The twenty-first century	二十一世纪
Advancing like the angel that had come	天使般挺进，降临到
To Constantine	君士坦丁面前
Constantine in his dream	君士坦丁陷在他的梦里
Oh this is your cross to bear	哦，这是你要背负的十字架
Oh Lord Oh Lord let me deliver	哦，主，哦，主，让我将
Hallowed adventure to all mankind	神圣的冒险带给未来的
In the future	全人类
Oh art cried the painter	哦，艺术，画家呼喊着
Oh art—Oh art—cried the angel	哦，艺术——哦，艺术——天使呼喊着
Art the great material gift of man	艺术是人类伟大的物质天赋
Art that hath denied	那曾拒绝过
The humble pleas of St. Francis	圣方济各谦卑恳求的艺术
Oh thou Artist	哦，你这艺术家

All shall crumble

一切都会崩塌

Into dust

化为尘埃

Oh thou navigator

哦，你这航海家

The terrible end of man

人类可怕的末日

This is your gift to mankind

这是你带给人类的礼物

This is your cross to bear

这是你要背负的十字架

And Columbus

哥伦布

Saw all of nature aflame

看到整个自然在燃烧

The apocalyptic night

世界末日之夜

And the dream

陷入困境的君主

Of the troubled King

他的梦境

Dissolved into light.

熔解在光里。

1 阿雷佐（Arezzo），位于意大利中部托斯卡纳大区，阿雷佐省的首府。

2 圣方济各，又称阿西西的圣方济各，动物、天主教运动、美国旧金山以及自然环境的守护圣人。他一生最有名的事件为，双膝跪于石边，在他的手掌与脚掌上接受钉于十字架上的耶稣基督的圣痕。佛兰德画家扬·凡·艾克的画作《接受圣痕的圣方济各》描绘了这一场景。

3 皮耶罗·德拉·弗朗切斯卡（Piero della Francesca，约 1415—1492），意大利文艺复兴早期画家兼理论家。1452 年为阿雷佐圣方济各教堂创作了湿壁画《十字架传奇》。

4 真十字架，基督教圣物之一，据信是钉死耶稣基督的十字架。在基督教传统中，真十字架作为耶稣为人类带来救赎的标志，具有极其重要的象征意义。

FUTURE AND FILM

未 来 与 电 影

Notes to the Future

What did we want
What did we ever want
To shake the fragile hands of time
To rip from their sockets
Deceiving eyes
To ride through the night
In a three cornered hat
Against the shadows
To cry Awake Awake
Wake up arms delicate feet
We are paramount then obsolete
Wake up throat wake up limbs
Our mantle pressed
from palm to palm
Wake up hearts dressed in rags
Costly garments fall away
Dangle now in truthful threads
That bind the breast
And wind the muscle
Of the soul and whole together

Listen my children and you shall hear
The sound of your own steps
The sound of your hereafter
Memory awaits and turns to greet you
Draping its banner across your wrists
Wake up arms delicate feet
For as one to march the streets
Each alone each part of another
Your steps shall ring
Shall raise the cloud
And they that will hear will hear
Voice of the one and the one and the one
As it has never been uttered before
For something greater yet to come
Than the hour of the prophets
In their great cities
For the people of Ninevah
Fell to their knees
Heeding the cry of Jonah
United covering themselves in sackcloth
And ashes and called to their God
And all their hearts were as one heart
And all their voices were as one voice
God heard them and his mind was moved
Yet something greater will come to pass
And who will call and what will they call
Will they call to God the air the fowl
It will not matter if the call is true
They shall call and this is known
One voice and each another
Shall enter the dead
The living flower
Enter forms that we know not
To be felt by sea by air by earth
And shall be an elemental pledge
This our birthright
This our charge
We have given over to others
And they have not done well
And the forests mourn the leaves fall
Swaddling babes watch and wonder
As the fathers of our spirit nations
Dance in the streets in celebration

As the mountains turn pale
From their nuclear hand
And they have not done well
Now my children
You must overturn the tables
Deliver the future from material rule
For the only rule to be considered
Is the eleventh commandment
To love one another
And this is our covenant
Across your wrist
This offering is yours
To adore adorn
To bury to burn
Upon a mound
To hail
To set away
It is merely a cloth merely our colors
Invested with the blood of a people
All their hopes and dreams
It has its excellence yet it is nothing
It shall not be a tyranny above us
Nor should God nor love nor nature
Yet we hold as our pleasure
This tender honor
That we acknowledge the individual
And the common ground formed
And if our cloth be raised and lowered
Half mast what does this tell us
An individual has passed
Saluted and mourned by his countrymen
This ritual extends to us all
For we are all the individual
No unknown no insignificant one
Nor insignificant labor nor act of charity
Each has a story to be told and retold
Which shall be as a glowing thread
In the fabric of man
And the children shall march
And bring the colors forward
Investing within them
The redeeming blood
Of their revolutionary hearts

致未来的笔记

我们想要的是什么

我们想要的到底是什么

握住时间脆弱的手

把他们充满欺骗的眼睛

从眼眶里扯出来

骑行穿过黑夜

戴着一顶三角帽

倚靠着阴影

哭喊着，醒来，醒来吧

唤醒手臂，柔嫩的脚

我们至高无上随后被遗忘

唤醒喉咙，唤醒四肢

我们的外表一掌接着

一掌被压扁

唤醒心灵，穿上破衣烂衫

昂贵的衣物消失了

挂在真诚的丝线上摇摇晃晃

把乳房捆绑住

把灵魂的肌肉

和整个身体缠绕一端

听着，我的孩子们，你们将听到

自己脚步的声音

你们来世的声音

记忆会等待着，转身迎接你

把它的旗帜缠绕在你手腕上

唤醒手臂，柔嫩的脚

结为一个整体去街道上游行

每个个体都是他人的一部分

你们的脚步会发出回响

会掀起云

那样他们就会听到，会听到

合一之声，合一之声，合一之声

这声音此前从未发出过

有些更伟大的事即将到来

胜过先知们的时刻

在他们伟大的城市里

尼尼微[1]的人民

跪倒在地

倾听约拿的呼喊

合为一体，用粗布衣和灰烬

遮盖身体，呼唤着他们的上帝

所有的心犹如一颗心

366

所有的声音犹如一个声音

上帝听到了他们，他的心灵被撼动

有些更伟大的事即将发生

谁会去呼唤，他们会呼唤什么

他们会向上帝呼唤吗，向空气，向禽鸟

只要这呼唤是真的，向谁呼唤都无关紧要

他们将呼唤，这一点确定无疑

一个声音接着另一个

会进入死者的身体

鲜活的花朵

进入我们不知晓的形态

会被大海，被空气，被土地感受到

会成为一种基本的誓言

这是我们与生俱来的权利

这是我们的控告

我们曾将这权利让与他人

他们却行使得不好

森林哀悼着树叶的坠落

襁褓中的婴儿看着，感到好奇

我们精神国度之父

在街道上起舞欢庆

当群山因他们掌控核能之手

而变得苍白时

他们没有将这权利行使好

现在我的孩子们

你们必须掀翻桌子

将未来从物质法则中解放出来

唯一应当考虑的法则

是第十一条诫命

去爱彼此

这就是我们的盟约

缠绕在你的手腕

这是你们的献祭

去崇拜，使它生色

去埋葬，去焚烧

在土堆上

去欢呼

动身出发

它不过是一块布，不过是我们的颜色

浸染着一个民族的鲜血

全部的希望与梦想

它有自己的卓越，然而它并不算什么

它不应该成为凌驾我们之上的暴政

上帝不应该，爱不应该，自然也不应该

然而我们仍以此为荣

这温柔的荣誉

我们认可个体

形成了共同基础

如果我们的旗帜升起后又降至

半旗，这告诉我们什么

有个人去世了

他的同胞向他致敬并哀悼

这仪式适用于我们所有人

因为我们每个人都是个体

没有不为人知，也没有微不足道的人

没有无关紧要的劳动，也不是慈善之举

每个人都有一个故事要讲述然后再重述

它会像一条闪闪发光的丝线

串起人类社会的织布

孩子们列队行进

将这颜色带到前面

投入他们当中

他们革命之心的

救赎之血

1 尼尼微，古代亚述帝国的重镇之一，位于底格里斯河东岸，在今日伊拉克北部城市摩苏尔附近。自公元前11世纪起尼尼微即为亚述帝国的首都。公元前605年，强盛一时的亚述帝国正式灭亡，尼尼微随之没落。

... Wim Wenders Film

no equation to explain the division of the senses

no sound to reflect the radiance of time

hands press against the sky, the soul foams

and light shoots from the face of the predator

in the beginning is dream

the milky corridor that shakes us out

and sends us reeling from site to site

forests and junkyards, halls of disorder

where we are swept to encircle dawn

strapped in a low car

racing thru silence

trumpeting bliss

you could kiss the world goodbye

or wake up

and kiss the world.

(Refrain)
    can you feel
    in the night
    the world turn
    round and round
    wander wander
    by the light
    turning turning
    in your eyes.

wander wander
guided by
endless eyes
endless light

Turning light

IT TAKES TIME

No equation to explain the division of the senses

No sound to reflect the radiance of time

In the beginning is dream halls of disorder

Where we are swept to encircle dawn

Strapped in a low car racing

Thru silence trumpeting bliss

You could kiss the world goodbye

Standing outside the courthouse in the rain

Seemed like a lost soul from the chapel of dreams

With a handful of images

Faces of children phases of the moon

One little thing you get wrong changes

The dimensions streets, swept memory

Diffused and lost like a prayer in the sun

Sometimes you can't tell

Whether you're waking up or going to sleep

Spiraling unnumbered streets

All the games cannot be yours

All the sights, the treasures of the eye

这需要时间

没有方程式能解释感官如何分配

没有声音能表达时间的光辉

最开始，是失去秩序的梦境大厅

在那里我们被黎明横扫着包围起来

困入一场消沉的赛车比赛

借由沉默大肆宣扬着幸福

你可以跟这世界吻别

站在雨中的法院门外

看起来像梦的小教堂外迷失的灵魂

握着一大把图片

孩子们的脸庞，盈亏的月相

一件小事，你找错了零钱

维度的街道，被清扫的记忆

像阳光下的祷告一样扩散并迷失

有时你无法分辨

自己究竟是醒着还是将入睡

蜿蜒曲折无法计数的街道

所有游戏都不是你的

所有的风景，眼中的珍宝

Does the divided soul remain the same?

No equation to explain

Destiny's hand moved, by love

Drawn by the whispering shadows

Into the mathematics of our desire

—for Wim Wenders's film To the End of the World

裂开的灵魂还能保持不变吗？

没有方程式能解释

命运之手因爱，而转动

被轻声低语的阴影所吸引

陷入我们欲望的数学运算

——写给维姆·文德斯的电影《直到世界尽头》

MERMAID SONG

美人鱼之歌

Do you remember me

你记得我吗

The ocean rolled

大海翻涌

Time was slow

时光缓动

We felt an energy

我们感受到一股能量

The cock was crowing

公鸡高啼

The rum was flowing

朗姆酒不停奔流

A mermaid burns to see

美人鱼迫不及待想看到

Beyond the sea

大海以外的地方

And if I could

假如我能够

Turn where you stood

转向你驻足之地

Would you feel me

你会感受到我吗

Would it be good

那会很美好吗

Would you remember

你会记得吗

So turn the little key

转动这把小钥匙

The ocean rolls

大海翻涌

Time is slow

时光缓动

Turn the little key

转动这把小钥匙

The cock is crowing

公鸡高啼

| The rum is flowing | 朗姆酒不停奔流 |

A mermaid burns to see	美人鱼迫不及待想看到
Beyond the sea	大海以外的地方
I long to see	我渴望去看一看
I long to see	我渴望去看一看
If there's a page for me	如果有一页留给我

Do you remember me	你还记得我吗
The ocean rolled	大海翻涌
Time was slow	时光缓动
We felt an energy	我们感受到一股能量
The cock was crowing	公鸡高啼
The rum was flowing	朗姆酒不停奔流

A mermaid burns to see	美人鱼迫不及待想看到
Beyond the sea	大海以外的地方
I long to see	我渴望去看一看
I long to see	我渴望去看一看
If there is a page for me	如果有一页留给我
A page for me	有一页留给我

In your diary.

—*for the film* Rum Diary

在你日记里。

——写给电影《朗姆酒日记》[1]

1《朗姆酒日记》(*The Rum Diary*),布鲁斯·罗宾逊执导、约翰尼·德普主演的影片,2011 年上映。

Rebellion is a heart	反叛是一颗心
breaking as the dawn	冲开一切如破晓
bursting into song	放声去歌唱
bursting into song	放声去歌唱
A bird in the hand	掌中一只小鸟
another role to play	有另一个角色要扮演
mocking as the jay	像鸟一样嘲笑
mocking as the jay	像鸟一样嘲笑
She's the silent one	她是那个沉默的人
in her soft boots	穿着她的软底靴
racing thru the flames	穿越火焰飞驰
racing thru the flames	穿越火焰飞驰
She's the silent one	她是那个沉默的人
in her soft boots	穿着她的软底靴
drawing her bow	拉起她的弓
and her only truth	和她唯一的真理
Rebellion is an arrow	反叛是一枚箭头

wired to the sun

igniting everyone

igniting everyone

A bird in the hand

another role to play

mocking as the jay

mocking as the jay

She's the silent one

in her soft boots

drawing her bow

and her only truth

Racing thru the flames

in her soft boots

mocking as the jay

and she be mocking you

—*for the film* Hunger Games: Catching Fire

与太阳连为一线

点燃每一个人

点燃每一个人

掌中一只小鸟

有另一个角色要扮演

像鸟一样嘲笑

像鸟一样嘲笑

她是那个沉默的人

穿着她的软底靴

拉起她的弓

和她唯一的真理

穿越火焰飞驰

她穿着软底靴

像鸟一样嘲笑

她在嘲笑你

——写给电影《饥饿游戏 2：星火燎原》

JUST KIDS

只是孩子 [1]

Wake up

醒来吧

Come—take my hand

过来——握住我的手

Truth was like a dictionary

真理如一本字典

Urgent and sublime

紧迫而崇高

We shook ourselves

我们摇晃着身体

Into the light

走进光里

Like washing on a line

像晾衣绳上刚洗好的衣服

Like a gleaming sari

像一条闪闪发光的纱丽 [2]

In the Indian wind

飘荡在印度的风里

Wrapped in one another

彼此缠绕在一起

Where pure hearts are kin

纯洁的心是同类

We ventured to the city

我们冒险闯到城里去

To the Chelsea Hotel

闯进切尔西酒店

A place to lay our heads

一个让我们大脑休憩之处

A bit of heaven in hell

地狱里的一角天堂

Entered the halls

进入我们新大学的

Of our new university

华丽大厅

They gave all the keys to you

他们把所有钥匙都给了你

And you offered them to me

你又把它们献给我

In the blue night	在蓝色的夜里
You were bluer still	你愈发忧郁
Your ankles tattooed with stars	脚踝上文着星星
We were so hungry	我们如此饥饿
We could not sleep	我们无法入睡
And another hunger ensued	另一种饥饿随之而来
And we called out to Morpheus	我们唤出梦神摩耳甫斯 [3]
To spread his cloak	铺展开他的斗篷
On the world of our ways	覆盖住我俩的世界
You walked without fear	你毫无畏惧地前行
Toward the golden ladder	朝向那金色的阶梯
And I watched you	我看着你
Climb rung by rung	一级又一级地攀登
Toward another kind of sun	向着别样的太阳而去
And I went for another cup	我又去拿了一杯酒
It ran all over my dress	洒得衣服上到处都是
And you drank it up	你把它全部喝净
Life to life	生命对生命

Scene to scene	场景到场景
Fortune's strife	命运的争斗
Dream upon dream	梦境叠盖着梦境
Love was love	爱就是爱
Art was art	艺术就是艺术
Comingling in the heart	心与心融并
Kids	孩子
Just kids	只是孩子

1 帕蒂·史密斯在 2010 年 1 月出版了题为《只是孩子》(Just Kids) 的回忆录。书中记录了她与艺术家、摄影师罗伯特·梅普尔索普从 1960 年代相识一直到 1989 年罗伯特去世之间两人的传奇经历。本诗作为附加曲目收录在专辑《斑迹》黑胶豪华版的 B 面。

2 纱丽，印度、孟加拉国、巴基斯坦、尼泊尔、斯里兰卡等国妇女的一种传统服装。

3 摩耳甫斯，希腊神话中的梦神。他能够以各种形态出现在人们的梦境里。

MERCY IS

仁慈是

Mercy is as mercy does

仁慈不在言而在行

Wandering the wild

徘徊荒野中

The stars are eyes watching you

群星如眼睛般注视着你

A breath upon a cloud

云层之上的一口呼吸

Two white doves

两只白鸽

Two white wings

两对白色翅膀

To carry you away

将你带去

To a land in memory

记忆中的土地

A land in memory

记忆中的土地

The sky is high

天空高远

The earth is green

大地青翠

And cool below your feet

你脚下的大地

So swiftly now

现在迅疾冷却

Beneath the bough

在大树枝底下

Your father waits for thee

你的父亲在等着你

To wrap you in

将你揽入

His healing arms

他疗愈的怀抱里

As the night sky weeps

夜空低声啜泣

For mercy is the healing wind

因为仁慈是那疗愈的风

That whispers as you sleep

在你入睡时它低语

That whispers you to sleep.

在你入睡时它低语。

—*for the film* Noah

——*写给电影*《诺亚方舟》

381

poor fellah
for john walker lindh

an american /with a vision/of a religion/pure in it's
extent/studied at the madrasah in a remote corner/of
pakistan/tall bearded/almost a man/a model student
seeking the devout muslim life/an absolute
system/mathematically pure/on the northwest frontier no
longer alone/slept on a bed/of indian rope/full of
hope/poor dope/the heat and dust of april/drove him
away/into the cooler mountains/still seeking islam's
fountain/seven months premature/poor fellah /and easter
and passover/passed over/he journeyed to afghanistan/in
search of the pure /he gave them everything/he gave
them his heart he was so sure/poor fellah/walker was a
young man/embracing islam/walking with the
taliban/they captured his heart/he went through the
fazes/learning all the phrases memorizing pages/of the
koran/emerging on a saturday/ through a ruined avenue
crept from the underground/pine trees and debris/abdul
hamid/six nights in darkness without his catholic
father/and buddhist mother/separating treason and
dissent 16 to be a koranic scholar/19 to yemen to learn
arabic/went to afghanistan/to search for cooler
climates/to study the koran/pale as the sky/it attracted
his heart/if you be american/exercising freedom/looking
for something so pure/you may have to go and do
somethings/that other men/would not endure/he went to
the training camps/joined his brothers in kashmir/walked
a thousand miles/with the taliban/taken prisoner/during
the siege of kunduz/and marched to the fort/of certain
death/on the muddy outskirts/of mazar-i-sharif/ his
brothers died in ditches/in the open courtyards/their
faces blown/no one knew what the fuck was going on/who
was the enemy and who was the friend/and he wept/for
their corpses/that lay beneath the willows/walker was a
young man/walking with the taliban/embracing islam/it
attracted his heart/have a heart/have a heart/if you be a
christian/ exercise your wisdom/ forgive him/ have a
heart/ have a heart/ a heart

可怜的家伙

写给约翰·沃克·林德[1]

一个美国人 / 怀着对宗教 / 的憧憬 / 心愿纯净 / 在巴基斯坦 / 一个偏远角落的伊斯兰学校求学 / 个子很高留着胡子 / 快要长成一个男人 / 一个追寻着虔诚穆斯林生活的模范学生 / 纯粹的系统 / 如数学般纯净 / 在西北边疆不再感到孤独 / 睡在 / 印度绳床上 / 充满希望 / 可怜的笨蛋 / 四月的炽热与灰尘 / 赶走了他 / 进入更凉爽的群山 / 仍在寻找着伊斯兰的源泉 / 七个月的早产儿 / 可怜的家伙 / 复活节和逾越节 / 已度过了 / 他去往阿富汗旅行 / 寻找那纯净 / 他给了他们一切 / 他给了他们他的心他是如此确定 / 可怜的家伙 / 沃克是个年轻人 / 皈依伊斯兰 / 与塔利班同行 / 他们俘获了他的心 / 他经历了磨难 / 学习所有语句背诵着 / 古兰经 / 在一个周六他出现了 / 穿越一片废墟从地下匍匐着爬出来 / 松树与瓦砾 / 阿卜杜勒·哈米德 / 黑暗中的六个夜晚身边没有他的天主教徒父亲 / 和佛教徒母亲 / 分离叛国罪和异见分子十六岁成为古兰经学者 / 十九岁去也门学习阿拉伯语 / 前往阿富汗 / 去寻找更凉爽的气候 / 去学习古兰经 / 如天空般苍白 / 那吸引了他的心 / 如果你是美国人 / 行使着自由 / 寻找如此纯粹的事物 / 你可能不得不离开去做一些 / 其他人 / 无法承受的事 / 他去了训练营 / 加入了他在克什米尔的兄弟们 / 跟塔利班一起 / 行走了上千英里 / 被俘获 / 在昆都士围攻期间 / 向要塞进攻 / 必死之战 / 在马扎里沙里夫 / 泥泞的郊外 / 他的兄弟们死在壕沟里 / 死在开放的院落里 / 他们的脸被打爆 / 没人知道他妈的发生了什么 / 谁是敌人谁又是朋友 / 他哭了 / 看着他们的尸体 / 瘫在柳树下面 / 沃克是个年轻人 / 与塔利班同行 / 皈依伊斯兰 / 那俘获了他的心 / 发发慈悲 / 发发慈悲 / 如果你是基督徒 / 行使你的智慧 / 原谅他 / 发发慈悲 / 发发慈悲 / 慈悲 / 慈悲

---

1 约翰·沃克·林德（John Walker Lindh, 1981—），美国公民，2001 年阿富汗战争期间与塔利班战士一起在阿富汗被捕，2002 年被判 20 年监禁，2019 年获释。在接受《新闻周刊》采访时，他表示自己认为塔利班是世界上唯一准确执行伊斯兰教法的政府，他认为他在阿富汗是在为真理而战。

QANA 加纳[1]

There's no one 村子里面

In the village 空无一人

Not a human 没有一个人类

Nor a stone 也没有一块石头

There's no one 村子里面

In the village 空无一人

Children are gone 孩子们已离开

And a mother rocks 一个母亲摇晃着

Herself to sleep 她自己入睡

Let it come down 让它崩塌吧

Let her weep 让她哭泣

The dead lay in strange shapes 死者以怪异的姿势躺倒在地

Some stay buried 有些人被埋葬

Others crawl free 其他人爬着寻找自由

Baby didn't make it 婴儿没能活下来

Screaming debris 空留尖叫的残骸

And a mother rocks 一个母亲摇晃着

Herself to sleep 她自己入睡

Let it come down 让它崩塌吧

Let her weep	让她哭泣
The dead lay in strange shapes	死者以怪异的姿势躺倒在地
Limp little dolls	无力的小洋娃娃
Caked in mud	在泥土中结成块
Small, small hands	小小，小小的手
Found in the road	在路上被发现
They're talking about	他们在谈论着
War aims	战争的目的
What a phrase	多么可怕的话
Bombs that fall	炸弹从天而降
American made	美国人制造出
The new middle east	新的中东
The rice woman squeaks	卖米的女人短促尖叫
The dead lay in strange shapes	死者以怪异的姿势躺倒在地
Little bodies	小小的尸体
Little bodies	小小的尸体

Tied head and feet	绑着头和脚
Wrapped in plastic	裹满塑料布
Laid out in the street	躺在大街上
The new middle east	新的中东
The rice woman squeaks	卖米的女人短促尖叫
The dead lay in strange shapes	死者以怪异的姿势躺倒在地
Water to wine	水变成酒
Wine to blood	酒变成血
Ahh qana	啊，加纳
The miracle	那奇迹
Is love	是爱

1 加纳为黎巴嫩南部的一个村庄。1996 年 4 月 18 日，在加纳附近，以色列国防军向一联合国营地发射炮弹，制造了 "加纳惨案"（The Qana Massacre）。

WITHOUT CHAINS

Five long years

was I a man

dreaming in chains

with the lights on

five long years

nothing to say

thoughts impure

at Guantanamo Bay

Now I'm learning

to walk without chains

I'm learning to walk

without chains

without chains

Born in Bremen

played guitar

a young apprentice

building ships

loved and married

heard the call

摆脱锁链

漫长的五年

我还是个人类

在持续点亮的灯下

戴着锁链做梦

漫长的五年

没有话可说

在关塔那摩湾 [1]

思想是不纯的

现在我正在学习

摆脱锁链的行走

我学习着行走

摆脱锁链

摆脱锁链

生于不来梅

会弹吉他

一个青年学徒

建造船只

相爱后结婚

听到了召唤

is attaining wisdom

a pursuit of fools?

Journeyed to Pakistan

to study Koran

taken in custody

no reason why

then a prison camp

no freedom to breathe

branded an enemy

an enemy

No fault was found

yet do they believe

then flown home

a version of free

chained to the floor

muzzled and bound

a last humiliation

left to endure

想获得智慧

这是愚人的追求吗？

旅行至巴基斯坦

学习古兰经

却被拘留

没有任何原因

继而被投入战俘营

失去了呼吸的自由

被打上敌人的烙印

一个敌人

没有发现过错

可他们相信吗

接着飞回家

一种被链条

锁在地板的自由

被蒙住，被捆绑

最后一次羞辱

丢给我忍受

They say I walk strange

well that may be so

it's been a long time

since I walked at all

Now I'm learning to walk

without chains

to talk without chains

to breathe without chains

to pray without chains

to live without chains

to love without chains

without chains

—for Murat Kunaz

他们说我走路的样子很奇怪

好吧，也许就是这样

距离我上次行走

已经过去了太久

现在我正学习行走

摆脱锁链

摆脱锁链讲话

摆脱锁链呼吸

摆脱锁链祷告

摆脱锁链活着

摆脱锁链去爱

摆脱锁链

——写给穆拉特·库尔纳兹[2]

1 关塔那摩湾，位于古巴东南端关塔那摩省。湾中设有属于美国海军的关塔那摩湾海军基地，该基地曾被美军用于拘留和审讯在阿富汗与伊拉克等地区的战事中捕获的恐怖活动嫌疑人、战俘。此地因属于租借的古巴领土，法理上受刑人的权利不受联邦法律保护与监管，受到媒体与民间人权团体的关注。

2 穆拉特·库尔纳兹（Murat Kunaz, 1982—），土耳其公民，德国合法居民，于2001年12月被美国先后拘禁在阿富汗坎大哈军事基地和古巴关塔那摩海军基地中，在两处都受到了酷刑对待。2002年初，美国及德国的情报官员得出结论，对库尔纳兹的指控毫无根据。他前后总计被关押约五年。

Child 13 his father gone	13 号孩子他的父亲已离去
Saw Jupiter ride	看到木星之旅
All the things	所有他父亲
His father had known	所知之事
Abided within him	一直住在他心里
Charity boy charity boy	慈善男孩，慈善男孩
You live you give	你活着，你付出
You groan you've grown	你叹息，你长大
My heart's a stone	我的心是一块磐石
Your heart's a throne	你的心是一顶王座
Child 13 dreamed	13 号孩子他梦到
He and his father did ride	自己和父亲在骑行
The beaten track	被踩出来的路
The unbeaten track	人迹罕至的路
The uncharted sky	未标明的天空
His radiant face	他容光焕发的脸庞
Felt his father's eyes cry	感受到父亲的双眼在流泪
Clarity boy, charity boy	清澈男孩，慈善男孩
You live, you give	你活着，你付出
You groan, you've grown	你叹息，你长大

My heart's a stone

我的心是一块磐石

Your heart's a throne

你的心是一顶王座

In your hand a wand

你手里握着一根魔杖

A pen to pen

一支笔对着一支笔

The physician within

其中有慰藉

I held you in my arms

我抱你在怀里

I held you in my arms

我抱你在怀里

I cradled you in my arms

我把你轻柔地抱在怀里

BURNING ROSES

Father I am burning roses

father only God shall know

what the secret heart discloses

the ancient dances with the doe

Father I have sorely wounded

father I shall wound no more

I have waltzed among the thorns

where roses burn upon the floor

Daughter may you turn in laughter

a candle dreams a candle draws

the heart that burns

shall burn thereafter

may you turn as roses fall

燃烧的玫瑰

父亲，我在燃烧玫瑰

父亲，只有上帝会知道

隐秘的心揭示出什么

与牝鹿一同跳起远古之舞

父亲，我深深地伤害过别人

父亲，我不会再去伤害谁了

我在荆棘丛中跳起华尔兹

那里玫瑰在地板上燃烧

女儿，愿你在笑声中转身

一根蜡烛做梦，一根蜡烛吸引

那燃烧的心

此后也会烧掉

愿你在玫瑰落下时转身

MARIGOLD

He had a face of long ago

driven and strange with sad, sad eyes

and a smile to raise paradise

She tended her flock upon a hill

watched him from a place above

obscured by light, blushing gold

The heart is its own, yet not as god plans

and ne'er will she know so fine a man

Providence speaks another tongue

he traced the path of star and sun

and caught the eyes of the beguiled one

Through field and flower the poor girl fled

she raised her face her bonnet slid

he traced the path of star and sun

signs that marked the beguiled one

Faith has a flair divining good

金盏花

他有一张历经沧桑的脸

长着陌生的悲伤的，悲伤的双眼

一个微笑令天堂升起

她在山上照看羊群

站在高高的地方望着他

被光线遮蔽住，泛红的金色

心属于它自己，并不是神的安排

她再也无法认识一个这么好的男人

上帝说着另一种语言

他追踪星辰与太阳的路线

吸引受诱骗之人的注目

可怜的女孩穿过田野和花丛逃走

她扬起脸来，软帽滑落

他追踪星辰与太阳的路线

标记下受诱骗之人的记号

信仰有一种预知美好的天赋

her bonnet swept where he stood

he smoothed it out with his healing hand

and made his way into the cold, cold wind

The heart is its own, yet not as god plans

and ne'er will she know so fine a man

她的软帽扫过他曾站立的地方

他用疗愈之手抚平它的褶皱

随后他走进了寒冷，寒冷的风中

心属于它自己，而不是神的安排

她再也无法认识一个这么好的男人

THE PRIDE MOVES SLOWLY

骄傲移动起来很缓慢

I heard you crying in your sleep

我听到你在睡梦中哭泣

and stood above your contour there

于是站在你的身影上

I saw the moon behind your ear

我看到你耳后的月亮

wrists as mine, my mother's hair

母亲的头发，缠绕在我手腕

I saw you with your father's arms

我看到你长着父亲的手臂

and so possess his blades,

因此也拥有了他的锋利

protruding like small wings

小翅膀一样伸出

I thought I'd never see again

我曾以为再无法见到这景象

The lamp of his boyhood glows,

来自他少年时代的灯发着光，

the pride moves slowly

骄傲移动起来很缓慢

as in a dream. Circling

如在梦里。绕着圈

the shade's lucent plain

树荫下的光亮平原

Bequeathed with certain calm,

带着遗赠而来的平静，

the outline of their forms

它们外形的轮廓

diffuse as memories stream

随记忆流动而四处扩散

sown in sadness, sleep

在悲伤中播种，沉睡

A WOMAN'S STORY

一个女人的故事

She stepped out from the caravan

她走出大篷车

Draped in white by attendants round

身披白色周围站满侍从

And a black top hat veiled in lace

一顶黑色大礼帽，蕾丝面纱

And read the faces she laid down

看着那些脸庞她躺下来

She sang in her sleep

她在睡梦中歌唱

A woman's story

一个女人的故事

Just a diviner shuffling time

讲完也不过是占卜师的洗牌时间

An image of a girl in a wedding gown

穿着结婚礼服的女孩

And her king his mane a crown

她的国王，他的鬃毛是一顶王冠

And she sang in her sleep

她在睡梦中歌唱

A woman's story

一个女人的故事

And the faces divined

那些被占卜的脸庞

Were their own

是她们自己的

She raced through the hall

她飞速穿过大厅

Like a young gazelle

像只年轻的瞪羚

Climbing the twilight painted sky

攀登黄昏彩绘过的天空

He drew her with a silken prayer

他用丝滑的祷告吸引了她

Into the calmness of his lair

走入他巢穴的宁静之中

And a garland of rubies for her hair

在她头发上戴上红宝石的花环

They drank from a cup never known

他们从无人见过的杯中饮酒

And her soul and his soul were as one	她的灵魂与他的灵魂合而为一
And they lie in their bed as ordained	他们躺在床上似乎一切都是命定
Wrapped in an emerald sea of dreams	包裹在梦幻的翡翠海中
And she lifted her pale limbs	她抬起苍白的肢体
To the sadness of horns	听着悲伤的号角
Sounding him	回荡在他体内
And he died in her bed	他死在她的床上
Like a swallow	像一只燕子
Beating to go home	着急要回家
But he just gave up	但他就那么放弃了
And fell thru the sky	从天空坠落而下
Like an arrow	像一枚箭头
Thru the night	穿越黑夜
Thru the infinite	穿越无限
And she sang in her sleep	她在睡梦中歌唱
A woman's story	一个女人的故事
And the faces divined	那些被占卜的脸庞
Were their own	是她们自己的

And her golden eyes sought

An emptiness

The twilight painted sky

Ruled by him

And to her life's

Only bliss

She returned

Like a lioness

她金色的眼睛在寻找

一片虚空

黄昏彩绘过的天空

由他统治

她生命里

唯一的幸福

她归来

仿佛一头雌狮

LAUGHARNE

It was the town of Laugharne

Behind a gate of stone

The Merlin ring

Another winding wall

Where the voices find

A triangle of vine

He limped into town

A three-legged dog

Struck by lines

Infusing the air

Mighty charms

Tossed carelessly

It's not the rock, the rock

It's not the dome, the dome

It's not the wall, the wall

It's just a wall that's all

It was a tad unnatural

And his kingdom came

Through the moaning trees

拉恩 [1]

那就是拉恩镇

在一座石门后面

梅林 [2] 之环

另一面蜿蜒城墙

声音在那里被找到

葡萄藤围的三角

他一瘸一拐走进城

一只三条腿的狗

被线条撞击

灌输进空气

强大的魅力

不经意地丢弃

不是岩石，岩石

不是穹顶，穹顶

不是墙壁，墙壁

只是一堵墙，仅此而已

这有点不自然

他的王国降临

穿过低吟的树丛

New Jerusalem	新耶路撒冷
The lamb but a babe	那羔羊不过是个婴儿
Stood by Raphael	站在拉斐尔身边
And the summer man	夏日的男人
Bared his hairy soul	裸露出他毛茸茸的灵魂
Through mythology	穿越神话
Through the mystic fire	穿越神秘火焰
The way of prophecy	预言的方式
Is not the grail, the grail	不是圣杯，圣杯
Is not the bow, the bow	不是弯弓，弯弓
Is not the wall, the wall	不是墙壁，墙壁
It's just a wall, that's all	只是一堵墙，仅此而已
Ah, but give me a whirl	啊，但是给我一次机会
Come from this and that	源于此，源于彼
You drop in my heart	你在我心里留下的
Just a linear tale	只是个线性讲述的故事
Clarity revealed	清晰地透露给
To a three-legged dog	一只三条腿的狗
In the town of Laugharne	在拉恩镇里

The new Jerusalem

With its solemn pines

And the small small homes

And an energy

Uncontained contained

新耶路撒冷

生着庄严的松树

小小，小小的房子

以及包含其中

无法驾驭的能量

It's not the rock, the rock

It's not the grail, the grail

It's not the wall, the wall

It's just a wall, that's all

不是岩石，岩石

不是圣杯，圣杯

不是墙壁，墙壁

只是一堵墙，仅此而已

1 拉恩（Laugharne）是位于威尔士卡马森郡南海岸的一个城镇。迪伦·托马斯 1949—1953 年在这里安家。

2 梅林（Merlin），英格兰及威尔士神话中的传奇魔法师，因扶助阿瑟王登位而闻名。曾为纪念在索尔斯伯利迎战撒克逊人而牺牲的 3000 名贵族战士建立环型石阵的纪念碑。

THE WRITER'S SONG

作家之歌

I laid my mat among the reeds	我把垫子铺入芦苇丛
I could hear the freemen call	我能听到自由人的呼唤
oh my life what does it matter	哦，我的生活，还有什么紧要
will the reed cease bending	芦苇会停止弯折吗
will the leper turn	被孤立者会回转吗
I had a horn I did not blow	我有一支不曾吹响的号角
I had a sake and another	我有一杯接一杯的清酒
I could hear the freemen	我能听到自由人
drunk with sky	迷醉于天空
what matter my cry	我的哭泣有什么紧要
will the moon swell	月亮会肿胀吗
will the flame shy	火焰会羞涩吗
Banzai banzai	万岁 万岁
it is better to write then die	与其去死，不如写作
In the blue crater	在蓝色的陨石坑里
set with straw	铺满稻草
I could hear	我能听到
the freemen call	自由人的呼唤

the way is hard	道路艰难
the gate is narrow	大门狭窄
what matter I say	我的话语有什么紧要
with the new mown hay	在我枕头里
my pillow	塞着新割的干草
I had a sake and another	我喝了一杯接一杯的清酒
I did not care to own nor rove	我不在乎拥有或流浪
I wrote my name upon the water	我把名字写在水上
nothing but nothing above	空无一物在其上
Banzai banzai	万岁 万岁
it is better to write then die	与其去死，不如写作
A thousand prayers	一千次祷告
and souvenirs	和纪念品
set away in earthenware	安放进陶器里
we draw the jars	我们从架子上
from the shelves	取下酒坛
drink our parting	为我们与自己的

from ourselves

So be we king
or be we bum
the reed still whistles
the heart still hums

离别而欢饮

让我们成为国王吧
要么就成为流浪汉
芦苇仍在吹着口哨
心仍然在嗡嗡哼响

the writers song

i placed my mat
among the reeds
i could hear the freeman
who were drunk cry out
what matter what i say
will the reed cease bending
will the leper turn

in the blue crator
set with yellow hay
i could hear the freemen
drunk with sky
what matter my cry
will the moon swell
will the flame shy

i had a saki
and another
bonsai
a thousand souvineers
and a thousand prayers
and be we kings
or be we slaves
the reed still whistles
the heart still raves
the hand still grasps
a cup of love
nothing but nothing
above

i had a saki
and another
it is better to write
then die
bonsai
some scrawl their name
on the face of the water
on vellum sheets
on heavens border
to breathe well
is all one can ask
and to perform a task
formed by no other

travel to its own
book and the scare
within him from
his journeys produced
a least one
mostly work.
a Thieves journal

《作家之歌》

致　谢

本书中的歌词是四十年合作创作的成果。其中除了我自己写作的一小部分音乐外，其余全部音乐由以下音乐家创作或联合创作：

莱尼·凯，伊万·克拉尔，查理德·索尔，杰伊·迪·多尔蒂，艾伦·拉尼尔，奥利弗·雷，汤姆·魏尔伦，布鲁斯·斯普林斯汀，弗雷德·索尼克·史密斯，杰西·帕里斯·史密斯，以及托尼·沙纳罕。

非常感谢加布里埃尔·杜布和庄雪（音）。

皇家打字机图片：© 奥利弗·雷。

《群马》封面照，34 页：© 罗伯特·梅普尔索普基金会，授权使用。

手写歌词及祷告者披肩图片，318 页，重印自作者个人档案。

© Robert Mapplethorpe Foundation

"听着。我相信我们梦想的一切
通过我们的联合均能实现"

一頁 folio

始于一页，抵达世界
Humanities · History · Literature · Arts

出 品 人　范　新

品牌总监　恰　恰

特约编辑　王韵沁

营销总监　张　延

营销编辑　闵　婕

新 媒 体　赵雪雨

版权总监　吴攀君

印制总监　刘玲玲

Folio (Beijing) Culture & Media Co., Ltd.
Bldg. 16C, Jingyuan Art Center,
Chaoyang, Beijing, China 100124

一頁 folio
微信公众号

官方微博: @一頁 folio ｜官方豆瓣: 一頁 folio ｜联系我们: rights@foliobook.com.cn